Robert Hunt

Popular Romances of the West of England

SALZWASSER
VERLAG

Robert Hunt

Popular Romances of the West of England

Reprint of the original, first published in 1865.

1st Edition 2022 | ISBN: 978-3-75258-937-5

Verlag (Publisher): Salzwasser Verlag GmbH, Zeilweg 44, 60439 Frankfurt, Deutschland
Vertretungsberechtigt (Authorized to represent): E. Roepke, Zeilweg 44, 60439 Frankfurt, Deutschland
Druck (Print): Books on Demand GmbH, In de Tarpen 42, 22848 Norderstedt, Deutschland

POPULAR ROMANCES

OF THE

WEST OF ENGLAND;

OR,

The Drolls, Traditions, and Superstitions of
Old Cornwall.

COLLECTED AND EDITED BY

ROBERT HUNT, F.R.S.

SECOND SERIES.

LONDON

1865.

CONTENTS.

THE SAINTS.

HOLY WELLS.

KING ARTHUR.

SORCERY AND WITCHCRAFT.

POPULAR SUPERSTITIONS.

MISCELLANEOUS STORIES.

APPENDIX.

ROMANCES AND SUPERSTITIONS

OF

HISTORIC TIMES.

THE SAINTS.

"With great pretended spiritual motions,
And many fine whimsical notions,
With blind zeal and large devotions."

Samuel Butler.

POPULAR ROMANCES AND SUPERSTITIONS OF THE WEST OF ENGLAND.

LEGENDS OF THE SAINTS.

"This ilkë monk let olde thingës pace,
And held after the newë world the trace.
He gave not of the text a pulled hen,
That saith, that hunters be not holy men,
Ne that a monk, when he is reckëless,
Is like to a fish that is waterless;
This is to say, a monk out of his cloister,
This ilkë text held he not worth an oyster,]
And I say his opinion was good."
The Canterbury Tales—CHAUCER.

THE process through which a man, who has made himself remarkable to his ignorant fellow-men, is passed after death—first, into the hero performing fabulous exploits, and eventually into the giant—is not difficult to understand.

The remembrance of great deeds, and the memory of virtues,—even in modern days, when the exaggerations of votaries are subdued by the influence of education,—ever tends to bring them out in strong contrast with the surrounding objects. The mass of men form the background, as it were, of the picture, and the hero or the saint stands forth in all his brightness of colour in the foreground.

Amidst the uneducated Celtic population who inhabited Old Cornwall, it was the practice, as with the Celts of other countries, to exalt their benefactors with all the adornments of that hyperbole which distinguishes their songs and stories. When the first Christian missionaries dwelt amongst this people, they impressed them with the daring which they exhibited by the persecution which they uncomplainingly endured and the holy lives they led.

Those who were morally so superior to the living men, were represented as physically so to their children, and every generation adorned the relation which it had received with the ornaments derived from their own imaginations, which had been tutored amidst the severer scenes of nature; and consequently the warrior, or the holy man, was transmuted into the giant.

If to this we add the desire which was constantly shewn by the earlier priesthood to persuade the people of their miraculous powers—of the direct interference of Heaven in their behalf—and of the violent conflicts which they were occasionally enduring with the enemy of the human race, there will be no difficulty in marking out the steps by which the ordinary man has become an extraordinary hero. When we hear of the saints to whose memories the parish churches are dedicated, being enabled to hurl rocks of enormous size through the air, to carry them in their pockets, and indeed to use them as playthings, we perceive that the traditions of the legitimate giants, have been transferred to, and mixed up with, the memories of a more recent people.

In addition to legends of the Titanic type, this section will include a few of the true monastic character. The only purpose I have in giving these is to preserve, as examples, some curious superstitions which have not yet entirely lost their hold on the people.

THE CROWZA STONES.

ST JUST, from his home in Penwith, being weary of having little to do, except offering prayers for the tinners and fishermen, went on a visit to the hospitable St Keverne, who had fixed his hermitage in a well-selected spot, not far from the Lizard headland. The holy brothers rejoiced together, and in full feeding and deep drinking they pleasantly passed the time. St Just gloried in the goodly chalice from which he drank the richest of wines, and envied St Keverne the possession of a cup of such rare value. Again and again did he pledge St Keverne; their holy bond of brotherhood was to be for ever; Heaven was to witness the purity of their friendship, and to the world they were to become patterns of ecclesiastical love.

The time came when St Just felt he must return to his flock; and repeating over again his vows, and begging St Keverne to return his visit, he departed—St Keverne sending many a blessing after his good brother.

The Saint of the west, had not left his brother of the south, many hours before the latter missed his cup. Diligent search was made in every corner of his dwelling, but no cup could be found. At length St Keverne could not but feel that he had been robbed of his treasure by his western friend. That one in whom he had placed such confidence—one to whom he had opened his heart, and to whom he had shewn the most unstinting hospitality—should have behaved so treacherously, overcame the serenity of the good man. His rage was excessive. After the first burst was over, and reason reasserted her power, St Keverne felt that his wisest course was to pursue the thief, inflict summary punishment on him, and recover his cup. The thought was followed by a firm resolve, and away St Keverne started in pursuit of

St Just. Passing over Crowza Down, some of the boulders of "Ironstone" which are scattered over the surface caught his eye, and presently he whipped a few of these stone pebbles into his pockets, and hastened onward.

When he drew near Tre-men-keverne he spied St Just. St Keverne worked himself up into a boiling rage, and toiled with increased speed up the hill, hallooing to the saintly thief, who pursued his way for some time in the well-assumed quiet of conscious innocence.

Long and loud did St Keverne call on St Just to stop, but the latter was deaf to all calls of the kind—on he went, quickening, however, his pace a little.

At length St Keverne came within a stone's throw of the dissembling culprit, and calling him a thief—adding thereto some of the most choice epithets from his holy vocabulary—taking a stone from his pocket, he let it fly after St Just.

The stone falling heavily by the side of St Just convinced him that he had to deal with an awkward enemy, and that he had best make all the use he could of his legs. He quietly untied the chalice, which he had fastened to his girdle, and let it fall to the ground. Then, still as if unconscious of his follower, he set off to run as fast as his ponderous body would allow his legs to carry him. St Keverne came up to where his cup glistened in the sunshine. He had recovered his treasure, he should get no good out of the false friend, and he was sadly jaded with his long run. Therefore he took, one by one, the stones from his pockets—he hurled them, fairly aimed, after the retreating culprit, and cursed him as he went.

There the pebbles remain where they fell,—the peculiarity of the stone being in all respects unlike anything around, but being clearly the Crowza stones,—attesting the truth of the legend; and their weights, each one being several hundred pounds, proving the power of the giant saint.

Many have been the attempts made to remove these stones. They are carried away easily enough by day, but they ever return to the spot on which they now repose, at night.

THE LONGSTONE.

THE GIANT'S HAT AND STAFF.

SOME say it was St Roach, others refer it to St Austell; but all agree in one thing, that the Longstone was once the staff of some holy man, and that its present state is owing to the malignant persecution of the demon of darkness. It happened after this manner. The good saint who had been engaged in some mission was returning to his cell across St Austell Downs. The night had been fine, the clearness of the sky and the brightness of the stars conduced to religious thoughts, and those of the saint fled heavenwards. The devil was wandering abroad that night, and maliciously he resolved to play a trick upon his enemy. The saint was wrapt in thought. The devil was working his dire spells. The sky became black, the stars disappeared, and suddenly a terrific rush of wind seized the saint, whirled him round and round, and at last blew his hat high into the air. The hat went ricocheting over the moor and the saint after it, the devil enjoying the sport. The long stick which the saint carried impeded his progress in the storm, and he stuck it into the ground. On went the hat, speedily followed the saint over and round the moor, until thoroughly wearied out, he at length gave up the chase. He, now exposed to the beat of the tempest bareheaded, endeavoured to find his way to his cell, and thought to pick up his staff on the way. No staff could be found in the darkness, and his hat was, he thought, gone irrecoverably. At length the saint reached his cell, he quieted his spirit by prayer, and sought the forgetfulness of sleep, safe under the protection of the holy cross, from all the tricks of the devil. The evil one, however, was at work on the wild moor, and by his incantations he changed the hat and the staff into two rocks. Morning came, the saint went abroad seeking for his lost covering and support. He found them both—one a huge circular boulder, and the other a long stone which remains to this day.*

The Saint's, or, as it was often called, the Giant's Hat was removed in 1798 by a regiment of soldiers who were encamped near it. They felt satisfied that this mysterious stone was the cause of the wet season which rendered their camp unpleasant, and consequently they resolved to remove the evil spell by destroying it.

ST SENNEN AND ST JUST.

THESE saints held rule over adjoining parishes; but, like neighbours, not unfrequently, they quarrelled. We know not the cause which made their angry passions rise; but no doubt the saints were occasionally exposed to the influences of the evil principle, which appears to be one of the ruling powers of the world. It is not often that we have instances of excess of passion in man or woman without some evidence of the evil resulting from it. Every tempest in the physical world leaves its mark on the face of the earth. Every tempest in the moral world, in a similar manner, leaves some scar to tell of its ravages on the soul. A most enduring monument in granite tells us of the rage to

* Another tradition affirms that one of the sons of Cyrus lies buried beneath the Longstone.

which those two holy men were the victims. As we have said, there is no record of the origin of the duel which was fought between St Just and St Sennen; but, in the fury of their rage, they tore each a rock from the granite mass, and hurled it onwards to destroy his brother. They were so well aimed that both saints must have perished had the rocks been allowed to travel as intended. A merciful hand guided them, though in opposite directions, in precisely the same path. The huge rocks came together; so severe was the blow of impact that they became one mass, and fell to the ground, to remain a monument of the impotent rage of two giants.

LEGENDS OF ST LEVEN.

I.—THE SAINT AND JOHANA.

THE walls of what are supposed to be the hut of St Leven are still to be seen at Bodellen. If you walk from Bodellen to St Leven Church, on passing near the stile in Rospletha you will see a three-cornered garden. This belonged to a woman who is only known to us as Johana. Johana's Garden is still the name of the place. One Sunday morning St Leven was passing over the stile to go as usual to his fishing-place below the church, to catch his dinner. Johana was in the garden picking pot-herbs at the time, and she lectured the holy man for fishing on a Sunday. They came to high words, and St Leven told Johana that there was no more sin in taking his dinner from the sea than she herself committed in taking hers from the garden. The saint called her foolish Johana, and said if another of her name was christened in his well she should be a bigger fool than Johana herself. From that day to this no child called Johana has been christened in St Leven. All parents who desire to give that name to their daughters, dreading St Leven's curse, take the children to Sennen.

II.—THE SAINT'S PATH.

The path along which St Leven was accustomed to walk from Bodellen, by Rospletha, on to St Leven's Rocks, as they are still called, may be yet seen; the grass grows greener wherever the good priest trod than in any other part of the fields through which the footpath passes.

III.—THE ST LEVEN STONE.

On the south side of the church, to the east of the porch, is a rock known by the above name. It is broken in two, and the fissure is filled in with ferns and wild flowers, while the grass grows rank around it. On this rock St Leven often sat to rest after the fatigue of fishing; and desiring to leave some enduring memento of himself in connexion with this his rude but favourite seat, he one day gave it a blow with his fist and cracked it through. He prayed over the rock, and uttered the following prophecy:—

> "When, with panniers astride,
> A packhorse one can ride
> Through St Leven's Stone,
> The world will be done."

This stone must have been venerated for the saint's sake when the church was built, or it would certainly have been employed for the building. It is more than fifty years since I first made acquaintance, as a child, with the St Leven Stone, and it may be a satisfaction to many to know that the progress of separation is an exceedingly slow one. I cannot detect the slightest difference in the width of the fissure now and then. At the present slow rate of opening, the pack-horse and panniers will not be able to pass through the rock for many thousands of years to come. We need not, therefore, place much reliance on those prophecies which give but a limited duration to this planet.*

IV.—THE TWO BREAMS.

Although in common with many of the churches in the remote districts of Cornwall, "decay's effacing fingers" have been allowed to do their work in St Leven Church, yet there still remains some of the ornamental work which once adorned it. Much of the carving is irremediably gone; but still the inquirer will find that it once told the story of important events in the life of the good St Leven. Two fishes on the same hook form the device, which appears at one time to have prevailed in this church. These are to commemorate a remarkable incident in St Leven's life. One lovely evening about sunset, St Leven was on his rocks fishing. There was a heavy pull upon his line, and drawing it in, he found two breams on the same hook. The good saint, anxious to serve both alike, to avoid, indeed, even the appearance of partiality, took both the fishes off the hook, and cast them back into the sea. Again they came to the hook, and again were they returned to their native elements. The line was no sooner cast a third time than the same two fishes hooked themselves once more. St Leven thought there must be some reason unknown to him for this strange occurrence, so he took both the fishes home with him. When the saint reached Bodellen, he found his sister, St Breage,† had

* See 1st Series, p. 198.

† St Breock or Briock, a bishop of a diocese in Armorica, is said to have been the patron saint of St Breage. But there is a Cornish distich, "Germow Mathern, Breaga Lavethas." Germoe was a king, Breaga a mid-wife, which rather favours the statement that St Breage was a sister of St Leven. Breage and Germoe are adjoining parishes, having the shores of the Mount's Bay for their southern boundaries. When the uncultivated

come to visit him with two children. Then he thought he saw the hand of Providence at work in guiding the fish to his hook.

Even saints are blind when they attempt to fathom the ways of the Unseen. The fish were, of course, cooked for supper; and the saint having asked a blessing upon their savoury meal, all sat down to partake of it. The children had walked far, and they were ravenously hungry. They ate their suppers with rapidity, and, not taking time to pick out the bones of the fish, they were both choked. The apparent blessing was thus transformed into a curse, and the bream has from that day forward ever gone by the name, amongst fishermen, of "choke children."

There are many disputes as to the fish concerned in this legend. Some of the fishermen of St Leven parish have insisted upon their being "chad," (the shad, *clupeida alosa ;*) while others, with the strong evidence afforded by the bony structure of the fish, will have it to have been the bream, (*cyprinus brama.*) My young readers warned by the name, should be equally careful in eating either of those fish.

SAINT KEYNE.

BRAGHAN, or Brechan, was a king in Wales, and the builder of the town of Brecknock. This worthy old king and saint was the happy father of twenty-six children,

inhabitants of this remote region regarded a wreck as a "God-send," and plundered without hesitation every body, living or dead, thrown upon the shore, these parishes acquired a melancholy notoriety. The sailors' popular prayer being,

"God keep us from rocks and shelving sands,
And save us from Breage and Germoe men's lands."

Happily those days are almost forgotten. The ameliorating influences of the Christian faith, which was let in upon a most benighted people by John Wesley, like a sunbeam, dispelled those evil principles, and gave birth to pure and simple virtues.

or, as some say, twenty-four. Of these fourteen or fifteen were sainted for their holiness, and their portraits are preserved within a fold of the kingly robe of the saint, their father, in the window at St Neot's Church, bearing the inscription, "Sante Brechane, cum omnibus sanctis, ora pro nobis," and known as the young women's window.

Of the holy children settled in Cornwall, we learn that the following gave their names to Cornish churches :—

1. John, giving	name to the	Church of	St Ive.
2. Endellient,	"	"	Endellion.
3. Menfre,	"	"	St Minver.
4. Tethe,	"	"	St Teath.
5. Mabena,	"	"	St Mabyn.
6. Merewenna,	"	"	Marham.
7. Wenna,	"	"	St Wenn.
8. KEYNE,	"	"	ST KEYNE.
9. Yse,	"	"	St Issey.
10. Morwenna,	"	"	Morwinstow.
11. Cleder,	"	"	St Clether.
12. Keri,	"	"	Egloskerry.
13. Helie,	"	"	Egloshayle.
14. Adwent,	"	"	Advent.
15. Lanent,	"	"	Lelant.*

Of this remarkable family St Keyne stands out as the brightest star. Lovely beyond measure, she wandered over the country safe, even in lawless times, from insult, by "the strength of her purity."

We find this virtuous woman performing miracles wherever she went. The district now known by the name of Keynsham, in Somersetshire, was in those days infested with serpents. St Keyne, rivaling St Hilda of the Northern Isle, changed them all into coils of stone, and there they are in the quarries at the present time to attest the truth of the legend. Geologists, with more learning than poetry, term

* Leland, cited by William of Worcester from the Cornish Calendar at St Michael's Mount. Michell's "Parochial History of Saint Neot's."

them Ammonites, deriving their name from the horn of Jupiter Ammon, as if the Egyptian Jupiter was likely to have charmed serpents in England. We are satisfied to leave the question for the consideration of our readers. After a life spent in the conversion of sinners, the building of churches, and the performance of miracles, this good woman retired into Cornwall, and in one of its most picturesque valleys, she sought and found that quiet which was conducive to a happy termination of a well-spent life. She desired, above all things, "peace on earth;" and she hoped to benefit the world, by giving to woman a chance of being equal to her lord and master. A beautiful well of water was near the home of the saint, and she planted, with her blessing, four trees around it—the withy, the oak, the elm, and the ash. When the hour of her death was drawing near, St Keyne caused herself to be borne on a litter to the shade which she had formed, and soothed by the influence of the murmur of the flowing fountain, she blessed the waters, and gave them their wondrous power, thus quaintly described by Carew:—
"Next, I will relate to you, another of the Cornish natural wonders—viz., St Keyne's Well; but lest you make wonder, first at the sainte, before you notice the well, you must understand that this was not Kayne the Manqueller, but one of a gentler spirit and milder sex—to wit, a woman. He who caused the spring to be pictured, added this rhyme for an explanation:—

'In name, in shape, in quality,
This well is very quaint;
The name to lot of Kayne befell,
No over-holy saint.
The shape, four trees of divers kind,
Withy, oak, elm, and ash,
Make with their roots an arched roof,
Whose floor this spring does wash.

The quality, that man or wife,
Whose chance or choice attains,
First of this sacred stream to drink,
Thereby the mastery gains.' "*

ST DENNIS'S BLOOD.

THE patron saint of the parish church of St Dennis was born in the city of Athens, in the reign of Tiberius. His name and fame have full record in the "History of the Saints of the Church of Rome." How his name was connected with this remote parish is not clearly made out. We learn, however, that the good man was beheaded at Montmartre, and that he walked after his execution, with his head under his arm, to the place in Paris which still bears his name. At the very time when the decapitation took place in Paris, *blood fell on the stones of this churchyard* in Cornwall. Previously to the breaking out of the plague in London, the stains of the blood of St Dennis were again seen; and during our wars with the Dutch, the defeat of the English fleet was foretold by the rain of gore in this remote and sequestered place. Hals, the Cornish historian, with much gravity, informs us that he had seen some of the stones with blood upon them. Whenever this phenomenon occurs again we may expect some sad calamity to be near.

Some years since a Cornish gentleman was cruelly murdered, and his body thrown into a brook. I have been very lately shewn stones taken from this brook with bright red spots of some vegetable growth on them. It is said that

* Carew's Survey, Lord Dedunstanville's edition, p. 305. See "The Well of St Keyne," by Robert Southey, in his "Ballads and Metrical Tales," vol. i.; or of Southey's collected works, vol. vi.

St Keyne, or St Kenna, is said to have visited St Michael's Mount, and imparted this peculiar virtue to a stone chair on the tower.

ever since the murder the stones in this brook are spotted with gore, whereas they never were so previously to this dreadful deed.

ST KEA'S BOAT.

ST KEA, a young Irish saint, stood on the southern shores of Ireland and saw the Christian missionaries departing to carry the blessed Word to the heathens of Western England. He watched their barks fade beneath the horizon, and he felt that he was left to a solitude which was not fitted to one in the full energy of young life, and burning with zeal.

The saint knelt on a boulder of granite lying on the shore, and he prayed with fervour that Heaven would order it so that he might diffuse his religious fervour amongst the barbarians of Cornwall. He prayed on for some time, not observing the rising of the tide. When he had poured out his full soul, he awoke to the fact, not only that the waves were washing around the stone on which he knelt, but that the stone was actually floating on the water. Impressed with the miracle, St Kea sprang to his feet, and looking towards the setting sun, with his cross uplifted, he exclaimed, "To Thee, and only to Thee, my God, do I trust my soul!"

Onward floated the granite, rendered buoyant by supernatural power. Floated hither and thither by the tides, it swam on; blown sometimes in one direction, and sometimes in another, by the varying winds, days and nights were spent upon the waters. The faith of St Kea failed not; three times a day he knelt in prayer to God. At all other times he stood gazing on the heavens. At length the faith of the saint being fairly tried, the moorstone boat floated steadily up the river, and landed at St Kea, which place he soon

Christianised, and there stands to this day this monument of St Kea's sincere belief.

ST GERMAN'S WELL.

THE good St German was, it would appear, sent into Cornwall in the reign of the Emperor Valentinian, mainly to suppress the Pelagian heresy. The inhabitants of the shores of the Tamar had long been schooled into the belief in original sin, and they would not endure its denial from the lips of a stranger. In this they were supported by the monks, who had already a firm footing in the land, and who taught the people implicit obedience to their religious instructors, faith in election, and that all human efforts were unavailing, unless supported by priestly aid. St German was a man with vast powers of endurance. He preached his doctrines of freewill, and of the value of good works, notwithstanding the outcry raised against him. His miracles were of the most remarkable character, and sufficiently impressive to convince a large body of the Cornish people that he was an inspired priest. St German raised a beautiful church, and built a monastic house for the relief of poor people. Yet notwithstanding the example of the pure life of the saint, and his unceasing study to do good, a large section of the priests and the people never ceased to persecute him. To all human endurance there is a limit, and even that of the saint weakened eventually, before the never-ceasing annoyances by which he was hemmed in.

One Sabbath morning the priest attended as usual to his Christian duties, when he was interrupted by a brawl amongst the outrageous people, who had come in from all parts of the country with a determination to drive him from the place of his adoption. The holy man prayed for his persecutors, and he entreated them to calm their angry passions and listen to his healing words. But no words could convey any healing balm to their stormy hearts. At length his brethren, fearing that his life was in danger, begged him to fly, and eventually he left the church by a small door near the altar, while some of the monks endeavoured to tranquillise the people. St German went, a sad man, to the cliffs at the Rame head, and there alone he wept in agony at the failure of his labours. So intense was the soul-suffering of this holy man, that the rocks felt the power of spirit-struggling, and wept with him. The eyes of man, a spiritual creation, dry after the outburst of sorrow, but when the gross forms of matter are compelled to sympathise with spiritual sorrow, they remain for ever under the influence; and from that day the tears of the cliffs have continued to fall, and the Well of St German attests to this day of the saint's agony. The saint was not allowed to remain in concealment long. The crowd of opposing priests and the peasantry were on his track. Hundreds were on the hill, and arming themselves with stones, they descended with shouts, determined to destroy him. St German prayed to God for deliverance, and immediately a rush, as of thunder, was heard upon the hills—a chariot surrounded by flames, and flashing light in all directions, was seen rapidly approaching. The crowd paused, fell back, and the flaming car passed on to where St German knelt. There were two bright angels in the chariot; they lifted the persecuted saint from the ground, and placing him between them, ascended into the air.

"Curse your persecutors," said the angels. The saint cursed them; and from that time all holiness left the church he had built. The saint was borne to other lands, and lived to effect great good. On the rocks the burnt tracks of the chariot wheels were long to be seen, and the Well of Tears still flows.

HOW ST PIRAN REACHED CORNWALL.

GOOD men are frequently persecuted by those whom they have benefited the most. The righteous Piran had, by virtue of his sanctity, been enabled to feed ten Irish kings and their armies for ten days together with three cows. He brought to life by his prayers the dogs which had been killed while hunting the elk and the boar, and even restored to existence many of the warriors who had fallen on the battle-field. Notwithstanding this, and his incomparable goodness, some of these kings condemned him to be cast off a precipice into the sea, with a millstone around his neck.

On a boisterous day, a crowd of the lawless Irish assembled on the brow of a beetling cliff, with Piran in chains. By great labour they had rolled a huge millstone to the top of the hill, and Piran was chained to it. At a signal from one of the kings, the stone and the saint were rolled to the edge of, and suddenly over, the cliff into the Atlantic. The winds were blowing tempestuously, the heavens were dark with clouds, and the waves white with crested foam. No sooner was Piran and the millstone launched into space, than the sun shone out brightly, casting the full lustre of its beams on the holy man, who sat tranquilly on the descending stone. The winds died away, and the waves became smooth as a mirror. The moment the millstone touched the water, hundreds were converted to Christianity who saw this miracle. St Piran floated on safely to Cornwall; he landed on the 5th of March on the sands which bear his name. He lived amongst the Cornish men until he attained the age of 206 years.*

* See Gilbert, vol. iii. p. 329. See Appendix A. The name of this saint is written Piran, Peran, and Perran.

ST PERRAN, THE MINERS' SAINT.

ST PIRAN, or St Perran, has sometimes gained the credit of discovering tin in Cornwall; yet Usher places the date of his birth about the year 352; and the merchants of Tyre are said to have traded with Cornwall for tin as early as the days of King Solomon.

There are three places in Cornwall to which the name of Perran is given:—

> Perran-Aworthall—*i. e., Perran on the noted River.*
> Perran-Uthno—*i. e., Perran the Little.*
> Perran-Zabuloe—*i. e., Perran in the Sands.*

This sufficiently proves that the saint, or some one bearing that name, was eminently popular amongst the people; and in St Perran we have an example—of which several instances are given—of the manner in which a very ancient event is shifted forward, as it were, for the purpose of investing some popular hero with additional reasons for securing the devotion of the people, and of drawing them to his shrine.*

Picrous, or Piecras, is another name which has been floated by tradition, down the stream of time, in connexion with the discovery of tin; and in the eastern portion of Cornwall, Picrous-day, the second Thursday before Christmas-day, is kept as the tinners' holiday.

* *See* Perran-Zabuloe, with an Account of the Past and Present State of the Oratory of St Piran in the Sands, and Remarks on its Antiquity. By the Rev. Wm. Haslam, B.A., and by the Rev. Collins Trelawney.

St Kieran, the favourite Celtic saint, reached Scotland from Ireland, the precursor of St Columba, (565 A.D.) "The cave of St Kieran is still shewn in Kintyre, where the first Christian teacher of the Western Highlands is believed to have made his abode."—*Wilson's Prehistoric Annals.*

There is a curious resemblance between the deeds and the names of those two saints.

The popular story of the discovery of tin is, however, given, with all its anachronisms.

THE DISCOVERY OF TIN.

St Piran, or St Perran, leading his lonely life on the plains which now bear his name, devoted himself to the study of the objects which presented themselves to his notice. The good saint decorated the altar in his church with the choicest flowers, and his cell was adorned with the crystals which he could collect from the neighbouring rocks. In his wanderings on the sea-shore, St Perran could not but observe the numerous mineral veins running through the slate rocks forming the beautiful cliffs on this coast. Examples of every kind he collected; and on one occasion, when preparing his humble meal, a heavy black stone was employed to form a part of the fireplace. The fire was more intense than usual, and a stream of beautiful white metal flowed out of the fire. Great was the joy of the saint; he perceived that God, in His goodness, had discovered to him something which would be useful to man. St Perran communicated his discovery to St Chiwidden. They examined the shores together, and Chiwidden, who was learned in the learning of the East, soon devised a process for producing this metal in large quantities. The two saints called the Cornish men together. They told them of their treasures, and they taught them how to dig the ore from the earth, and how, by the agency of fire, to obtain the metal. Great was the joy in Cornwall, and many days of feasting followed the announcement. Mead and metheglin, with other drinks, flowed in abundance; and vile rumour says the saints and their people were rendered equally unstable thereby. "Drunk as a Perraner," has certainly passed into a proverb from that day.

The riot of joy at length came to an end, and steadily, seriously, the tribes of Perran and St Agnes set to work. They soon accumulated a vast quantity of this precious metal; and when they carried it to the southern coasts, the merchants from Gaul eagerly purchased it of them. The noise of the discovery, even in those days, rapidly extended itself; and even the cities of Tyre learned that a metal precious to them, was to be obtained in a country far to the west. The Phœnician navigators were not long in finding out the Tin Islands; and great was the alarm amidst the Cornish Britons lest the source of their treasure should be discovered. Then it was they intrenched the whole of St Agnes beacon; then it was they built the numerous hill castles, which have puzzled the antiquarian; then it was that they constructed the Rounds,—amongst which the Perran Round remains as a remarkable example,—all of them to protect their tin ground. So resolved were the whole of the population of the district to preserve the tin workings, that they prevented any foreigner from landing on the mainland, and they established tin markets on the islands on the coast. On these islands were hoisted the standard of Cornwall, a white cross on a black ground, which was the device of St Perran and St Chiwidden, symbolising the black tin ore and the white metal.*

ST NEOT, THE PIGMY.

WHENCE came the saint, or hermit, who has given his name to two churches in England, is not known.

Tradition, however, informs us that he was remarkably small in stature, though exquisitely formed. He could not, according to all accounts, have been more than fifteen inches

* See Appendix B.

high. Yet, though so diminutive a man, he possessed a soul which was giant-like in the power of his faith. The Church of St Neot, which has been built on the ancient site of the hermit's cell, is situated in a secluded valley, watered by a branch of the river Fowey. The surrounding country is, even now, but very partially cultivated, and it must have been, a few centuries since, a desert waste; but the valley is, and no doubt ever has been, beautifully wooded. Not far from the church is the holy well, in which the pious anchorite would stand immersed to his neck, whilst he repeated the whole Book of Psalms. Great was the reward for such an exercise of devotion and faith. Out of numerous miracles we select only a few, which have some especial character about them.

ST NEOT AND THE FOX.

One day the holy hermit was standing in his bath chanting the Psalms, when he heard the sound of huntsmen approaching. Whether the saint feared ridicule or ill-treatment, we know not; but certainly he left some psalms unsung that day, and hastily gathering up his clothes, he fled to his cell.

In his haste the goodman lost his shoe, and a hungry fox having escaped the hunters, came to the spring to drink. Having quenched the fever of thirst, and being hungry, he spied the saint's shoe, and presently ate it. The hermit despatched his servant to look for his shoe; and, lo, he found the fox cast into a deep sleep, and the thongs of the shoe hanging out of his vile mouth. Of course the shoe was pulled out of his stomach, and restored to the saint.

ST NEOT AND THE DOE.

Again, on another day, when the hermit was in his fountain, a lovely doe, flying from the huntsmen, fell down on the edge of the well, imploring, with tearful eyes and anxious pantings, the aid of St Neot. The dogs followed in full chase, ready to pounce on the trembling doe, and eager to tear her in pieces. They saw the saint, and one look from his holy eyes sent them flying back into the woods, more speedily, if possible, than they rushed out of it.

The huntsman too came on, ready to discharge his arrow into the heart of the doe; but, impressed with the sight he saw, he fell on his knees, cast away his quiver, and became from that day a follower of the saint's, giving him his horn to hang, as a memorial, in the church, where it was long to be seen. The huntsman became eventually one of the monks of the neighbouring house of St Petroch.

ST NEOT AND THE THIEVES.

When St Neot was abbot, some thieves came by night and stole the oxen belonging to the farm of the monastery. The weather was most uncertain,—the seed-time was passing away,—and a fine morning rendered it imperative that the ploughs should be quickly employed. There were no oxen. Great was the difficulty, and earnest were the abbot's prayers. In answer to them, the wild stags came in from the forests, and tamely offered their necks to the yoke. When unyoked in the evening, they resorted to their favourite pastures, but voluntarily returned each morning to their work. The report of this event reached the ears of the thieves. They became penitent, and restored the oxen to the monastery. Not only so, but they consecrated their days to devotional exercises. The oxen being restored, the stags were dismissed; but they bore for ever a white ring, like a yoke, about their necks, and they held a charmed life, safe from the shafts of the hunters.

ST NEOT AND THE FISHES.

On one occasion, when the saint was at his devotions, an angel appeared unto him, and shewing him three fishes in the well, he said, "These are for thee; take one each day for thy daily food, and the number shall never grow less: the choice of one of three fishes shall be thine all the days of thy life." Long time passed by, and daily a fish was taken from the well, and three awaited his coming every morning. At length the saint, who shared in human suffering notwithstanding his piety, fell ill; and being confined to his bed, St Neot sent his servant Barius to fetch him a fish for his dinner. Barius being desirous of pleasing, if possible, the sick man's taste, went to the well and caught two fishes. One of these he broiled, and the other he boiled. Nicely cooked, Barius took them on a dish to his master's bedside, who started up alarmed for the consequences of the act of his servant, in disobedience to the injunctions of the angel. So good a man could not allow wrath to get the mastery of him; so he sat up in his bed, and, instead of eating, he prayed with great earnestness over the cooked fish. At last the spirit of holiness exerted its full power. St Neot commanded Barius to return at once and cast the fish into the well. Barius went and did as his master had told him to do; and, lo, the moment the fishes fell into the water they recovered life, and swam away with the third fish, as if nothing had happened to them.

All these things and more are recorded in the windows of St Neot's Church.*

* See Appendix C.

PROBUS AND GRACE.

EVERY one is acquainted with the beautiful tower of Probus Church. If they are not, they should lose no time in visiting it. Various are the stories in connexion with those two saints, who are curiously connected with the church, and one of the fairs held in the church-town. A safe tradition tells us that St Probus built the church, and failing in the means of adding a tower to his building, he petitioned St Grace to aid him. Grace was a wealthy lady, and she resolved at her own cost to build a tower, the like of which should not be seen in the "West Countrie." Regardless of the expense, sculptured stone was worked by the most skilful masons, and the whole put together in the happiest of proportions. When the tower was finished, St Probus opened his church with every becoming solemnity, and took to himself all the praise which was lavished on the tower, although he had built only a plain church. When, however, the praise of Probus was at the highest, a voice was heard slowly and distinctly exclaiming,

> "Saint Probus and Grace,
> Not the first, but the last;"

and thus for ever have Probus and Grace been united as patron saints of this church.

Mr Davies Gilbert remarks, however, in his "Parochial History:" "Few gentlemen's houses in the west of Cornwall were without the honour of receiving Prince Charles during his residence in the county about the middle part of the civil wars; and he is said to have remained for a time longer than usual with Mr Williams, who, after the Restoration, waited on the king with congratulations from the parish; and, on being complimented by him with the question whether he could do anything for his friends, answered that the parish would esteem themselves highly honoured and distinguished by the grant of a fair, which was accordingly done for the 17th September. This fair coming the last in succession after three others, has acquired for itself a curious appellation, derived from the two patron saints, and from the peculiar pronunciation in that neighbourhood of the word last, somewhat like laest,—

> 'Saint Probus and Grace,
> Not the first, but the last,'—

and from this distinction it is usually called Probus and Grace Fair." We are obliged, therefore, to lean on the original tradition for the true meaning of this couplet.

ST NECTAN'S KIEVE AND THE LONELY SISTERS.

FAR up the deep and rocky vale of Trevillet, in the parish of Tintagel,* stands on a pile of rocks the little chapel of the good St Nectan. No holy man ever selected a more secluded, or a more lovely spot in which to pass a religious life. From the chapel rock you look over the deep valley full of trees. You see here and there the lovely trout-stream, running rapidly towards the sea; and, opening in the distance, there rolls the mighty ocean itself. Although this oratory is shut in amongst the woods, so as to be invisible to any one approaching it by land, until they are close upon it, it is plainly seen by the fishermen or by the sailor far off at sea; and in olden time the prayers of St Nectan were sought by all whose business was in the "deep waters."

* TINTAGEL is the usual name. Gilbert, in his "Parochial History," has it, "DUNDAGELL, *alias* DYNDAGELL, *alias* BOSITHNEY;" in "Doomsday-book" it is called "DUNECHEINE." Tonkin writes "Dindagel or Daundagel," and sometimes DUNGIOGEL. "A King Nectan, or St Nectan, is said to have built numerous churches in several parts of Scotland, as well as in other parts of the kingdom of the Northern Picts."—*Wilson's Prehistoric Annals of Scotland.*

The river runs steadily along within a short distance of St Nectan's Chapel, and then it suddenly leaps over the rock—a beautiful fall of water—into St Nectan's Kieve. This deep rock-basin, brimming with the clearest water, overflows, and another waterfall carries the river to the lower level of the valley. Standing here within a circular wall of rocks, you see how the falling fluid has worked back the softer slate-rock until it has reached the harder masses, which are beautifully polished by the same agent. Mosses, ferns, and grasses decorate the fall, fringing every rock with a native drapery of the most exquisite beauty. Here is one of the wildest, one of the most untrained, and, at the same time, one of the most beautiful spots in Cornwall, full of poetry, and coloured by legend. Yet here comes prosaic man, and by one stroke of his everyday genius, he adds, indeed, a colour to the violet. You walk along the valley, through paths trodden out of the undergrowth, deviously wandering up hill, or down hill, as rock or tree has interposed. Many a spot of quiet beauty solicits you to loiter, and loitering, you feel that there are places from which the winds appear to gather poetry. You break the spell, or the ear, catching the murmur of the waters, dispels the illusions which have been created by the eye, and you wander forward anxious to reach the holy "Kieve,"—to visit the saint's hermitage. Here, say you, is the place to hold "commune with Nature's works, and view her charms unrolled," when, lo, a well-made door painted lead colour, with a real substantial lock, bars your way, and Fancy, with everything that is holy, flies away before the terrible words which inform you that trespassers will be punished, and that the key can be obtained at ——. Well was it that Mr Wilkie Collins gave "up the attempt to discover Nighton's Kieve;"* for had he, when he had found

* It is called indifferently Nectan, Nathan, Nighton, or Knighton's Kieve.

it, discovered this evidence of man's greedy soul, it would have convinced him that the "evil genius of fairy mythology," who so cautiously hid "the nymph of the waterfall," was no other than the farmer, who, as he told me, "owns the fee," and one who is resolved also, to pocket the fee, before any pilgrim can see the oratory and the waterfall of St Nectan. Of course this would have turned the placid current of the thoughts of "the Rambler beyond Railways," which now flow so pleasantly; into a troubled stream of biliary bitterness.

St Nectan placed in the little bell-tower of his secluded chapel a silver bell, the notes of which were so clear and penetrating that they could be heard far off at sea. When the notes came through the air, and fell on the ears of the seamen, they knew that St Nectan was about to pray for them, and they prostrated themselves before Heaven for a few minutes, and thus endeavoured to win the blessing.

St Nectan was on the bed of death. There was strife in the land. A severe struggle was going on between the Churchmen, and endeavours were being made to introduce a new faith.

The sunset of life gave to the saint the spirit of prophecy, and he told his weeping followers that the light of their religion would grow dim in the land; but that a spark would for ever live amidst the ashes, and that in due time it would kindle into a flame, and burn more brightly than ever. His silver bell, he said, should never ring for others than the true believer. He would enclose it in the rock of the Kieve; but when again the true faith revived, it should be recovered, and rung, to cheer once more the land.

One lovely summer evening, while the sun was slowly sinking towards the golden sea, St Nectan desired his attendants to carry him to the bank which overhung the "Kieve," and requested them to take the bell from the tower and bring it to him.

There he lay for some time in silent prayer, waiting as if for a sign, then slowly raising himself from the bed on which he had been placed, he grasped the silver bell. He rang it sharply and clearly three times, and then he dropped it into the transparent waters of the Kieve. He watched it disappear, and then he closed his eyes in death. On receiving the bell the waters were troubled, but they soon became clear as before, and the bell was nowhere to be seen. St Nectan died, and two strange ladies from a foreign land came and took possession of his oratory, and all that belonged unto the holy man. They placed—acting, as it was believed, on the wishes of the saint himself—his body, all the sacramental plate, and other sacred treasures, in a large oak chest. They turned the waters of the fall aside, and dug a grave in the river bed, below the Kieve, in which they placed this precious chest. The waters were then returned to their natural course, and they murmur ever above the grave of him who loved them. The silver bell was concealed in the Kieve, and the saint with all that belonged to his holy office rested beneath the river bed. The oratory was dismantled, and the two ladies, women evidently of high birth, chose it for their dwelling. Their seclusion was perfect. "Both appeared to be about the same age, and both were inflexibly taciturn. One was never seen without the other. If they ever left the house, they only left it to walk in the more unfrequented parts of the wood; they kept no servant; they never had a visitor; no living soul but themselves ever crossed the door of their cottage." * The berries of the wood, a few roots which they cultivated, with snails gathered from the rocks

* Rambles beyond Railways. By Wilkie Collins. Mr Collins was curiously misled by those who told him the tradition. The building which these strange solitary women inhabited was St Nectan's, or, as he and many others write it, St Nighton's, Chapel, and not a cottage. They died, as Mr

and walls, and fish caught in the stream, served them for food. Curiosity was excited, the mystery which hung around this solitary pair became deepened by the obstinate silence which they observed in everything relating to themselves. The result of all this was an anxious endeavour, on the part of the superstitious and ignorant peasantry, to learn their secret. All was now conjecture, and the imagination commonly enough filled in a wild picture: devils or angels, as the case might be, were seen ministering to the solitary ones. Prying eyes were upon them, but the spies could glean no knowledge. Week, month, year passed by, and ungratified curiosity was dying through want of food, when it was discovered that one of the ladies had died. The peasantry went in a body to the chapel; no one forbade their entering it now. There sat a silent mourner leaning over the placid face of her dead sister. Hers was, indeed, a silent sorrow—no tear was in her eye, no sigh hove her chest, but the face told all that a remediless woe had fallen on her heart. The dead body was eventually removed, the living sister making no sign, and they left her in her solitude alone. Days passed on; no one heard of, no one probably inquired after, the lonely one. At last a wandering child, curious as children are, clambered to the window of the cell and looked in. There sat the lady; her handkerchief was on the floor, and one hand hung strangely, as if endeavouring to pick it up, but powerless to do so. The child told its story—the people again flocked to the chapel, and they found one sister had followed the other. The people buried the last beside the first, and they left no mark to tell us where,

Collins describes it; but either he, or those from whom he learned the tale, has filled in the picture from imagination. I perceive, on referring to Mr Walter White's admirable little book, "A Londoner's Walk to the Land's-End," that he has made the same mistake about the cottage.

unless the large flat stone which lies in the valley, a short distance from the foot of the fall, and beneath which, I was told, "some great person was buried," may be the covering of their tomb. No traces of the history of these solitary women have ever been discovered.

Centuries have passed away, and still the legends of the buried bell and treasure are preserved. Some long time since a party of men resolved to blast the "Kieve," and examine it for the silver bell. They were miners, and their engineering knowledge, though rude, was sufficient to enable them to divert the course of the river above the falls, and thus to leave the "Kieve" dry for them to work on when they had emptied it, which was an easy task. The "borer" now rung upon the rock, holes were pierced, and, being charged, they were blasted. The result was, however, anything but satisfactory, for the rock remained intact. Still they persevered, until at length a voice was heard amidst the ring of the iron tools in the holes of the rock. Every hand was stayed, every face was aghast, as they heard distinctly the ring of the silver bell, followed by a clear solemn voice proclaiming, "The child is not yet born who shall recover this treasure."

The work was stopped, and the river restored to its old channel, over which it will run undisturbed until the day of which St Nectan prophesied shall arrive.

When, in the autumn of 1863, I visited this lovely spot, my guide, the proprietor, informed me that very recently a gentleman residing, I believe, in London, dreamed that an angel stood on a little bank of pebbles, forming a petty island, at the foot of a waterfall, and, pointing to a certain spot, told him to search there and he would find gold and a mummy. This gentleman told his dream to a friend, who at once declared the place indicated to be St Nectan's waterfall. Upon this, the dreamer visited the West, and, upon being led by the owner of the property to the fall, he at once recognised the spot on which the angel stood.

A plan was then and there arranged by which a search might be again commenced, it being thought that, as an angel had indicated the spot, the time for the recovery of the treasure had arrived.

Let us hope that the search may be deferred, lest the natural beauties of the spot should be destroyed by the meddling of men, who can threaten trespassers,—fearing to lose a sixpence,—and who have already endeavoured to improve on nature, by cutting down some of the rock and planting rhododendrons.

The Rev. R. S. Hawker, of Morwenstow, has published in his "Echoes of Old Cornwall" a poem on this tradition, which, as it is but little known, and as it has the true poetic ring, I transcribe to adorn the pages of my Appendix.*

THEODORE, KING OF CORNWALL.

RIVIERE, near Hayle, now called Rovier, was the palace of Theodore, the king, to whom Cornwall appears to have been indebted for many of its saints. This Christian king, when the pagan people sought to destroy the first missionaries, gave the saints shelter in his palace. St Breca, St Iva, St Burianna, and many others, are said to have made Riviere their residence. It is not a little curious to find traditions existing, as it were, in a state of suspension between opinions. I have heard it said that there was a church at Rovier—that there was once a great palace there; and again, that Castle Cayle was one vast fortified place, and Rovier another. Mr Davies Gilbert quotes Whitaker on this point :—

"Mr Whitaker, who captivates every reader by the brilliancy of his style, and astonishes by the extent of his multifarious reading, draws, however, without reserve, on his fertile imagination, for whatever facts may be requisite to construct the fabric of a theory. He has made Riviere the palace and residence of Theodore, a sovereign prince of Cornwall, and conducts St Breca, St Iva, with several companions, not only into Hayle and to this palace, after their voyage from Ireland, but fixes the time of their arrival so exactly, as to make it take place in the night. In recent times the name of Riviere, which had been lost in the common pronunciation, Rovier, has revived in a very excellent house built by Mr Edwards on the farm, which he completed in 1791." †

* Appendix D. † Parochial History, vol. iii. p. 423.

HOLY WELLS.

"A well there is in the west country,
And a clearer one never was seen."

ROBERT SOUTHEY.

SUPERSTITIONS OF THE WELLS.

WELL-WORSHIP.

> "One meek cell,
> Built by the fathers o'er a lonely well,
> Still breathes the Baptist's sweet remembrance round
> A spring of silent waters."
>
> *Echoes from Old Cornwall*—R. S. HAWKER.

A SPRING of water has always something about it which gives rise to holy feelings. From the dark earth there wells up a pellucid fluid, which in its apparent tranquil joyousness gives gladness to all around. The velvet mosses, the sword-like grasses, and the feathery ferns, grow with more of that light and vigorous nature which indicates a fulness of life, within the charmed influence of a spring of water, than they do elsewhere.

The purity of the fluid impresses itself, through the eye, upon the mind, and its power of removing all impurity is felt to the soul. "Wash and be clean," is the murmuring call of the waters, as they overflow their rocky basins, or grassy vases, and deeply sunk in depravity must that man be who could put to unholy uses one of nature's fountains. The inner life of a well of waters, bursting from its grave in the earth, may be religiously said to form a type of the soul purified by death, rising into a glorified existence and the fulness of light. The tranquil beauty of the rising waters, whispering the softest music, like the healthful breathing of a sleeping infant, sends a feeling of happiness through the soul of the thoughtful observer, and the inner man is purified by its influence, as the outer man is cleansed by ablution.

Water cannot be regarded as having an inanimate existence. Its all-pervading character and its active nature, flowing on for ever, resting never, removes it from the torpid elements, and places it, like the air, amongst those higher creations which belong to the vital powers of the earth. The spring of water rises from the cold dark earth, it runs, a silver cord glistening in the sunshine, down the mountain-side. The rill (prettily called by Drayton "a rillet") gathers rejoicingly other waters unto itself, and it grows into a *brooklet* in its course. At length, flowing onward and increasing in size, the *brook* state of being is fairly won; and then, by the gathering together of some more dewdrops, the full dignity of a stream is acquired. Onwards the waters flow, still gleaning from every side, and wooing new *runlets* to its bosom, eager as it were to assume the state which, in America, would be called a "run" of water. Stream gathers on stream, and run on run; the union of waters becomes a *river;* rolling in its maturity, swelling in its pride, it seeks the ocean, and there is absorbed in the eternity of waters. Has ever poet yet penned a line which in any way conveys to the mind a sense of the grandeur, the immensity of the sea? I do not remember a verse which does not prove the incapacity of the human mind to embrace in its vastness the gathering together of the waters in the mighty sea. Man's mind is tempered, and his pride subdued, as he stands on the sea-side and looks on the undulating expanse to which, to him, there is no end. A material eternity of rain-drops gathered into a mass which is from Omnipotence and is omnipotent. The influences of heaven falling on the sheeted waters, they rise at their bidding and float in air, making the skies more beautiful or more sublime, according to the spirit of the hour. Whether the clouds float over the earth, illumined by sun-rays, like the cars of loving angels; or rush wildly onward, as if bearing demons of vengeance, they are subdued by the mountains, and fall reluctantly as mists around the rocks, condense solemnly as dews upon the sleeping flowers, sink to earth resignedly as tranquil rains, or splash in tempestuous anger on its surface. The draught, in whatever form it comes, is drunk with avidity, and, circulating through the subterranean recesses of the globe, it does its work of re-creation, and eventually reappears a bubbling spring, again to run its round of wonder-working tasks.

Those minds which saw a God in light, and worshipped a Creator in the sun, felt the power of the universal solvent, and saw in the diffusive nature of that fluid which is everywhere, something more than a type of the regenerating Spirit, which all, in their holier hours, feel necessary to clear off the earthiness of life. Man has ever sought to discover the spiritual in the material, and, from the imperfections of human reason, he has too frequently reposed on the material, and given to it the attributes which are purely spiritual. Through all ages the fountains of the hills and valleys have claimed the reverence of men; and waters presenting themselves, under aspects of beauty, or of terror, have been regarded with religious feelings of hope or of awe.

As it was of old, so is it to-day. It was but yesterday that I stood near the font of Royston Church, and heard the minister read with emphasis, "None can enter into the kingdom of God except he be regenerate and born anew of water." Surely the simple faith of the peasant mother who, on a spring morning, takes her weakly infant to some holy well, and three times dipping it in its clear waters, uttering an earnest prayer at each immersion, is but another form of the prescribed faith of the educated churchman.

Surely the practice of consulting the waters of a sacred spring, by young men and maidens, is but a traditional faith derived from the early creeds of Greece—a continuance of the *Hydromancy* which sought in the Castalian fountain the divination of the future.

THE WELL OF ST CONSTANTINE.

IN the parish of St Merran, or Meryn, near Padstow, are the remains of the Church of St Constantine, and the holy well of that saint. It had been an unusually hot and dry summer, and all the crops were perishing through want of water. The people inhabiting the parish had grown irreligious, and many of them sadly profane. The drought was a curse upon them for their wickedness. Their church was falling into ruin, their well was foul, and the arches over it were decayed and broken. In their distress, the wicked people who had reviled the Word of God, went to their priest for aid.

"There is no help for thee, unless thou cleansest the holy well."

They laughed him to scorn.

The drought continued, and they suffered want.

To the priest they went again.

"Cleanse the well," was his command, "and see the power of the blessing of the first Christian emperor." That cleansing a dirty well should bring them rain they did not believe. The drought continued, the rivers were dry, the people suffered thirst.

"Cleanse the well—wash, and drink," said the priest, when they again went to him.

Hunger and thirst made the people obedient. They went to the task. Mosses and weeds were removed, and the filth cleansed. To the surprise of all, beautifully clear water welled forth. They drank the water and prayed, and then washed themselves, and were refreshed. As they bathed their bodies, parched with heat, in the cool stream which flowed from the well, the heavens clouded over, and presently rain fell, turning all hearts to the true faith.

THE WELL OF ST LUDGVAN.

ST LUDGVAN, an Irish missionary, had finished his work. On the hill-top, looking over the most beautiful of bays, the church stood with all its blessings. Yet the saint, knowing human nature, determined on associating with it some object of a miraculous character, which should draw people from all parts of the world to Ludgvan. The saint prayed over the dry earth, which was beneath him, as he knelt on the church stile. His prayer was for water, and presently a most beautiful crystal stream welled up from below. The holy man prayed on, and then, to try the virtues of the water, he washed his eyes. They were rendered at once more powerful, so penetrating, indeed, as to enable him to see microscopic objects. The saint prayed again, and then he drank of the water. He discovered that his powers of utterance were greatly improved, his tongue formed words with scarcely any effort of his will. The saint now prayed, that all children baptized in the waters of this well might be protected against the hangman and his hempen cord; and an angel from heaven came down into the water, and promised the saint that his prayers should be granted. Not long after this, a good farmer and his wife brought their babe to the saint, that it might derive all the blessings belonging to this holy well. The priest stood at the baptismal font, the parents, with their friends around. The saint proceeded with the baptismal ceremonial, and at length the time arrived when he took the tender babe into his holy arms. He signed the sign of the cross over the child, and when he sprinkled water on the face of the infant its face glowed with a divine intelligence. The priest then proceeded with the prayer; but, to the astonishment of all, whenever he used the name of Jesus, the child, who had received the miraculous power of speech, from the water, pronounced distinctly the name of the devil, much to the consternation of all present. The saint knew that an evil spirit had taken possession of the child, and he endeavoured to cast him out; but the devil proved stronger than the saint for some time. St Ludgvan was not to be beaten; he knew that the spirit was a restless soul, which had been exorcised from Treassow, and he exerted all his energies in prayer. At length the spirit became obedient, and left the child. He was now commanded by the saint to take his flight to the Red Sea. He rose, before the terrified spectators, into a gigantic size, he then spat into the well; he laid hold of the pinnacles of the tower, and shook the church until they thought it would fall. The saint was alone unmoved. He prayed on, until, like a flash of lightning, the demon vanished, shaking down a pinnacle in his flight. The demon, by spitting in the water destroyed the spells of the water upon the eyes* and the tongue too; but it fortunately retains its virtue of preventing any child baptized in it from being hanged with a cord of hemp. Upon a cord of silk it is stated to have no power.

* It is curious that the farm over which some of this water flows is called "Collurian" to this day.

This well had nearly lost its reputation once—a Ludgvan woman was hanged, under the circumstances told in the following narrative :—

A small farmer, living in one of the most western districts of the county, died some years back of what was supposed at that time to be "English cholera." A few weeks after his decease his wife married again. This circumstance excited some attention in the neighbourhood. It was remembered that the woman had lived on very bad terms with her late husband, that she had on many occasions exhibited strong symptoms of possessing a very vindictive temper, and that during the farmer's lifetime she had openly manifested rather more than a Platonic preference for the man whom she subsequently married. Suspicion was generally excited; people began to doubt whether the first husband had died fairly. At length the proper order was applied for, and his body was disinterred. On examination, enough arsenic to have poisoned three men was found in the stomach. The wife was accused of murdering her husband, was tried, convicted on the clearest evidence, and hanged. Very shortly after she had suffered capital punishment horrible stories of a ghost were widely circulated. Certain people declared that they had seen a ghastly resemblance of the murderess, robed in her winding-sheet, with the black mark of the rope round her swollen neck, standing on stormy nights upon her husband's grave, and digging there with a spade, in hideous imitation of the actions of the men who had disinterred the corpse for medical examination. This was fearful enough; nobody dared go near the place after nightfall. But soon another circumstance was talked of in connexion with the poisoner, which affected the tranquillity of people's minds in the village where she had lived, and where it was believed she had been born, more seriously than even the ghost story itself. The well of

St Ludgvan, celebrated among the peasantry of the district for its one remarkable property, that every child baptized in its water (with which the church was duly supplied on christening occasions) was secure from ever being hanged.

No one doubted that all the babies fortunate enough to be born and baptized in the parish, though they might live to the age of Methuselah, and might during that period commit all the capital crimes recorded in the "Newgate Calendar," were still destined to keep quite clear of the summary jurisdiction of Jack Ketch. No one doubted this until the story of the apparition of the murderess began to be spread abroad, then awful misgivings arose in the popular mind.

A woman who had been born close by the magical well, and who had therefore in all probability been baptized in its water, like her neighbours of the parish, had nevertheless been publicly and unquestionably hanged. However, probability is not always the truth. Every parishioner determined that the baptismal register of the poisoner should be sought for, and that it should be thus officially ascertained whether she had been christened with the well water or not. After much trouble, the important document was discovered—not where it was at first looked after, but in a neighbouring parish. A mistake had been made about the woman's birthplace; she had not been baptized in St Ludgvan church, and had therefore not been protected by the marvellous virtue of the local water. Unutterable was the joy and trinmph of this discovery. The wonderful character of the parish well was wonderfully vindicated; its celebrity immediately spread wider than ever. The peasantry of the neighbouring districts began to send for the renowned water before christenings; and many of them actually continue, to this day, to bring it corked up in bottles to their churches, and to beg particularly that it may be used whenever they present their children to be baptized.*

GULVAL WELL.

A YOUNG woman, with a child in her arms, stands by the side of Gulval Well, in Fosses Moor. There is an expression of extreme anxiety in her interesting face, which exhibits a considerable amount of intelligence. She appears to doubt, and yet be disposed to believe in, the virtues of this remarkable well. She pauses, looks at her babe, and sighs. She is longing to know something of the absent, but she fears the well may indicate the extreme of human sorrow. While she is hesitating, an old woman advances towards her, upon whom the weight of eighty years was pressing, but not over heavily; and she at once asked the young mother if she wished to ask the well after the health of her husband.

"Yes, Aunt Alcie," she replied; "I am so anxious. I have not heard of John for six long months. I could not sleep last night, so I rose with the light, and came here, determined to ask the well; but I am afraid. O Aunt Alcie, suppose the well should not speak, I should die on the spot!"

"Nonsense, cheeld," said the old woman; "thy man is well enough; and the well will boil, if thee 'lt ask it in a proper spirit."

"But, Aunt Alcie, if it sends up puddled water, or if it remains quiet, what would become of me?"

"Never be foreboding, cheeld; troubles come quick without running to meet 'em. Take my word for it, the fayther

* See another story of this wretched woman in the section devoted to Demons and Spectres. 1st Series.

of thy little un will soon be home again. Ask the well! ask the well!"

"Has it told any death or sickness lately?" asked the young mother.

"On St Peter's eve Mary Curnew questioned the water about poor Willy."

"And the water never moved?"

"The well was quiet; and verily I guess it was about that time he died."

"Any sickness, Aunt Alcie?"

"Jenny Kelinach was told, by a burst of mud, how ill her old mother was; but do not be feard, all is well with Johnny Thomas."

Still the woman hesitated; desire, fear, hope, doubt, superstition, and intelligence struggled within her heart and brain.

The old creature, who was a sort of guardian to the well, used all her rude eloquence to persuade Jane Thomas to put her question, and at length she consented. Obeying the old woman's directions, she knelt on the mat of bright green grass which grew around, and leaning over the well so as to see her face in the water, she repeated after her instructor,

> "Water, water, tell me truly,
> Is the man I love duly
> On the earth, or under the sod,
> Sick or well,—in the name of God!"

Some minutes passed in perfect silence, and anxiety was rapidly turning cheeks and lips pale, when the colour rapidly returned. There was a gush of clear water from below, bubble rapidly followed bubble, sparkling brightly in the morning sunshine. Full of joy, the young mother rose from her knees, kissed her child, and exclaimed, "I am happy now!"*

* Hals, speaking of Gulval Well, thus describes it and its virtues:—"In Fosses Moor, part of this manor of Lanesly, in this parish, is that well-

THE WELL OF ST KEYNE.

ST Keyne came to this well about five hundred years before the Norman Conquest, and imparted a strange virtue to its waters—namely, that whichever of a newly-married couple should first drink thereof, was to enjoy the sweetness of domestic sovereignty ever after.

Situated in a thickly-wooded district, the well of St Keyne presents a singularly picturesque appearance. "Four trees of divers kinds," grow over the well, imparting a delightful shade, and its clear waters spread an emerald luxuriance around. Once, and once only, have I paid a visit to this sacred spot. Then and there I found a lady drinking of the waters from her thimble, and eagerly contending with her husband, that the right to rule was hers. The man, however, mildly insisted upon it that he had had the first drink, as he had rushed before his wife, and dipping his fingers into the waters, had sucked them. This the lady

known fountain called Gulval Well. To which place great numbers of people, time out of mind, have resorted for pleasure and profit of their health, as the credulous country people do in these days, not only to drink the waters thereof, but to inquire after the life or death of their absent friends; where, being arrived, they demanded the question at the well whether such a person by name be living, in health, sick, or dead. If the party be living and in health, the still quiet water of the well-pit, as soon as the question is demanded, will instantly bubble or boil up as a pot, clear crystalline water; if sick, foul and puddle waters; if the party be dead, it will neither bubble, boil up, nor alter its colour or still motion. However, I can speak nothing of the truth of those supernatural facts from my own sight or experience, but write from the mouths of those who told me they had seen and proved the veracity thereof. Finally, it is a strong and courageous fountain of water, kept neat and clean by an old woman of the vicinity, to accommodate strangers, for her own advantage, by blazing the virtues and divine qualities of those waters."—*Hals, quoted by Gilbert, Parochial History of Cornwall*, vol. ii. p. 121.

contended was not drinking, and she, I have no doubt, through life had the best of the argument.

Tonkin says, in his "History of Cornwall," "Did it retain this wondrous quality, as it does to this day the shape, I believe there would be to it a greater resort of both sexes than either to Bath or Tunbridge; for who would not be fond of attaining this longed-for sovereignty?" He then adds, "Since the writing of this, the trees were blown down by a violent storm, and in their place Mr Rashleigh, in whose land it is, has planted two oaks, an ash, and an elm, which thrive well; but the wonderful arch is destroyed." The author can add to this that (as he supposes, owing to the alteration made in the trees) the sovereign virtues of the waters have perished.

Southey's ballad will be remembered by most readers:—

"A well there is in the west country,
And a clearer one never was seen;
There is not a wife in the west country
But has heard of the Well of St Keyne.

"An oak and an elm-tree stand beside,
And behind doth an ash-tree grow,
And a willow from the bank above
Droops to the water below."

It has been already stated that, sitting in St Michael's Chair, on the tower of the church of St Michael's Mount, has the same virtue as the waters of this well; and that this remarkable power was the gift of the same St Keyne who imparted such wonderful properties to this well.

MADDERN OR MADRON WELL.

> "Plunge thy right hand in St Madron's spring,
> If true to its troth be the palm you bring;
> But if a false digit thy fingers bear,
> Lay them at once on the burning share."

OF the holy well at St Maddern, Carne * writes thus:—

"It has been contended that a virgin was the patroness of this church—that she was buried at Minster—and that many miracles were performed at her grave. A learned commentator, however, is satisfied that it was St Motran, who was one of the large company that did come from Ireland with St Buriana, and he was slain at the mouth of the Hayle; the body was begged, and afterwards buried here. Near by was the miraculous Well of St Maddern, over which a chapel was built, so sacred was it held. (This chapel was destroyed by the fanaticism of Major Ceely in the days of Cromwell.) It stood at no great distance on the moor, and the soil around it was black and boggy, mingled with a gray moorstone. . . .

"The votaries bent awfully and tremblingly over its sedgy bank, and gazed on its clear bosom for a few minutes ere they proved the fatal ordeal; then an imploring look was cast towards the figure of St Motran, many a crossing was repeated, and at last the pin or pebble held aloof was dropped into the depth beneath. Often did the rustic beauty fix her eye intently on the bubbles that rose, and broke, and disappeared; for in that moment the lover was lost, or the faithful husband gained. It was only on particular days, however, according to the increase or decrease of the moon, that the hidden virtues of the well were consulted." †

* "Tales of the West," by the author of "Letters from the East."

† The tale of "The Legend of Pacorra."

MADRON WELL.

Of this well we have the following notice by William Scawen, Esq., Vice-Warden of the Stannaries. The paper from which we extract it, was first printed by Davies Gilbert, Esq., F.R.S., as an appendix to his "Parochial History of Cornwall." Its complete title is, "Observations on an Ancient Manuscript, entitled 'Passio Christo,' written in the Cornish Language, and now preserved in the Bodelian Library; with an Account of the Language, Manners, and Customs of the People of Cornwall, (from a Manuscript in the Library of Thomas Artle, Esq., 1777)":—

"Of St Mardren's Well, (which is a parish west to the Mount,) a fresh true story of two persons, both of them lame and decrepit, thus recovered from their infirmity. These two persons, after they had applied themselves to divers physicians and chirurgeons, for cure, and finding no success by them, they resorted to St Mardren's Well, and according to the ancient custom which they had heard of, the same which was once in a year—to wit, on Corpus Christi evening, to lay some small offering on the altar there, and to lie on the ground all night, drink of the water there, and in the morning after to take a good draught more, and to take and carry away some of the water, each of them in a bottle, at their departure. This course these two men followed, and within three weeks they found the effect of it, and, by degrees their strength increasing, were able to move themselves on crutches. The year following they took the same course again, after which they were able to go with the help of a stick; and at length one of them, John Thomas, being a fisherman, was, and is at this day, able to follow his fishing craft. The other, whose name was William Cork, was a soldier under the command of my kinsman, Colonel William Godolphin, (as he has often told me,) was able to perform his duty, and died in the service of his majesty King Charles. But herewith take also this:—

"One Mr Hutchens, a person well known in those parts, and now lately dead, being parson of Ludgvan, a near neighbouring parish to St Mardren's Well, he observed that many of his parishioners often frequented this well superstitiously, for which he reproved them privately, and sometimes publicly, in his sermons; but afterwards he, the said Mr Hutchens, meeting with a woman coming from the well with a bottle in her hand, desired her earnestly that he might drink thereof, being then troubled with cholical pains, which accordingly he did, and was eased of his infirmity. The latter story is a full confutation of the former; for, if the taking the water accidentally thus prevailed upon the party to his cure, as it is likely it did, then the miracle which was intended to be by the ceremony of lying on the ground and offering is wholly fled, and it leaves the virtue of the water to be the true cause of the cure. And we have here, as in many places of the land, great variety of salutary springs, which have diversity of operations, which by natural reason have been found to be productive of good effects, and not by miracle, as the vain fancies of monks and friars have been exercised in heretofore.

Bishop Hale, of Exeter, in his "Great Mystery of Godliness," says:—"Of which kind was that noe less than miraculous cure, which, at St Maddern's Well, in Cornwall, was wrought upon a poore cripple; whereof, besides the attestation of many hundreds of the neighbours, I tooke a strict and impartial examination in my last triennial visitation there. This man, for sixteen years, was forced to walke upon his hands, by reason of the sinews of his leggs were soe contracted that he cold not goe or walke on his feet, who upon monition in a dream to wash in that well, which accordingly he did, was suddainly restored to the use of his limbs; and I sawe him both able to walk and gett his owne maintenance. I found here was neither art or collusion,—the cure done, the author our invisible God," &c.

In Madron Well—and, I have no doubt, in many others—may be found frequently the pins which have been dropped by maidens desirous of knowing "when they were to be married." I once witnessed the whole ceremony performed by a group of beautiful girls, who had walked on a May morning from Penzance. Two pieces of straw, about an inch long each, were crossed and the pin run through them. This cross was then dropped into the water, and the rising bubbles carefully counted, as they marked the number of years which would pass ere the arrival of the happy day. This practice also prevailed amongst the visitors to the well at the foot of Monacuddle Grove, near St Austell.

On approaching the waters, each visitor is expected to throw in a crooked pin; and, if you are lucky, you may possibly see the other pins rising from the bottom to meet the most recent offering. Rags and votive offerings to the genius of the waters are hung around many of the wells. Mr Couch says:—"At Madron Well, near Penzance, I observed the custom of hanging rags on the thorns which grew in the enclosure."

Crofton Croker tells us the same custom prevails in Ireland; and Dr O'Connor, in his "Travels in Persia," describes the prevalence of this custom.

Mr Campbell,* on this subject, writes:—"Holy healing wells are common all over the Highlands, and people still leave offerings of pins and nails, and bits of rag, though few would confess it. There is a well in Islay where I myself have, after drinking, deposited copper caps amongst a hoard of pins and buttons, and similar gear, placed in chinks in the rocks and trees at the edge of the 'Witches' Well.' There is another well with similar offerings freshly placed beside it, in an island in Loch Maree, in Ross-shire, and many similar wells are to be found in other places in Scotland. For example, I learn from Suther-

* "Popular Tales of the West Highlands," by J. F. Campbell. (See page 134, vol. ii.)

land that 'a well in the Black Isle of Cromarty, near Rosehaugh, has miraculous healing powers. A country woman tells me, that about forty years ago, she remembers it being surrounded by a crowd of people every first Tuesday in June, who bathed and drank of it before sunrise. Each patient tied a string or rag to one of the trees that overhung it before leaving. It was sovereign for headaches. Mr —— remembers to have seen a well, here called Mary's Well, hung round with votive rags.'"

Well-worship is mentioned by Martin. The custom, in his day, in the Hebrides, was to walk south round about the well.

Sir William Betham, in his "Gael and Cymbri," (Dublin: W. Curry, Jun., & Co., 1834,) says, at page 235:—"The Celtæ were much addicted to the worship of fountains and rivers as divinities. They had a deity called Divona, or the river-god."

THE WELL AT ALTAR-NUN.

CURE OF INSANITY.

AMONGST the numerous holy wells which exist in Cornwall, that of Alternon, or Altar-Nun, is the only one, as far as I can learn, which possessed the virtue of curing the insane.

We are told that Saint Nunne or Nuanita was the daughter of an Earl of Cornwall, and the mother of St David; that the holy well, which is situated about a mile from the cathedral of St David, was dedicated to her; and that she bestowed on the waters of the Cornish well those remarkable powers, which were not given to the Welsh one, from her fondness for the county of her birth.

Carew, in his "Survey of Cornwall," thus describes the practice:—

"The water running from St Nun's well fell into a square and enclosed walled plot, which might be filled at what depth they listed. Upon this wall was the frantic person put to stand, his back towards the pool, and from thence, with a sudden blow in the breast, tumbled headlong into the pond; where a strong fellow, provided for the nonce, took him, and tossed him up and down, alongst and athwart the water, till the patient, by foregoing his strength, had somewhat forgot his fury. Then was he conveyed to the church, and certain masses said over him: upon which handling, if his right wits returned, St Nun had the thanks; but if there appeared small amendment, he was bowssened again and again, while there remained in him any hope of life or recovery."

The 2d of March is dedicated to St Nun, and the influence of the water is greatly exalted on that day.

Although St Nun's well has been long famous, and the celebrity of its waters extended far, yet there was a belief prevailing amidst the uneducated, that the sudden shock produced by suddenly plunging an insane person into water was most effective in producing a return to reason.

On one occasion, a woman of weak mind, who was suffering under the influence of a religious monomania, consulted me on the benefit she might hope to receive from electricity. The burden of her ever-melancholy tale was, that "she had lost her God;" and she told me, with a strange mixture of incoherence and reason, that her conviction was that a sudden shock would cure her. She had herself proposed to her husband and friends that they should take her to a certain rock on St Michael's Mount, stand her on it, with her back to the sea, when "the waters were the strongest, at the flowing of the tide;" and after having prayed with her, give her the necessary blow on the chest, and thus plunge her into the waters below. I know not that the experiment was ever made in the case of this poor woman, but I have heard of several instances where this sudden plunge had been tried as a cure for insanity.

Mr T. Q. Couch thus describes the present condition of this well in a paper on "Well-Worship:"—*

* Notes and Queries.

"On the western side of the beautiful valley through which flows the Trelawney River, and near Hobb's Park, in the parish of Pelynt, Cornwall, is St Nun's, or St Ninnie's Well. Its position was, until lately, to be discovered by the oak-tree matted with ivy, and the thicket of willow and bramble which grew upon its roof. The front of the well is of a pointed form, and has a rude entrance about four feet high, and spanned above by a single flat stone, which leads into a grotto with arched roof. The walls on the interior are draped with luxuriant fronds of spleenwort, hart's tongue, and a rich undercovering of liverwort. At the further end of the floor is a round granite basin, with a deeply moulded brim, and ornamented on its circumference with a series of rings, each enclosing a cross or a ball. The water weeps into it from an opening at the back, and escapes again by a hole in the bottom. This interesting piece of antiquity has been protected by a tradition which we could wish to attach to some of our cromlechs and circles in danger of spoliation."

According to the narrative given by Mr Bond in his "History of Looe," the sacred protection given must have been limited in time, as the following story will prove :—

"KIPPISCOMBE LANE,

Probably so called from a consecrated well on the right hand side of the road. The titular saint of this well is supposed to have been St Cuby, now corrupted into Keby's Well. The spring flows into a circular basin or reservoir of granite, or of some stone like it, two feet four inches at its extreme diameter at top, and about two feet high. It appears to have been neatly carved and ornamented in its lower part with the figure of a griffin, and round the edge with dolphins, now much defaced. The water was formerly carried off by a drain or hole at the bottom, like those usually seen in fonts and piscinas. This basin (which I take to be an old font) was formerly much respected by the neighbours, who conceived some great misfortune would befall the person who should attempt to remove it from where it stood, and that it required immense power to remove it. A daring fellow, however, (says a story,) once went with a team of oxen for the express purpose of removing it. On his arrival at the spot, one of the oxen fell down dead, which so alarmed the fellow that he desisted from the attempt he was about to make. There are several loose stones scattered round this basin or reservoir, perhaps the remains of some building which formerly enclosed it—a small chapel likely. The last time I saw this reservoir it had been taken many feet from where it used to stand, and a piece of the brim of it had been recently struck off."

ST GUNDRED'S WELL AT ROACH ROCK.

CAREW, in his "Survey of Cornwall," p. 139, (p. 324, Lord Dunstanville's edit.,) tells us, "near this rock there is another which, having a pit in it, containeth water which ebbs and flows as the sea does. I was thereupon very curious to inspect this matter, and found it was only a hole artificially cut in a stone, about twelve inches deep and six broad; wherein after rayne, a pool of water stands, which afterwards with fair weather vanisheth away, and is dried up; and then again, on the falling of rain, water is replenished accordingly, which with dry weather abates as aforesaid, (for upon those occasions I have seen it to have water in its pit, and again to be without it,) which doubtless gave occasion to the feigned report that it ebbs and flows as the sea:" of all which premisses thus speaks Mr Carew further, out of the Cornish "Wonder Gatherer":—

"You neighbour scorners, holy, proud,
Goe people Roache's cell,
Far from the world and neer to the heavens;
There hermitts may you dwell.

"Is 't true the springe in rock hereby
Doth tidewise ebb and flowe?
Or have we fooles with lyars met?
Fame says its, be it soe."

The last tradition of this hermitage chapel is, that when it was kept in repair, a person diseased with a grievous leprosy, was either placed or fixed himself therein, where he lived until the time of his death, to avoid infecting others. He was daily attended with meat, drink, and washing by his daughter, named Gunnett or Gundred, and the well hereby from whence she fetched water for his use is to this day shewn, and called by the name of St Gunnett's Well, or St Gundred's Well.

It is not possible to give even the names of the wells which are still thought to have "some healing virtue" in them. The typical wells have alone been mentioned, and to these brief notices of a few others may be added.

ST CUTHBERT'S OR CUBERT'S WELL.

HAL thus describes this famous place:—"In this parish is that famous and well-known spring of water, called Holy-well, (so named, the inhabitants say, for that the virtues of this water was first discovered on All-Hallows day.) The same stands in a dark cavern of the seacliff rocks, beneath full seamark on spring-tides, from the top of which cavern falls down or distills continually drops of water from the white, blue, red, and green veins of those rocks. And accordingly, in the place where those drops of water fall, it swells to a lump of considerable bigness, and there petrifies to the hardness of ice, glass, or freestone, of the several colours aforesaid, according to the nature of those veins in the rock from whence it proceeds, and is of a hard, brittle nature, apt to break like glass.

"The virtues of this water are very great. It is incredible what numbers in summer-season frequent this place and waters from counties far distant." *

RICKETY CHILDREN.

THE practice of bathing rickety children on the first three Wednesdays in May is still far from uncommon in the outlying districts of Cornwall. The parents will walk many miles for the purpose of dipping the little sufferers in some well, from which the "healing virtue" has not entirely departed. Among these holy wells, Cubert, just named, is far-famed. To this well the peasantry still resort, firm in the faith that there, at this especial season, some mysterious virtue is communicated to its waters. On these occasions, only a few years since, the crowd assembled was so large, that it assumed the character of a fair.

CHAPELL UNY.

ON the first three Wednesdays in May, children suffering from mesenteric diseases are dipped three times in this well, *against the sun*, and *dragged* three times around the well on the grass, in the same direction.

* Gilbert, vol. i. p. 291.

PERRAN WELL.

CHILDREN were cured of several diseases by being bathed in this well. They were also carried to the sea-shore, and passed through a cleft in a rock on the shore at Perranzabalo. In the autumn of 1863 I sought for these holy waters. I was informed that some miners, in driving an adit, had tapped the spring and drained it. There is not, therefore, a trace of this once most celebrated well remaining. It was with difficulty that its site could be discovered. I have since learned that the cut stone-work which ornamented this holy place, was removed to Chiverton, for the purpose of preserving it.

REDRUTH WELL.

NO child christened in this well has ever been hanged. Saint Ruth, said to have been called Red Ruth, because she always wore a scarlet cloak, especially blessed, to this extent, those waters. I believe the population in this large parish cares but little now, whether their children be baptized with this well water or any other; but, half a century since, it was very different. Then, many a parent would insist on seeing the water taken from the well and carried to the font in the church.

HOLY WELL AT LITTLE CONAN.

ON Palm Sunday the people resorted to the well sacred to "Our Lady of Nant's," with a cross of palm, and after making the priest a present, they were allowed to throw the cross into the well; if it swam the thrower was to outlive the year, if it sank he was not.*

* Carew.

THE PRESERVATION OF HOLY WELLS.

IT is a very common notion amongst the peasantry, that a just retribution overtakes those who wilfully destroy monuments, such as stone circles, crosses, wells, and the like. Mr Blight writes me—"Whilst at Boscaswell, in St Just, a few weeks since, an old man told me, that a person who altered an old Holy Well there, was drowned the next day in sight of his home, and that a person who carried away the stones of an ancient chapel, had his house burned down that very night." We hope the certainty of punishment will prevent any further spoliation. Cannot we do something towards the preservation of our antiquities? I quote from a local paper the following :—

"If the attention of the members of the Penzance Antiquarian Society were directed to the state of the 'Holy Well' at Laneast, and the remains of the Old Chapel Park, St Clether, they might perhaps induce the proprietors of these 'remnants of antiquity' to bestow a little care on the same, and arrest their further ruin and destruction. Many other 'objects of interest' are in a sad state of neglect, and fast 'fading away.' Slaughtor Bridge, near Camelford, has completely vanished. This is much to be regretted, and is a double loss—first, to those who delight in these 'memorials of the past,' and also to the town and neighbourhood, depriving them of an attraction that has induced many strangers of taste to pay them a visit."

KING ARTHUR.

"There is a place within
  The winding shore of Severne sea
On mids of rock, about whose foote
  The tydes turne—keeping play.
A towery-topped castle here,
  Wide blazeth over all,
Which Corineus ancient broode
  Tintagel Castle call."

Old Poet—Translated by CAMDEN.

ROMANCES OF ARTHUR.

ARTHUR LEGENDS.

"For there was no man knew from whence he came;
But after tempest, when the long wave broke
All down the thundering shores of Bude and Boss,
There came a day as still as heaven, and then
They found a naked child upon the sands
Of wild Dundagil by the Cornish sea;
And that was Arthur."
Idyls of the King—TENNYSON.

THE scarcity of traditions connected with King Arthur is not a little remarkable in Cornwall, where he is said to have been born, and where we believe him to have been killed. In the autumn of last year (1863) I visited Tintagel and Camelford. I sought with anxiety for some stories of the British king, but not one could be obtained. The man who has charge of the ruins of the castle—was very sorry that he had lent a book which he once had, and which contained many curious stories, but he had no story to tell me.

We hear of Prince Arthur at the Land's End, and of his fights with the Danes in two or three other places. Merlin, who may be considered as especially associated with Arthur, has left indications of his presence here and there, in prophetic rhymes not always fulfilled; but of Arthur's chieftains we have no folk-lore. All the rock markings, or rock peculiarities, which would in West Cornwall have been given to the giants, are referred to King Arthur in the eastern districts.

Jack the Giant Killer and Thomas Thumb—the former having been tutor, in his own especial calling, to King Arthur's only son,* and the latter the king's favourite dwarf †—are, except in story-books, unknown. Jack Hornby,‡—if he ever lived near the Land's End, unless he is the same with "Little Jack Horner,"—has been so long a stranger, that his name is forgotten.

The continuance of a fixed belief in the existence of Arthur is easily explained. The poets and the romance writers have made the achievements of a British chieftain familiar to all the people; and Arthur has not only a name, but a local habitation given to him equally in Scotland, England, Wales, and Ireland.

Mr Campbell, in his "West Highland Tales," gives a "Genealogy Abridgment of the very ancient and noble family of Argyle, 1779." The writer says this family began with Constantine, grandfather to King Arthur; and he informs us that Sir Moroie Mor, a son of King Arthur, of whom great and strange things are told in the Irish traditions—who was born at Dumbarton Castle, and who was usually known as "The Fool of the Forest"—was the real progenitor of "Mac Callen Mor." From this Moroie Mor was derived the mighty Diarmaid, celebrated in many a Gaelic lay—"to whom all popular traditions trace the Campbell clan."

* "Popular Rhymes and Nursery Tales," by James O. Halliwell.

† See "Thomas of the Thumb, or *Tòmas na h'ordaig,*" Tale lxix. "Popular Tales of the West Highlands," by J. F. Campbell.

‡ "Popular Rhymes and Nursery Tales," by James O. Halliwell.

"Arthur and Diarmaid," writes Mr Campbell, "primeval Celtic worthies, whose very existence the historian ignores, are thus brought together by a family genealogist."

"Was the Constantine grandfather to Arthur one of the five tyrants named by Gildas?"—I quote from Camden * and Milton.†

Constantinus, son of Cador, Duke of Cornwall, Arthur's half-brother by the mother's side, "a tyrannical and bloody king."

Aurelius Conanus, who "wallowed in murder and adultery."

Vortipore, "tyrant of the Dimeta."

Cuneglas, "the yellow butcher."

Maglocunes, "the island dragon."

It is curious to find a Scotch genealogist uniting in one bond the Arthur of Dundagel and the ancestors of the Argyles of Dumbarton.

May we not after this venture to suggest that, in all probability, the parish of Constantine, pronounced, however, *Cus-ten-ton,*) between Helstone and Penryn, may derive its name from this Constantinus, rather than from the first Christian emperor.

Again, the family of Cossentine has been often said to be offsets from Constantine, the descendant of the Greek emperors, who was buried in Landulph church. Seeing that the name has been known for so long a period in Cornwall, may not this family rather trace their origin up to this Constantine the Tyrant?

* Camden's "Britannica," by Gough, vol. i., p. 139. From this author we do not learn much. Indeed he says—"As to that Constantine, whom Gildas calls 'that tyrannical whelp of the impure Danmonian lioness,' and of the disforesting of the whole country under King John, before whose time it was all forest, let historians tell—it is not to my purpose." vol. i. p. 8.

† Milton's "History of Britain," edit. 1678, p. 155.

THE BATTLE OF VELLAN-DRUCHAR.*

THE Sea Kings, in their predatory wanderings, landed in Genvor Cove, and, as they had frequently done on previous occasions, they proceeded to pillage the little hamlet of Escols. On one occasion they landed in unusually large numbers, being resolved, as it appeared, to spoil many of the large and wealthy towns of Western Cornwall, which they were led to believe were unprotected. It fortunately happened that the heavy surf on the beach retarded their landing, so that the inhabitants had notice of their threatened invasion.

That night the beacon fire was lit on the chapel hill, another was soon blazing on Castle-an-dinas, and on Trecrobben. Carn Brea promptly replied, and continued the signal-light, which also blazed lustrously that night on St Agnes Beacon. Presently the fires were seen on Belovely Beacon, and rapidly they appeared on the Great Stone, on St Bellarmine's Tor, and Cadbarrow, and then the fires blazed out on Roughtor and Brownwilly, thus rapidly conveying the intelligence of war to Prince Arthur and his brave knights, who were happily assembled in full force at Tintagel to do honour to several native Princes who were at that time on a visit to the King of Cornwall. Arthur, and nine other kings, by fórced marches, reached the neighbourhood of the Land's-End at the end of two days. The Danes crossed the land down through the bottoms to the sea on the northern side of the promontory, spreading destruction in their paths. Arthur met them on their return, and gave them battle near Vellan-Druchar. So terrible was the slaughter, that the mill was worked with blood that day. Not a single Dane of the vast army that had landed escaped. A few had been left in charge of the ships, and as soon as

* Vellan (mill), druchar (wheel.)

they learned the fate of their brethren, they hastened to escape, hoping to return to their own northern land. A holy woman, whose name has not been preserved to us, "brought home a west wind" by emptying the Holy Well against the hill, and sweeping the church from the door to the altar. Thus they were prevented from escaping, and were all thrown by the force of a storm and the currents either on the rocky shore, or on the sands, where they were left high and dry. It happened on the occasion of an extraordinary spring-tide, which was yet increased by the wind, so that the ships lay high up on the rocks, or on the sands; and for years the birds built their nests in the masts and rigging.

Thus perished the last army of Danes who dared to land upon our western shores.

King Arthur and the nine kings pledged each other in the holy water from St Sennen's Well, they returned thanks for their victory in St Sennen's Chapel, and dined that day on the Table-men.

Merlin, the prophet, was amongst the host, and the feast being ended, he was seized with the prophetic afflatus, and in the hearing of all the host proclaimed—

"The northmen wild once more shall land,
And leave their bones on Escol's sand.
The soil of Vellan-Druchar's plain,
Again shall take a sanguine stain;
And o'er the mill wheel roll a flood
Of Danish mixed with Cornish blood.
When thus the vanquished find no tomb,
Expect the dreadful day of doom."

ARTHUR ATTHE LAND'S-END.

BOLERIUM, or *Bellerium,* is the name given by the ancients to the Land's-End. Diodorus writes, Belerium; Ptolemy, Bolerium. Milton adopts this name in his

"Lycidas," and leads his readers to infer that it was derived from the Giant Bellerus. It is quite possible that in Milton's time the name of one of the numerous giants who appear to have made the Land's-End district their dwelling-place, might have still lived in the memories of men. Certain it is no such a giant is remembered now.*

In a map of Saxon England we find the Land's-End called Penƿiðſteoꞃt, and in some early English books this promontory is named *Penrhin-guard*, and *Penrlien-gard*, said to signify the "Headland of Blood."† The old Cornish people called this promontory "Pen-von-las," the "End of the Earth," hence we derive the name of the Land's-End. May not this sanguinary name have been derived from a fact, and that actually several battles were fought by the Britons under the command of Arthur, with the Saxons or the Danes, in this neighbourhood? We have not far off the *Field of Slaughter*, "Bollait," where the ancient people of Cornwall made their final stand against the Saxons. On this field flint arrow-heads have frequently been found. The tradition of Vellan-Druchar, which is but one of several I have heard of a similar character, points to the same idea. Arthur, according to one story, held possession of Trereen Castle for some time. Another castle on the north coast is said to have been occupied by him. An old man living in Pendean once told me that the land at one time "swarmed with giants, until Arthur, the good king, vanished them all with his cross-sword."

* Carew says, "a promontory, (by *Pomp. Mela*, called Bolerium; by *Diodorus*, Velerium; by *Volaterane*, Helenium; by the Cornish, Pedn an laaz; and by the English, the Land's-End.)"—*Survey of Cornwall.*

† Penƿiðſteoꞃt.—The name of the Land's-End in the Saxon map; in the text, Camden prints Penƿihtſteoꞃt.

TRADITIONS OF THE DANES IN CORNWALL.

THE Danes are said to have landed in several places around the coast, and have made permanent settlements in some parts. We have already spoken of the battle of Vellandruchar. In Sennen Cove there was for a long period a colony of red-haired people,—indeed, I am iuformed some of them still live on the spot,—with whom the other inhabitants of the district refused to marry. Up to a very recent period, in several of the outlying villages, a red-haired family was "looked down" upon. "Oh, he or she is a red-haired Daäne," was a common expression of contempt.

There are several hills which bear the names of Danes' castles—as Castle-an-Dinas, near Penzance, and another in St Columb.* Another very remarkable earthwork in Perran Zabula (*Caer-Dane*) is described by Hals.†

* "CASTELL-AN-DINAS.—In the parish of St Colomb Major stands a castle of this name. Near this castle, by the highway, stands the Coyt, a stony tumulus so called, of which sort there are many in Wales and Wiltshire, as is mentioned in the 'Additions to Camden's Britannia' in these places, commonly called the Devil's Coyts. It consists of four long stones of great bigness, perpendicularly pitched in the earth contiguous with each other, leaving only a small vacancy downwards, but meeting together at the top; over all which is laid a flat stone of prodigious bulk and magnitude, bending towards the east in way of adoration, (as Mr Lhuyd concludes of all those Coyts elsewhere,) as the person therein under it interred did when in the land of the living; but how or by what art this prodigious flat stone should be placed on the top of the others, amazeth the wisest mathematicians, engineers, or architects to tell or conjecture. Colt, in Belgic-British, is a cave, vault, or cott-house, of which coyt might possibly be a corruption."—*Gilbert's Parochial History.*

† In the Manor of Lambourn is an ancient barrow, called Creeg Mear, the Great Barrow, which was cut open by a labourer in search of stones to build a hedge. He came upon a small hollow, in which he found nine urns filled with ashes; the man broke them, supposing they were only old pitchers, good for nothing; but Tonkin, who saw them, believes them to have been Danish, containing the ashes of some chief commanders slain in battle; and, says he, on a small hill just under this barrow is a Danish

Eventually the Danes are said to have made permanent settlements in Cornwall, and to have lived on friendly terms with the Britons.

The Danes and the Cornish are reported to have concentrated their forces to oppose Egbert the Saxon. In 835 the combined body are reported to have met, and fought a pitched battle on Hengistendane, (now Hengistondown,) near Callington. The Cornish were so totally routed, that Egbert obliged the Danes to retire to their ships, and passed a law "that no Briton should in future cross the Tamar, or set foot on English ground, on pain of death."*

In 997 the Danes, sailing about Penwrith-steort, landed in several places, foraged the country, burnt the towns, and destroyed the people.†

Many of the traditions which are given in different parts of these volumes have much of the Danish element in them.‡

KING ARTHUR IN THE FORM OF A CHOUGH.

I QUOTE the following as it stands:—§

"In Jarvis's translation of "Don Quixote," book ii., chap. v., the following passage occurs:—

encampment, called Castle Caer Dane, vulgo Castle Caer Don,—*i.e.*, the Danes' Camp,—consisting of three entrenchments finished, and another begun, with an intent to surround the inner three, but not completed; and opposite to this, about a bowshot, the river only running between, on another hill is another camp or castle, called Castle Kaerkief, castrum simile, from Kyfel similis, alike alluding to Castle Caer Dane. But this is but just begun, and not finished in any part, from which I guess there were two different parties, the one attacking the other before the entrenchments were finished.

* C. S. Gilbert's Historical Survey. † Gilbert.

‡ See Popular Tales from the Norse. By George Webbe Dasent, D.C.L. Legends of Iceland, collected by Jón Arnason. Translated by George E. J. Powell and Eirékur Magnússon.

§ *Notes and Queries*, vol. viii. p. 618.

"'Have you not read, sir,' answered Don Quixote, 'the annals and histories of England, wherein are recorded the famous exploits of King Arthur, whom, in our Castilian tongue, we always call King Artus; of whom there goes an old tradition, and a common one all over that kingdom of Great Britain, that this king did not die, but that, by magic art, he was turned into a raven; and that, in process of time, he shall reign again and recover his kingdom and sceptre, for which reason it cannot be proved that, from that time to this, any Englishman has killed a raven?'

"My reason for transcribing this passage is to record the curious fact that the legend of King Arthur's existence in the form of a raven was still repeated as a piece of folk lore in Cornwall about sixty years ago. My father, who died about two years since, at the age of eighty, spent a few years of his youth in the neighbourhood of Penzance. One day he was walking along Marazion Green with his fowling-piece on his shoulder, he saw a raven at a distance, and fired at it. An old man who was near immediately rebuked him, telling him that he ought on no account to have shot at a raven, for that King Arthur was still alive in the form of that bird. My father was much interested when I drew his attention to the passage which I have quoted above.

"Perhaps some of your Cornish or Welsh correspondents may be able to say whether the legend is still known among the people of Cornwall or Wales.

"EDGAR MACCULLOCH."

"GUERNSEY."

I have been most desirous of discovering if any such legend as the above exists. I have questioned people in every part of Cornwall in which King Arthur has been reported to have dwelt or fought, and especially have I inquired in the neighbourhood of Tintagel, which is reported to have been Arthur's stronghold. Nowhere do I find the raven associated with him, but I have been told that bad luck would follow the man who killed a Chough, for Arthur was transformed into one of these birds.

THE CORNISH CHOUGH.

THE tradition relative to King Arthur and his transformation into a raven, is fixed very decidedly on the Cornish Chough, from the colour of its beak and talons. The—

"Talons and beak all red with blood"

are said to mark the violent end to which this celebrated chieftain came.

SLAUGHTER BRIDGE.

HISTORIANS and poets have made the world familiar with King Arthur. We know how Merlin deceived, by his magic, the beautiful Igerna, so that she received King Uter as her husband. We know also that Uter Pendragon died, and that his son, by Igerna, reigned King of Britain. How Arthur ruled, and how he slaughtered all the enemies of Britain, is told in the chronicles. But even at Tintagel* all is silent respecting the king or his celebrated Round Table.

* "I shall offer a conjecture touching the name of this place, which I will not say is right, but only probable. *Tin* is the same as *Din*, *Dinas*, and *Diseth*, deceit; so that *Tindixel*, turned, for easier pronunciation, to *Tintagel*, *Dindagel*, or *Daundagel*, signifies *Castle of Deceit*, which name might be aptly given to it from the famous deceit practised here by Uter Pendragon by the help of Merlin's enchantment."—*Tonkin*.

"Mr Hals says this place is called *Donechenïv* in 'Domesday Survey.' *Dunechine* would mean the fortress of the chasm, corresponding precisely with its situation."—*Davies Gilbert*.

"In the days of King Arthur the Mount of Cornwall was kept by a monstrous giant," is familiar to us all; and it is curious to find a tradition that the extirpation of these Titans was due to Arthur and Christianity, as already related. At Slaughter Bridge I heard the story, but it did not sound like a tradition; the true native character was not in the narrative. That in 824 the Cornish and Saxons fought so bloody a battle that the river ran red with blood. On Slaughter Bridge Arthur is said to have killed his nephew, Modred, but that, previously to this last fight, Modred wounded his uncle with a poisoned sword, nearly in front of Worthyvale House. A single stone laid over a stream, having some letters cut on its lower surface, is believed to mark the exact spot where Arthur received his death-wound.

CAMELFORD AND KING ARTHUR.

AT the head of this river Alan is seated Camelford, otherwise written Galleford, a small town. It was formerly called Kambton, according to Leland, who tells us that "Arthur, the British Hector," was slain here, or in the valley near it. He adds, in support of this, that "pieces of armour, rings, and brass furniture for horses are sometimes digged up here by the countrymen; and after so many ages, the tradition of a bloody victory in this place is still preserved." There are also extant some verses of a Middle Age poet about "Camels" running with blood after the battle of Arthur against Modred.*

"Camulus is another name of the god of war, occurring in two of Gruter's inscriptions."†

Seeing that Arthur's great battles were fought near this

* Gilbert, vol. ii. p. 402, *et seq.*

† Gruter's Collection of Ancient Inscriptions, quoted by J. C. Pritchard.

town, and on the banks of the river, may not the names given to the town and river be derived from Camulus?

> "O'er Cornwall's cliffs the tempest roar'd,
> High the screaming sea-mew soar'd;
> On Tintagel's topmost tower
> Darksome fell the sleety shower;
> Round the rough castle shrilly sung
> The whirling blast, and wildly flung
> On each tall rampart's thundering side
> The surges of the tumbling tide:
> When Arthur ranged his red cross ranks
> On conscious Camlan's crimson'd banks."
>
> *The Grave of King Arthur*—WHARTON.

In a Welsh poem it is recited that Arthur, after the battle of Camlan in Cornwall, was interred in the Abbey of Glastonbury, before the high altar, without any external mark. Henry II. is said to have visited the abbey, and to have ordered that the spot described by the bard should be opened. We are told that at twenty feet deep they found the body deposited under a large stone, with Arthur's name inscribed thereon.

Glastonbury Abbey is said to have been founded by Joseph of Arimathea, in a spot anciently called the island or valley of Avolmia or Avolon.

Bale, in his "Acts of English Votaries," attests to the finding of the remains of Arthur:—

"In Avallon, anno 1191, there found they the flesh bothe of Arthur and of hys wyfe Guenever turned all into duste, wythin theyr coffines of strong oke, the bones only remaynynge. A monke of the same abbeye, standyng and behouldyng the fine broydinges of the wommanis heare as *yellow as golde* there still to remayne. As a man ravyshed, or more than halfe from his wyttes, he leaped into the graffe, xv fote depe, to have caugte them sodenlye. But he fayled of his purpose. For so soon as they were touched they fell all to powder."

DAMELIOCK CASTLE.

THIS ancient British castle once stood in savage grandeur a rival to Tintagel. Its ruins, which can scarcely be traced, are in the parish of St Tudy. Here Gothlois of the Purple Spear, Earl of Cornwall, fortified himself against Uter Pendragon's soldiery, and here he was slain. Gothlois, or Gothlouis, was the husband of Igerna, who was so cruelly deceived by Uter, and who became the mother of Arthur.

CARLIAN IN KEA.

ONE of the most celebrated of Arthur's knights, Sir Tristram, is said to have been born in this parish. A tradition of this is preserved in the parish, but it is probably derived from the verses of Thomas of Erceldoune, better known as Thomas the Rhymer.

SORCERY AND WITCHCRAFT.

"And, wow! Tam saw an unco sight—
Warlocks and witches in a dance."
Tam o' Shanter—BURNS.

ROMANCES OF WITCHES, ETC.

THE "CUNNING MAN."

> "And as he rode over the more,
> Hee see a lady where shee sate
> Betwixt an oke and a greene hollen;
> She was cladd in red scarlett.
>
> "Then there as shold have stood her mouth,
> Then there was sett her eye;
> The other was in her forhead fast,
> The way that she might see.
>
> "Her nose was crook'd and turn'd outward,
> Her mouth stood foule awry;
> A worse-form'd lady then shee was,
> Never man saw with his eye."
>
> *The Marriage of Sir Gawaine.*

THAT a deep-rooted belief in the power of the witch still lingers in the remote districts of Cornwall cannot be denied. A gentleman, who has for many years been actively engaged in a public capacity, gives me, in reply to some questions which I put to him relative to a witch or conjurer, much information, which is embodied in this section.

A "cunning man" was long resident in Bodmin, to whom the people from all parts of the country went to be relieved of spells, under the influence of which either themselves or their cattle were supposed to be suffering. Thomas ——, who resided at Nanstallan, not far from the town of Bodmin, was waylaid, robbed, and well thrashed on his way home from market. This act, which was accompanied by some appearance of brutality, was generally referred to one of the dupes of his cunning. Howbeit, Thomas —— appears to have felt that the place was getting too hot for him, for he migrated to one of the parishes on the western side of the Fowey river. Numerous instances are within my knowledge of the belief which existed amongst the peasantry that this man really possessed the power of removing the effects of witchcraft. Thomas —— took up his abode for some time with a small farmer, who had lost some cattle. These losses were attributed to the malign influences of some evil-disposed person; but as Thomas —— failed to detect the individual, he with the farmer made many journeys to Exeter, to consult the "White Witch," who resided in that city. Whether the result was satisfactory or otherwise, I have never learned. Thomas ——, it must be remembered, was only a "witch." The term is applied equally to men as to women. I never heard any uneducated person speak of a "wizard." There appears to be, however, some very remarkable distinctions between a male and a female witch. The former is almost always employed to remove the evil influences exerted by the latter. Witches, such as Thomas, had but limited power. They could tell who had been guilty of ill-wishing, but they were powerless to break the spell and "unbewitch" the sufferer. This was frequently accomplished by the friends of the bewitched, who, in concert with Thomas ——, would perform certain ceremonies, many of them of an obscene, and usually of a blasphemous, character. The "White Witch" was supposed to possess the higher power of removing the spell, and of punishing the individual by whose wickedness the wrong had been inflicted.

Jenny Harris was a reputed witch. This woman, old, poor, and, from the world's ill usage, rendered malicious, was often charged with the evils which fell upon cattle, children, or, indeed, on men and women. On one occasion, a robust and rough-handed washerwoman, who conceived that she was under the spell of Jenny Harris, laid violent hands on the aged crone, being resolved to "bring blood from her." The witch's arm was scratched and gouged from the elbow to the wrist, so that a sound inch of skin did not exist. This violent assault became the subject of inquiry before the magistrates, who fined the washerwoman five pounds for the assault.

My correspondent writes :—" I was also present at a magistrates' meeting at the Porcupine Inn, near Tywardreath, some years ago, when an old woman from Golant was brought up for witchcraft. One farmer, who appeared against her, stated that he had then six bullocks hanging up in chains in his orchard, and he attributed their disease and death to the poor old woman's influence. The case was dismissed, but it afforded a good deal of merriment. There was a dinner at the inn after the meeting, and some of the farmers present were disposed to ridicule the idea of witchcraft. I said, well knowing their real views and opinions, 'Gentlemen, it is all well enough to laugh, but it appears to me to be a serious matter.' Upon which Mr ——, a farmer of ——, said, 'You are right, Mr ——; I'll tell of two cases in which one family suffered severely,' and he gave us the details of the cases. All the others present had a case or two, each one within his own experience to vouch for, and the whole afternoon was spent telling witch stories."

The extent to which this belief was carried within a comparatively recent period, may be inferred from the fact that, on one occasion when the visitors were assembled at the county asylum, a man residing at Callington came with the mother of a poor imbecile patient, and sent his card to the boardroom. This was inscribed with his name and M.A. Upon being asked how he became a Master of Arts, he replied that he was a "Master of Black Arts." The object of this fellow's visit was, having persuaded the mother of his power, to propose to the visitors that they should place the imbecile girl in his care, upon his undertaking, on their paying him five pounds, to cure her. Of course this was not listened to. This fellow imposed upon people to such an extent, that he was eventually tried at the sessions, under an almost forgotten Act of Parliament, for witchcraft. The impression on the mind of my informant is that the case broke down.

NOTES ON WITCHCRAFT.

IN confirmation of the melancholy facts related of the continuance of the belief in witchcraft, I would give the accompanying cuttings from the *West Briton* newspaper of a very recent date :—

GROSS SUPERSTITION.

"During the week ending Sunday last, a 'wise man' from Illogan has been engaged with about half-a-dozen witchcraft cases, one a young tradesman, and another a sea-captain. It appears that the 'wise man' was in the first place visited at his home by these deluded people at different times, and he declared the whole of them to be spell-bound. In one case he said that if the person had not come so soon, in about a fortnight he would have been in the asylum; another would have had his leg broken; and in every case something very direful would have happened. Numerous incantations have been performed. In the case of a captain of a vessel, a visit was paid to the sea-side, and while the 'wise man' uttered some unintelligible gibberish, the captain had to throw a stone into the sea. So heavy was the spell under which he laboured, and which immediately fell upon the 'wise man,' that the latter pretended that he could scarcely walk back to Hayle. The most abominable part of the incantations is performed during the hours of midnight, and for that purpose the wretch sleeps with his victims, and for five nights following he had five different bed-fellows. Having no doubt reaped a pretty good harvest during the week, he returned to his home on Monday; but such was the pretended effect produced by the different spells and witchcraft that fell upon him from his many dupes, that two of the young men who had been under his charge were obliged to obtain a horse and cart and carry him to the Hayle station. One of the men, having had 'two spells' resting on him, the 'wise man' was obliged to sleep with him on Saturday and Sunday nights, having spent the whole of the Sunday in his diabolical work. It is time that the police, or some other higher authorities, should take the matter up, as the person alluded to is well known, and frequently visited by the ignorant and superstitious."

THE CASE OF GROSS SUPERSTITION AT HAYLE.

"In the *West Briton* of the 27th ult. we gave some particulars of several cases of disgraceful fraud and delusion which had been practised by a pretended 'wise man' from Illogan, and of gross superstition and gullibility on the part of his dupes. A correspondent has furnished us with the following particulars relative to the antecedents of the pretended conjurer. He states that James Thomas, the conjurer from the parish of Illogan, married some time since the late celebrated Tammy Blee, of Redruth, who afterwards removed to Helston and carried on as a fortune-teller, but parted from her husband, James Thomas, on account of a warrant for his apprehension having been issued against him by the magistrates of St Ives, for attempting to take a spell from Mrs Paynter, through her husband, William Paynter, who stated before the magistrates that he wanted to commit a disgraceful offence. Thomas then absconded, and was absent from the west of Cornwall for upwards of two years. His wife then stated that the virtue was in her and not in him; that she was of the real 'Pellar' blood; and that he could tell nothing but through her. His greatest dupes have been at St Just and Hayle, and other parts of the west of Cornwall. He has been in the habit of receiving money annually for keeping witchcraft from vessels sailing out of Hayle. He slept with several of his dupes recently; and about a fortnight since he stated that he must sleep with certain young men at Copperhouse, Hayle, in order to protect them from something that was hanging over them, one of them being a mason and another a miner, the two latter lately from St Just. He said himself this week at Truro that he had cured a young man of St Erth, and was going on Saturday again to take a spell from the father, a tin smelter. He has caused a great disturbance amongst the neighbours, by charging some with having bewitched others. He is a drunken, disgraceful, beastly fellow, and ought to be sent to the treadmill. One of the young men is now thoroughly ashamed of himself to think he has been duped so by this scoundrel. We have purposely withheld the names of a number of Thomas's egregious dupes, with which our correspondent has furnished us, believing that the badgering which they have doubtless received from their friends has proved a sufficient punishment to them, and that their eyes are now thoroughly opened to the gross and disgraceful imposture that has been practised upon them."

The following is from the *Western Morning News* :—

CALLING A WOMAN A WITCH.

"At the Liskeard police court, on Monday, Harriet King appeared before the sitting magistrates charged with an assault on Elizabeth Wellington. The complainant had called the mother of defendant a witch, and said she had ill-wished a person, and the ill wish fell on the cat, and the cat died. This annoyed the daughter, who retaliated by bad words and blows. The magistrates expressed surprise at the cause of the assault, but as that had been proved, they fined defendant 1s. and the costs, £1 in all."

ILL-WISHING.

I GIVE the following notices as I receive them :—"I caant altogether exackly bleve in wiches at al," said a good dame to us ; "but this I can tell ee, our John's wife quarrelled once with her next door neighbor's wife, and when John come home, like a husband always should, he took up for his wife, 'northin but nat'r'l chiel was a.' Well, the woman took a nif, and for a long time never spoke to our John ; at laast, after a bit, she used to speak to un, and like as if a was all over, and she used to speak quite sochebl' like. Well, John alleas was very well when he used to meet her, but as soon as ever he got underground, he was tooken ill to wonce ; when a dedn't meet her, a was well enuf. Well, John was advised to go to the 'Peller,' and off he went to Helstun sure nuf, and the 'Peller' towld un to come so many times in three months, and do something anorther, and towld un who a was that hoverlooked un, and a was that vere woman. Well, the 'Peller' towld John that if a dedn't do it, a would very likely die sudden. Our John, dear fellow, came home, and got unbelieving, and dedn't do as a was towld. Wat was the konsikense? Why, in less than three months a was a dead man. Not as I believe the woman 's a witch—no, not I; but she had a evil mind, and what 's so bad as a evil mind?"

"I used to have a woman meeting me," said a fisherman, "when I went a-fishing; and she used to wish me 'a good catch' every time she seed me, and I was always sure to have no luck whenever I met her; luck used to be good enough other times. Well, I went to the 'Peller,' and done what he told me I done, and the woman came and begged my pardon, and my luck was good enough after that." To what purpose he had been lucky I could not divine, for he was miserably clad, and I learned that his family were, like himself, miserable and degraded.

In a certain cordwainer's workshop, which we could name, the following important information was afforded by a lady customer. The worthy tradesman was bewailing the loss of a good-sized pig that had sickened, and being afraid it would die, he had drowned it, to make its death easier:—"If thee'st only towld me afore, tha peg wud a bean wel enuf in a week, I knaw. That peg wus begruged thee, thas the way a wudn' thrive. I 'll tel ee wat mi faathur dun wonse. He wont hof to pausans* an' bot a bra purty letle peg, an' as a wus cumin home wed'en, a womun seed un, an' axed faathur to sell un to hur fur five shelins fur his bargin. Shaan't sell un, saze faathur. Mite sa wel, saze she, an' off she went. Faathur tendud un an' tended un, an' a wudn'

* The Parson's.

grough a mossel. Wy? A was begruged, thas wot a was. Wel, faathur wen' off, an' he wos towld to go hom an fill a botel with waater, an' beré un in the cawl. Faathur dun so, an' a wuden long afore the wumun caame to faathur an' axed un wat had a dun by hur, for she suffered agonies; an' if heed only *forgive* hur, she'd nevur do so nevur no mure. So faathur went to the cawl hus, an' brok the botel. She was at once relieved, an' the peg got wel enuf aftur. I can tel ee, ef thee's honle dun that, a wud ben wel enuf, if a wusn'd pisind."

"Well," said one of the company, "I believe I was ill-wished once. I had a great beautiful cage, full of pretty canaries. I hung them out one Sunday morning, and a woman came along and asked me to let her have one of my birds. 'Yes,' said I, 'for half-a-crown.' She said she shouldn't buy none. I told her I would not give her one, and off she went. That day week I had not a bird left; everybody said they was bethought me, and I suppose they were; but this I do know, I lost all my canaries."

Carne, in his "Legend of Pacorra," well expresses the belief in the power of ill wishes:—"Thriven!" said the woman, with a bitter laugh; "not if my curse could avail, should they thrive! and it has availed," she continued, in a lower tone. "You know the wasting illness that's fallen on all that cruel faggot, Dame Tredray's children, that said they ought to thraw me from the head of Tol-y-pedden, and that I should neither be broken nor drowned; and the hard squire of Pendine, that would ha' had me burned in the great bonfire upon the bicking,* because King Harry had a son born,—has he ever left his bed since, or will he ever again, ken ye?"

* The Beacon.

THE "PELLER."

A MAN who has resided at several places on the south coast was known by this name. He is said to be in possession of no end of charms, and to possess powers, of no common order, over this and the other world. "He is able," writes a friend, "to put ghosts, hobgoblins, and, I believe, even Satan himself, to rest. I have known farmers, well informed in many other matters, and members of religious bodies, go to the 'Peller' to have the 'spirits that possessed the calves' driven out; for they, the calves, 'were so wild, they tore down all the wooden fences and gates, and must be possessed with the devil.'

"The 'Peller' always performs a cure; but as the evil spirits must go somewhere, and as it is always to be feared that they may enter into other calves or pigs, or, it may be, even possess the bodies of their owners themselves, the 'Peller' makes it imperative that a stone wall shall be built around the calves, to confine them for three times seven days, or until the next moon is as old as the present one. This precaution always results in taming the devils and the calves, and consequently in curing them—the 'Peller' usually sending the spirits to some very remote region, and chaining them down under granite rocks."

An old woman had long suffered from debility; but she and her friends were satisfied that she had been ill-wished. So she went to the "Peller." He told her to buy a bullock's heart, and get a packet of pound pins. She was to stick the heart as full of pins as she could, and "the body that ill-wished her felt every pin run into the bullock's heart same as if they had been run into her." The spell was taken off, and the old woman grew strong.

An old man living on Lady Downs had a lot of money stolen from his house. He, too, went to the "Peller." In this case the magician performed the spells, and the man was told the money would be returned. After a few days, it was so; the money, during the night, was tied to the handle of the door, and found there by the owner in the morning.

BEWITCHED CATTLE.

A FARMER, who possessed broad acres, and who was in many respects a sensible man, was greatly annoyed to find that his cattle became diseased in the spring. Nothing could satisfy him but that they were bewitched, and he was resolved to find out the person who had cast the evil eye on his oxen. According to an anciently-prescribed rule, the farmer took one of his bullocks and bled it to death, catching all the blood on bundles of straw. The bloody straw was then piled into a heap, and set on fire. Burning with a vast quantity of smoke, the farmer expected to see the witch, either in reality or in shadow, amidst the smoke.

In this particular case he was to some extent gratified. An old woman who lived in the adjoining village noticing the fire and smoke,—with all a woman's curiosity,—went to Farmer ——'s field to see what was going on. She was instantly pounced on by this superstitious man, and he would no doubt have seriously ill-treated her, had not the poor, and now terrified, old soul, who roused her neighbours by her cries, been rescued by them. Every person knew this poor woman to be a most inoffensive and good creature, and consequently the farmer was only laughed at for sacrificing thus foolishly one of his oxen.

Another farmer living in one of the western parishes was constantly losing his cattle in the spring. Many persons said this was because they were nearly starved during the winter, but he insisted upon it that he was ill-wished, and that a blight was upon him.

At length, to break the spell, and discover the witch, he betook himself to a conjuror (white witch) who lived near the Lizard Point. This learned person, of whom several other facts are told in these pages, told the farmer to bleed the next animal when taken ill, and to receive the blood upon straw, being careful not to lose any of it. Then the straw and blood were to be burnt, and whilst the blood was burning he would be certain of seeing the witch pass through the smoke.

A young steer fell ill first; it was bled as ordered, the blood caught upon the straw, and both carefully burnt. While this was going on, female curiosity induced a poor weak old woman to go into the field and see what was going on. She was well known to all, and as guiltless as a child of ill-wishing any body, but she was seen through the smoke darted upon by the farmer, and cruelly ill-treated.

HOW TO BECOME A WITCH.

TOUCH a Logan stone nine times at midnight, and any woman will become a witch. A more certain plan is said to be—To get on the Giant's Rock at Zennor Church-Town nine times without shaking it. Seeing that this rock was at one time a very sensitive Logan stone, the task was somewhat difficult.

CORNISH SORCERERS.

THE powers of the sorcerer appear to have been passed on from father to son through a long succession of generations. There are many families—the descendants from the ancient Cornish people—who are even yet supposed to possess remarkable powers of one kind or another. Several families, which have become extinct, are more especially reputed by tradition to have had dealings with the bad spirits, and many of them to have made compacts with the Evil One himself. Amongst the most curious of the stories once told,—I believe they are nearly all forgotten,—are those connected with Pengerswick Castle. A small tower alone remains to note the site of a once famous fortified place. This castle was said to have been occupied, in the time of Henry VIII., by a man who had committed some great crime; but long previous to that period the place was famous for its wickedness.*

HOW PENGERSWICK BECAME A SORCERER.

THE first Pengerswick, by whom the castle, which still bears his name, was built, was a proud man, and desired to ally himself with some of the best families of Cornwall. He wished his son to wed a lady who was very much older than himself, who is said to have been connected with the Godolphin family. This elderly maiden had a violent desire either for the young man or the castle—it is not very clear which. The young Pengerswick gave her no return for the manifestations of love which she lavished upon him. Eventually, finding all her attempts to win the young man's love were abortive, and that all the love potions brewed for her by the Witch of Fraddam were of no avail, she married the old lord—mainly, it is said, to be revenged on the son.

The witch had a niece who, though poor, possessed considerable beauty; she was called Bitha. This young girl was frequently employed by her aunt and the lady of Godol-

* See Appendix E.

phin to aid them in their spells on the young Pengerswick, and, as a natural consequence, she fell desperately in love with him herself. Bitha ingratiated herself with the lady of Pengerswick, now the stepmother of the young man, and was selected as her maid. This gave her many opportunities of seeing and speaking to young Pengerswick, and her passion increased. The old stepdame was still passionately fond of the young man, and never let a chance escape her which she thought likely to lead to the excitement of passion in his heart towards her. In all her attempts she failed. Her love was turned to hate; and having seen her stepson in company with Bitha, this hate was quickened by the more violent jealousy. Every means which her wicked mind could devise were employed to destroy the young man. Bitha had learned from her aunt, the Witch of Fraddam, much of her art, and she devoted herself to counteract the spells of her mistress.

The stepmother, failing to accomplish her ends, resolved to ruin young Pengerswick with his father. She persuaded the old man that his son really entertained a violent passion for her, and that she was compelled to confine herself to her tower in fear. The aged woman prevailed on Lord Pengerswick to hire a gang of outlandish sailors to carry his son away and sell him for a slave, giving him to believe that she should herself in a short time present him with an heir.

The young Pengerswick escaped all their plots, and at his own good time he disappeared from the castle, and for a long period was never heard of.

The mistress and maid plotted and counter-plotted to secure the old Pengerswick's wealth; and when he was on his death-bed, Bitha informed him of the vile practices of his wife, and consoled him with the information that he was dying from the effects of poison given him by her.

The young lord, after long years, returned from some Eastern lands with a princess for his wife, learned in all the magic sciences of those enchanted lands. He found his stepmother shut up in her chamber, with her skin covered with scales like a serpent, from the effects of the poisons which she had so often been distilling for the old lord and his son. She refused to be seen, and eventually cast herself into the sea, to the relief of all parties.

Bitha fared not much better. She lived on the Downs in St Hilary; and from the poisonous fumes she had inhaled, and from her dealings with the devil, her skin became of the colour of that of *a toad*.

THE LORD OF PENGERSWICK AN ENCHANTER.

THE Lord of Pengerswick came from some Eastern clime, bringing with him a foreign lady of great beauty. She was considered by all an "outlandish" woman; and by many declared to be a "Saracen."* No one, beyond the selected servants, was ever allowed within the walls of Pengerswick Castle; and they, it was said, were bound by magic spells. No one dared tell of anything transacted within the walls; consequently all was conjecture amongst the neighbouring peasantry, miners, and fishermen. Certain it was, they said, that Pengerswick would shut himself up for days together in his chamber, burning strange things, which sent their strong odours,—not only to every part of the castle,—but for miles around the country. Often at night, and especially in stormy weather, Pengerswick was heard for hours together calling up the spirits, by reading from his books in some unknown tongue. On those occasions his voice would roll through the halls louder than the surging waves which beat against the neighbouring rocks, the spirits replying like the

* See Appendix F, "*Saracen.*"

roar of thunder. Then would all the servants rush in fright from the building, and remain crowded together, even in the most tempestuous night, in one of the open courts. Fearful, indeed, would be the strife between the man and the demons; and it sometimes happened that the spirits were too powerful for the enchanter. He was, however, constantly and carefully watched by his wife; and whenever the strife became too serious, her harp was heard making the softest, the sweetest music. At this the spirits fled; and they were heard passing through the air towards the Land's-End, moaning like the soughing of a departing storm. The lights would then be extinguished in the enchanter's tower, and all would be peace. The servants would return to their apartments with a feeling of perfect confidence. They feared their master, but their mistress inspired them with love. Lady Pengerswick was never seen beyond the grounds surrounding the castle. She sat all day in lonely state and pride in her tower, the lattice-window of her apartment being high on the seaward side. Her voice accompanying the music of her harp was rarely heard, but when she warbled the soft love strains of her Eastern land. Often at early dawn the very fishes of the neighbouring bay would raise their heads above the surface of the waters, enchanted by the music and the voice; and it is said that the mermaids from the Lizard, and many of the strange spirits of the waters, would come near to Pengerswick cove, drawn by the same influence. On moonlight nights the air has often seemed to be full of sound, and yet the lady's voice was seldom louder than that of a warbling bird. On these occasions, men have seen thousands of spirits gliding up and down the moonbeams, and floating idly on the silvered waves, listening to, and sometimes softly echoing, the words which Lady Pengerswick sang. Long did this strange pair inhabit this lonely castle; and although the Lord of Pengerswick frequently rode abroad on a most magnificent horse—which had the reputation of being of Satanic origin, it was at once so docile to its master and so wild to any other person,—yet he made no acquaintance with any of the neighbouring gentry. He was feared by all, and yet they respected him for many of the good deeds performed by him. He completely enthralled the Giants of the Mount; and before he disappeared from Cornwall, they died, owing, it was said, to grief and want of food.

Where the Lord of Pengerswick came from, no one knew; he, with his lady, with two attendants, who never spoke in any but an Eastern tongue, which was understood by none around them, made their appearance one winter's day, mounted on beautiful horses, evidently from Arabia or some distant land.

They soon—having gold in abundance—got possession of a cottage; and in a marvellously short time the castle, which yet bears his name, was rebuilt by this lord. Many affirm that the lord by the force of his enchantments, and the lady by the spell of her voice, compelled the spirits of the earth and air to work for them; and that three nights were sufficient to rear an enormous pile, of which but one tower now remains.

Their coming was sudden and mysterious; their going was still more so. Years had rolled on, and the people around were familiarised with those strange neighbours, from whom also they derived large profits, since they paid whatsoever price was demanded for any article which they required. One day a stranger was seen in Market-Jew, whose face was bronzed by long exposure to an Eastern sun. No one knew him; and he eluded the anxious inquiries of the numerous gossips, who were especially anxious to learn something of this man, who, it was surmised by every one, must have some connexion with Pengerswick or his lady; yet no one could assign any reason for such a supposition. Week after week passed away, and the stranger remained in the town, giving no sign. Wonder was on every old woman's lips, and expressed in every old man's eyes; but they had to wonder on. One thing, it was said, had been noticed; and this seemed to confirm the suspicions of the people. The stranger wandered out on dark nights—spent them, it was thought, on the sea-shore; and some fishermen said they had seen him seated on the rock at the entrance of the valley of Pengerswick. It was thought that the lord kept more at home than usual, and of late no one had heard his incantation songs and sounds; neither had they heard the harp of the lady. A very tempestuous night, singular for its gloom—when even the ordinary light, which, on the darkest night, is evident to the traveller in the open country, did not exist—appears to have brought things to their climax. There was a sudden alarm in Market-Jew, a red glare in the eastern sky, and presently a burst of flames above the hill, and St Michael's Mount was illuminated in a remarkable manner. Pengerswick Castle was on fire; the servants fled in terror; but neither the lord nor his lady could be found. From that day to the present they were lost to all.

The interior of the castle was entirely destroyed; not a vestige of furniture, books, or anything belonging to the "Enchanter" could be found. He and everything belonging to him had vanished; and, strange to tell, from that night the bronzed stranger was never again seen. The inhabitants of Market-Jew naturally crowded to the fire; and when all was over they returned to their homes, speculating on the strange occurrences of the night. Two of the oldest people always declared that, when the flames were at the highest, they saw two men and a lady floating in the midst of the fire, and that they ascended from amidst the falling walls, passed through the air like lightning, and disappeared.

THE WITCH OF FRADDAM AND THE ENCHANTER OF PENGERSWICK.

AGAIN and again had the Lord of Pengerswick reversed the spells of the Witch of Fraddam, who was reported to be the most powerful weird woman in the west country. She had been thwarted so many times by this "white witch," that she resolved to destroy him by some magic more potent than anything yet heard of. It is said that she betook herself to Kynance Cove, and that there she raised the devil by her incantations, and that she pledged her soul to him in return for the aid he promised. The enchanter's famous mare was to be seduced to drink from a tub of poisoned water placed by the road-side, the effect of which was to render him in the highest degree restive, and cause him to fling his rider. The wounded Lord of Pengerswick was, in his agony, to be drenched, by the old witch, with some hell-broth, brewed in the blackest night, under the most evil aspects of the stars; by this he would be in her power for ever, and she might torment him as she pleased. The devil felt certain of securing the soul of the Witch of Fraddam, but he was less certain of securing that of the enchanter. They say, indeed, that the sorcery which Pengerswick learned in the East was so potent, that the devil feared him. However, as the proverb is, he held with the hounds and ran with the hare. The witch collected with the utmost care all the deadly things she could obtain, with which to brew her famous drink. In the darkest night, in the midst of the wildest storms, amidst the flashings of lightnings and the bellowings of the thunder, the witch was seen riding on her black ram-cat over the moors and mountains in search of her poisons. At length all was complete—the horse drink was boiled, the hell-broth was brewed. It was in March, about the time of the equinox; the night was dark, and the King of Storms was abroad. The witch planted her tub of drink in a dark lane, through which she knew the Lord of Pengerswick must pass, and near to it she sat, croning over her crock of broth. The witch-woman had not long to wait; amidst the hurrying winds was heard the heavy tramp of the enchanter's mare, and soon she perceived the outline of man and horse defined sharply against the line of lurid light which stretched along the western horizon. On they came; the witch was scarcely able to contain herself—her joy and her fears, struggling one with the other, almost overpowered her. On came the horse and his rider: they neared the tub of drink; the mare snorted loudly, and her eyes flashed fire as she looked at the black tub by the road-side. Pengerswick bent him over the horse's neck and whispered into her ear; she turns round, and, flinging out her heels, with one kick she scattered all to the wild winds. The tub flew before the blow; it rushed against the crock, which it overturned, and striking against the legs of the old Witch of Fraddam, she fell along with the tub, which assumed the shape of a coffin. Her terror was extreme: she who thought to have unhorsed the conjuror, found herself in a carriage for which she did not bargain. The enchanter raised his voice and gave utterance to some wild words in an unknown tongue, at which even his terrible mare trembled. A whirlwind arose, and the devil was in the midst of it. He took the coffin in which lay the terrified witch high into the air, and the crock followed them. The derisive laughter of Pengerswick, and the savage neighing of the horse, were heard above the roar of the winds. At length, with a satisfied tone, he exclaimed,

"She is settled till the day of doom," gave the mare the spurs, and rode rapidly home.

The Witch of Fraddam still floats up and down, over the seas, around the coast, in her coffin, followed by the crock, which seems like a punt in attendance on a jolly-boat. She still works mischief, stirring up the sea with her laddle and broom till the waves swell into mountains, which heave off from their crests, so much mist and foam, that these wild wanderers of the winds can scarcely be seen through the mist. Woe to the mariner who sees the witch!

The Lord of Pengerswick alone had power over her. He had but to stand on his tower, and blow three blasts on his trumpet, to summon her to the shore, and compel her to peace.

TREWA, OR TREWE; THE HOME OF WITCHES.

AS we walk from Nancledrea Bottoms towards Zennor we pass Trewa, (pronounced *Truee,*) which is said to have been the place where at midsummer all the witches of the west met. Here are the remains of very ancient tin stream works, and these, I was informed, "were the remains of bals which had been worked before the deluge; there was nothing so old anywhere else in Cornwall." Around us, on the hill-sides and up the bottoms, huge boulders of granite are most fantastically scattered. All these rocks sprang from the ground at the call of the giants. At Embla Green we still see the ruins of the Giant's House, but all we know of this Titan is that he was the king. On one side we have the "Giant's Well," and not far off the "Druid's Well," and a little before us is Zennor coit or cromlech.

From this point the scenery is of the wildest description. The granite cairns are spread around in every direction, and many of those masses are so strangely fashioned by the atmospheric influences ever acting on them, that fancy can readily fashion them into tombs and temples. Rock basins abound on these hills, and of ruined cromlechs there are many. Whatever the local historians may say, local traditions assure us that on Midsummer Eve all the witches in Penwith gathered here, and that they lit fires on every cromlech, and in every rock basin, until the hills were alive with flame, and renewed their vows to the evil ones from whom they derived their power. Hence, to this day this place is called Burn Downs. Amidst these rock masses there was one pile remarkable amidst all the others for its size, and—being formed of cubical masses—for its square character. This was known as the Witches' Rock, and here it was said they assembled at midnight to carry on their wicked deeds. This rock has been removed, and with it the witches have died; the last real witch in Zennor having passed away, as I have been told, about thirty years since, and with her, some say, the fairies fled. I have, however, many reasons for believing that our little friends have still a few haunts in this locality. There is but one reason why we should regret the disappearance of the Witches' Rock. *Any one touching this rock nine times at midnight was insured against bad luck.*

KENIDZHEK WITCH.

ON the tract called the "Gump," near Kenidzhek, is a beautiful well of clear water, not far from which was a miner's cot, in which dwelt two miners with their sister. They told her never to go to the well after daylight; they would fetch the water for her. However, on one Saturday night she had forgotten to get in a supply for the morrow, so she went off to the well. Passing by a gap in a broken down hedge (called a *gurgo*) near the well, she saw an old woman sitting down, wrapped in a red shawl; she asked her what she did there at that time of night, but received no reply; she thought this rather strange, but plunged her pitcher in the well; when she drew it up, though a perfectly sound vessel, it contained no water; she tried again and again, and, though she saw the water rushing in at the mouth of the pitcher, it was sure to be empty when lifted out. She then became rather frightened; spoke again to the old woman, but receiving no answer, hastened away, and came in great alarm to her brothers. They told her that it was on account of this old woman they did not wish her to go to the well at night. What she saw was the ghost of old Moll, a witch who had been a great terror to the people in her lifetime, and had laid many fearful spells on them. They said they saw her sitting in the gap by the wall every night when going to bed.

THE WITCHES OF THE LOGAN STONE.

WHO that has travelled into Cornwall but has visited the Logan Stone? Numerous Logan rocks exist on the granite hills of the county, but that remarkable mass which is poised on the cubical masses forming its Cyclopean support, at Trereen, is beyond all others "The Logan Stone."

A more sublime spot could not have been chosen by the Bardic priesthood for any ordeal connected with their worship; and even admitting that nature may have disposed the huge mass to wear away, so as to rest delicately poised on a pivot, it is highly probable that the wild worship of the untrained tribes, who had passed to those islands from the shores of the Mediterranean Sea, may have led them to believe that some superhuman power belonged to such a strangely-balanced mass of rock.

Nothing can be more certain than that through all time, passing on from father to son, there has been a wild reverence of this mass of rock; and long after the days when the Druid ceased to be, there is every reason for believing that the Christian priests, if they did not encourage, did not forbid, the use of this and similar rocks to be used as places of ordeal by the uneducated and superstitious people around.

Hence the mass of rock on which is poised the Logan Stone has ever been connected with the supernatural. To the south of the Logan Rock is a high peak of granite, towering above the other rocks; this is known as the Castle Peak.

No one can say for how long a period, but most certainly for ages, this peak has been the midnight rendezvous for witches. Many a man, and woman too, now sleeping quietly in the churchyard of St Levan, would, had they the power, attest to having seen the witches flying into the Castle Peak on moonlight nights, mounted on the stems of the ragwort, (*Senécio Jacobæa Linn,*) and bringing with them the things necessary to make their charms potent and strong.

This place was long noted as the gathering-place of the army of witches who took their departure for Wales, where they would luxuriate at the most favoured seasons of the year upon the milk of the Welshmen's cows. From this peak many a struggling ship has been watched by a malignant crone, while she has been brewing the tempest to destroy it; and many a rejoicing chorus has been echoed, in horror, by the cliffs around, when the witches have been croaking their miserable delight over the perishing crews, as they have watched man, woman, and child drowning, whom they were presently to rob of the treasures they were bringing home from other lands.

Upon the rocks behind the Logan Rock it would appear that every kind of mischief which can befall man or beast was once brewed by the St Levan witches.

MADGY FIGGY'S CHAIR.

ALL those who have visited the fine piles of rocks in the vicinity of the so-called "St Levan," Land's-End, called Tol-pedden-Penwith,—and infinitely finer than anything immediately surrounding the most western promontory itself,—cannot have failed to notice the arrangement of cubical masses of granite piled one upon the other, known as the *Chair Ladder*.

This remarkable pile presents to the beat of the Atlantic waves a sheer face of cliff of very considerable height, standing up like a huge basaltic column, or a pillar built by the Titans, the horizontal joints representing so many steps in the so-called "Ladder." On the top is placed a stone of somewhat remarkable shape, which is by no great effort of the imagination converted into a chair. There it was that Madgy Figgy, one of the most celebrated of the St Levan and Burian witches, was in the habit of seating herself when she desired to call up to her aid the spirits of the storm. Often has she been seen swinging herself to and fro on this dizzy height when a storm has been coming home upon the shores, and richly-laden vessels have been struggling with the winds. From this spot she poured forth her imprecations on man and beast, and none whom she had offended could escape those withering spells; and from this "chair," which will ever bear her name, Madgy Figgy would always take her flight. Often, starting like some huge bird, mounted on a stem of ragwort, Figgy has headed a band of inferior witches, and gone off rejoicing in their iniquities to Wales or Spain.

This old hag lived in a cottage not far from Raftra, and she and all her gang, which appears to have been a pretty numerous crew, were notorious wreckers. On one occasion, Madgy from her seat of storms lured a Portuguese Indiaman into Perloe Cove, and drowned all the passengers. As they were washed on shore, the bodies were stripped of everything valuable, and buried by Figgy and her husband in the green hollow, which may yet be seen, just above Perloe Cove, marking the graves with a rough stone placed at the head of the corpse. The spoils on this occasion must have been large, for all the women were supplied for years with rich dresses, and costly jewels were seen decking the red arms of the girls who laboured in the fields. For a long time gems and gold continued to be found on the sands. Howbeit, amongst the bodies thrown ashore was one of a lady richly dressed, with chains of gold about her. "Rich and rare were the gems she wore," and not only so, but valuable treasure was fastened around her, she evidently hoping, if saved, to secure some of her property. This body, like all the others, was stripped; but Figgy said there was a mark on it which boded them evil, and she would not allow any of the gold or gems to be divided, as it would be sure to bring bad luck if it were separated. A dreadful quarrel ensued, and bloodshed was threatened; but the diabolical old Figgy was more than a match for any of the men, and the power of her impetuous will was superior to them all.

Everything of value, therefore, belonging to this lady was gathered into a heap, and placed in a chest in Madgy Figgy's hut. They buried the Portuguese lady the same evening; and after dark a light was seen to rise from the grave, pass along the cliffs, and seat itself in Madgy's chair at Tol-Pedden. Then, after some hours, it descended, passed back again, and, entering the cottage, rested upon the chest. This curious phenomenon continued for more than three months,—nightly,—much to the alarm of all but Figgy, who said she knew all about it, and it would all be right in time. One day a strange-looking and strangely-attired man arrived at the cottage. Figgy's man (her husband) was at home alone. To him the stranger addressed himself by signs,—he could not speak English, so he does not appear to have spoken at all,—and expressed a wish to be led to the graves. Away they went, but the foreigner did not appear to require a guide. He at once selected the grave of the lady, and sitting down upon it, he gave vent to his pent-up sorrows. He sent Figgy's man away, and remained there till night, when the light arose from the grave more brilliant than ever, and proceeded directly to the hut, resting as usual on the chest, which was now covered up with old sails, and all kinds of fishermen's lumber.

The foreigner swept these things aside, and opened the chest. He selected everything belonging to the lady, refusing to take any of the other valuables. He rewarded the wreckers with costly gifts, and left them—no one knowing from whence he came nor whither he went. Madgy Figgy was now truly triumphant. "One witch knows another witch, dead or living," she would say; "and the African would have been the death of us if we hadn't kept the treasure, whereas now we have good gifts, and no gainsaying 'em." Some do say they have seen the light in Madgy Figgy's chair since those times.

OLD MADGE FIGGEY AND THE PIG.

MADGE FIGGEY once lived in St Leven, but she removed to Burian Church-town. She had a neighbour, Tom Trenoweth, who had a very fine sow, and the old creature took it into her head to desire this sow. The pig was worth a pound of any man's money, but Madge offered Tom five shillings for it.

"No," says Tom, "I shan't sell the sow to you, nor to anybody else. I am going to put her in the house, and feed her for myself against winter."

"Well," said old Madge, nodding her head, and shaking her finger at Tom, "you will wish you had."

From that time the sow ceased to "goody" (thrive.) The more corn the sow ate, the leaner she became. Old Madge came again, "Will ye sell her now, Tom?"

"No! and be —— to you," said Tom.

"Arreah, Tom! you will wish you had, before another week is ended, I can tell ye."

By next week the sow was gone to skin and bone, yet eating all the time meat enough for three.

At last Tom took the sow out of the house, and prepared to drive her to Penzance market, and sell her for what she would fetch.

The rope was put round her leg, but more for fashion's sake than anything else. The poor pig could scarcely stand on her legs, consequently there was little chance of her running away. Well, Tom and his pig were no sooner on the highroad than the sow set off like a greyhound, and never stopped, racing over hedges and ditches, until she reached Leah Lanes. Tom kept hold of the rope till his arm was almost dragged from his body, and he was fairly "out of breath." He dropped the rope, piggy went on "as quiet as a lamb," but only the way which pleased her best. At last Tom and the sow arrived at Tregenebris Downs. At the corner of the roads, where they divide,—one going to Sancreed, and the other to Penzance,—Tom again laid hold of the rope, and said to himself, "I'll surely get thee to Penzance yet."

The moment they came to the market-road, the sow made a bolt, jerked the rope out of Tom's hand, and ran off at full speed, never stopping until she got in under Tregenebris Bridge. Now that bridge is more like a long drain—locally a bolt—than anything else, and is smallest in the middle; so when the sow got half way in, she stuck fast; she couldn't go forward—she wouldn't come back. Tom fired all the stones he could find,—first at the pig's head, and then at her tail,—and all he got for his pains was a grunt. There he stopped, watching the sow till near sunset; he had eaten nothing since five in the morning, and was starving. He saw no chance of getting the sow out, so he swore at her, and prepared to go home, when who should come by but old Madge Figgey, with her stick in one hand and basket in the other.

"Why, Tom, is that you? What in the world are ye doing here at this time o' day?"

"Well," says Tom, "I'm cussed if I can tell; look under the bridge, if you're a mind to know."

"Why, I hear the sow grunting, I declare. What will ye sell her for now?"

"If you can get her out, take her," says Tom; "but hast anything to eat in your basket?"

Madge gave him a twopenny loaf.

"Thank ye," says Tom. "Now the devil take the both of ye!"

"Cheat! cheat! cheat!" says Madge. Out came the sow, and followed her home like a dog.

MADAM NOY AND OLD JOAN.

THEY say that, a long time since, there lived an old witch down by Alsia Mill, called Joan. Everybody feared to offend the old woman, and gave her everything she looked for, except Madam Noy, who lived in Pendrea.

Madam Noy had some beautiful hens of a new sort, with "cops" on their heads.

One morning early, Joan comes up to Pendrea, so as to catch Madam Noy going out into the farmyard, with her basket of corn to feed the poultry, and to collect the eggs.

Joan comes up nodding and curtsying every step. "Good morrow to your honour; how well you are looking, Madam Noy; and, oh, what beautiful hens. I've got an old hen that I do want to set; will you sell me a dozen of eggs? Those with the 'cops' I'd like to have best."

Madam turned round half offended, and said, "I have none to sell, neither with the cops nor yet without the cops, whilst I have so many old clucking hens about, and hardly an egg to be found."

"You surely wouldn't send me home empty as I came, madam dear?"

"You may go home the same way you came, for you aren't wanted here."

"Now," croaked Joan, hoarse with passion, "as true as I tell you so, if you don't sell me some eggs, you will wish your cakes dough."

As the old witch said this, she perched herself on the stile, shaking her finger and "nodling" her head.

Madam Noy was a bit of a virago herself, so she took up

a stone and flung it at Joan; it hit her in the face, and made her jaws rattle.

As soon as she recovered, she spinned forth :—

> "Madam Noy, you ugly old bitch,
> You shall have the gout, the palsy, and itch;
> All the eggs your hens lay henceforth shall be addle;
> All your hens have the pip, and die with the straddle;
> And ere I with the mighty fine madam have done,
> Of her favourite 'coppies' she shan't possess one."

From that day forward, madam was always afflicted. The doctor from Penzance could do little for her. The fowls' eggs were always bad; the hens died, and madam lost all her "coppies." This is the way it came about—in the place of cops the brains came out—and all by the spells of old Joan.

This forms the subject of one of the old Cornish drolls, which ran in an irregular jingle, such as the above, and was half sung, half said by the droll-teller.

THE WITCH OF TREVA.

ONCE on a time, long ago, there lived at Treva, a hamlet in Zennor, a wonderful old lady deeply skilled in necromancy. Her charms, spells, and dark incantations made her the terror of the neighbourhood. However, this old lady failed to impress her husband with any belief in her supernatural powers, nor did he fail to proclaim his unbelief aloud.

One day this sceptic came home to dinner and found, being exceedingly hungry, to his bitter disappointment, that not only was there no dinner to eat, but that there was no meat in the house. His rage was great, but all he could get from his wife was, "I couldn't get meat out of the stones, could I?" It was in vain to give the reins to passion, the old woman told him, and he must know "that hard words buttered no parsnips." Well, at length he resolved to put his wife's powers to the proof, and he quietly but determinedly told her that he would be the death of her if she did not get him some dinner ; but if in half an hour she gave him some good cooked meat, he would believe all she had boasted of her power, and be submissive to her for ever. St Ives, the nearest market-town, was five miles off; but nothing doubting, the witch put on her bonnet and cloak, and started. Her husband watched her from their cottage door, down the hill, and at the bottom of the hill he saw his wife quietly place herself on the ground and disappear. In her place a fine hare ran on at its full speed.

He was not a little startled, but he waited, and within the half hour in walked his wife with "good flesh and taties all ready for aiting." There was no longer any doubt, and the poor husband lived in fear of the witch of Treva to the day of her death.

This event took place after a few years, and it is said the room was full of evil spirits, and that the old woman's skrieks were awful to hear. Howbeit, peace in the shape of pale-faced death came to her at last, and then a black cloud rested over the house when all the heavens were clear and blue.

She was borne to the grave by six aged men, carried, as is the custom, under hand. When they were about half way between the house and the church, a hare started from the roadside and leaped over the coffin. The terrified bearers let the corpse fall to the ground, and ran away. Another lot of men took up the coffin and proceeded. They had not gone far when puss was suddenly seen seated on the coffin, and again the coffin was abandoned. After long consultation, and being persuaded by the parson to carry the old woman very quickly into the churchyard, while he walked before, six others made the attempt, and as the parson never ceased to repeat the Lord's Prayer, all went on quietly. Arrived at the church stile, they rested the corpse, the parson paused to commence the ordinary burial service, and there stood the hare, which, as soon as the clergyman began "I am the resurrection and the life," uttered a diabolical howl, changed into a black, unshapen creature, and disappeared.

HOW MR LENINE GAVE UP COURTING.

MR LENINE had been, as was his wont, spending his evening hours with the lady of his love. He was a timid man, and always returned to Tregenebris early. Beyond this, as the lady was alone, she deemed it prudent to let the world know that Mr Lenine left her by daylight.

One evening, it was scarcely yet dark, and our lover was returning home through Leah Lanes. His horse started at an old woman, who had crept under the hedge for shelter from a passing shower. As Mr Lenine saw a figure moving in the shade he was terrified.

"Tu-whit, tu-whoo, ho," sang an owl.

"It 's only me—Mr Lenine of Tregenebris," said he, putting the spurs to his horse.

Something followed him, fast as he might go, and he forced his horse up the hill by Leah vean.

"Tu-whit, tu-whoo, ho," sang the owl.

"It 's only me—Aunt Betty Foss," screamed the old woman.

"Tu-whit, tu-whoo, ho, ho," sang the owl again.

"Don't ye be afeard, Mr Lenine," shrieked Aunt Betty, almost out of breath.

"Tu-whit, tu-whoo, ho, ho, ho," also shrieked the owl.

"Oh, it's only John Lenine of Tregenebris," stammered the frightened lover, who had, however, reached home.

He went no more a-courting. He was fully persuaded that either a highwayman and his crew, or the devil and his imps, were upon him. He died a bachelor, and the charming lady became a peevish old maid, and died in solitude; all owing to the hooting owl.

Some do say Betty Foss was a witch, and the owl her familiar.

THE WITCH AND THE TOAD.

AN old woman called Alsey—usually Aunt Alsey—occupied a small cottage in Anthony, one of a row which belonged to a tradesman living in Dock—as Devonport was then designated, to distinguish it from Plymouth. The old woman possessed a very violent temper, and this, more than anything else, fixed upon her the character of being a witch. Her landlord had frequently sought his rent, and as frequently he received nothing but abuse. He had, on the special occasion to which our narrative refers, crossed the Tamar and walked to Anthony, with the firm resolve of securing his rent, now long in arrear, and of turning the old termagant out of the cottage. A violent scene ensued, and the vicious old woman, more than a match for a really kind-hearted and quiet man, remained the mistress of the situation. She seated herself in the door of her cottage and cursed her landlord's wife, "the child she was carrying," and all belonging to him, with so devilish a spite that Mr —— owned he was fairly driven away in terror.

On returning home, he, of course, told his wife all the circumstances; and while they were discoursing on the subject, —the whole story being attentively listened to by their daughter, then a young girl, who is my informant,—a woman came into the shop requiring some articles which they sold.

"Sit still, father," said Mrs —— to her husband; "you must be tired. I will see to the shop."

So she went from the parlour into the shop, and, hearing the wants of her customer, proceeded to supply them; gossiping gaily, as was her wont, to interest the buyer.

Mrs —— was weighing one of the articles required, when something falling heavily from the ceiling of the shop, struck the beam out of her hand, and both—the falling body and the scales—came together with much noise on to the counter. At the same instant both women screamed;—the shopkeeper calling also "Father! father!"—meaning her husband thereby—with great energy.

Mr —— and his daughter were in the shop instantly, and there, on the counter, they saw an enormous and most ugly toad sprawling amidst the chains of the scales. The first action of the man was to run back to the parlour, seize the tongs, and return to the shop. He grasped the swollen toad with the tongs, the vicious creature spitting all the time, and, without a word, he went back and flung it behind the block of wood which was burning in the grate. The object of terror being removed, the wife, who was shortly to become the mother of another child, though usually a woman who had great command over her feelings, fainted.

This circumstance demanding all their attention, the toad was forgotten. The shock was a severe one; and although Mrs —— was restored in a little time to her senses, she again and again became faint. Those fits continuing, her medical attendant, Dr ——, was sent for, and on his arrival he ordered that his patient should be immediately placed in bed, and the husband was informed that he must be prepared for a premature birth.

The anxiety occasioned by these circumstances, and the desire to afford every relief to his wife, so fully occupied Mr ——, that for an hour or two he entirely forgot the cause of all this mischief; or, perhaps satisfying himself that the toad was burnt to ashes, he had no curiosity to look after it. He was, however, suddenly summoned from the bedroom, in which he was with his wife, by his daughter calling to him, in a voice of terror,—

"O father, the toad, the toad!"

Mr —— rushed down-stairs, and he then discovered that the toad, though severely burnt, had escaped destruction. It must have crawled up over the log of wood, and from it have fallen down amongst the ashes. There it was now making useless struggles to escape, by climbing over the fender.

The tongs were again put in requisition, with the intention this time of carrying the reptile out of the house. Before, however, he had time to do so, a man from Anthony came hastily into the shop with the information that Aunt Alsey had fallen into the fire, as the people supposed, in a fit, and that she was nearly burnt to death. This man had been sent off with two commissions—one to fetch the doctor, and the other to bring Mr —— with him, as much of the cottage had been injured by fire, communicated to it by the old woman's dress.

In as short a time as possible the parish surgeon and Mr —— were at Anthony, and too truly they found the old woman most severely burnt—so seriously, indeed, there was no chance that one so aged could rally from the shock which her system must have received. However, a litter was carefully prepared, the old woman was placed in it, and carried to the workhouse. Every attention was given to her situation, but she never recovered perfect consciousness, and during the night she died.

The toad, which we left inside the fender in front of a blazing fire, was removed from a position so trying to any cold-blooded animal, by the servant, and thrown, with a "hugh" and a shudder, upon one of the flower-beds in the small garden behind the house.

There it lay the next morning dead, and when examined by Mr ——, it was found that all the injuries sustained by the toad corresponded with those received by the poor old wretch, who had no doubt fallen a victim to passion.

As we have only to deal with the mysterious relation which existed between the witch and the toad, it is not necessary that we should attend further to the innocent victim of an old woman's vengeance, than to say that eventually a babe was born—that that babe grew to be a handsome man, was an officer in the navy, and having married, went to sea, and perished, leaving a widow with an unborn child to lament his loss. Whether this was a result of the witch's curse, those who are more deeply skilled in witchcraft than I am may perhaps tell.

THE SAILOR WIZARD.

THIS appears to have been, and it may still be, a very common superstition. I have lately received from Mr T. Q. Couch of Bodmin the story of some sailors, who had reason to suspect that one of their body was a wizard. This was eventually proved to have been the case, by circumstances in every way resembling those of our old witch. There had been a quarrel, and revenge had been talked of. The sailors were all grouped together in the forepart of the ship, except the suspected one, and a toad fell sprawling amongst them. One of the men flung the creature into the fire in the caboose. It struggled for a moment in the fire, and then by a convulsive effort flung itself out. Immediately the toad was caught up by one of the men, and flung into the sea.

In the course of some little time the absent sailor made his appearance dripping wet. In a drunken frolic he had first fallen into the fire at a low beer shop or "Kiddle-e-Wink," and subsequently he fell out of the boat into the sea.

THE MINERS.

"To us our Queen, who in the central earth,
Midst fiery lavas or basaltine seas,
Deep-throned the illimitable waste enjoys,
Enormous solitude, has given these
Her subterraneous realms; bids us dwell here,
In the abyss of darkness, and exert
Immortal alchymy.

"Each devious cleft, each secret cell explore,
And from its fissures draw the ductile ore."

The Mine: a Dramatic Poem—
JOHN SARGENT.

ROMANCES OF THE MINERS.

TRADITIONS OF TINNERS.

> "An ancient story I 'll tell you anon,
> Which is older by far than the days of King John;
> But this you should know, that that red-robed sinner
> Robbed the Jew of the gold he had made as a tinner."
>
> *Old Cornish Song.*

THERE is scarcely a spot in Cornwall where tin is at present found, that has not been worked over by the "old men," as the ancient miners are always called.

Every valley has been "streamed"—that is, the deposits have been washed for tin; over every hill where now a tin mine appears, there are evidences, many of them most extensive, of actual mining operations having been carried on to as great a depth as was possible in the days when the appliances of science were unknown.

Wherever the "streamer" has been, upon whatever spot the old miner has worked, there we are told the "Finician" (*Phœnician*) has been, or the Jew has mined.*

* "They maintaine these works to have been verie auncient, and first wrought by the *Jewes* with Pickaxes of Holme-Boxe and Hartshorne. They prove this by the name of those places yet enduring, to wit, *Attall Sarazin*, in English, the *Jewes Offcast*, and by those tooles daily found amongst the rubble of such workes."—*Survey of Cornwall. Carew.* (Appendix F.)

There is much confusion in these traditions. The Jew, and the Saracen, and the Phœnician are regarded as terms applied to the same people. Whereas the Phœnicians, who are recorded to have traded with the Cornish Britons for tin, and the Jews, who were the great tin miners and merchants in the days of King John, are separated by wide periods of time; and the "Saracens," who some suppose to have been miners who came from Spain when that country was under the dominion of the Moors, occupy a very undefined position. Tradition, however, tells us that the old Cornish miners shipped their tin at several remarkable islands round the coast. St Michael's Mount has been especially noticed, but this arises from the circumstance that it still retains the peculiar character which it appears to have possessed when Diodorus wrote. But Looe Island, St Nicholas's Island in Plymouth Sound, the island at St Ives, the Chapel Rock at Perran, and many other insular masses of rock, which are at but a short distance from the coast, are said to have been shipping-places.

Tradition informs us that the Christian churches upon Dartmoor, which are said to have been built about the reign of John, were reared by the Jews. Once, and once only, I heard the story told in more detail. They, the Jews, did not actually work in the tin streams and mines of the Moor, but they employed tinners, who were Christians; and the king imposed on the Jew merchants the condition that they should build churches for their miners.

That the Phœnicians came to Cornwall to buy tin has been so often told, that there is little to be added to the story. It was certainly new, however, to be informed by the miners in Gwennap—that there could be no shade of doubt but that St Paul himself came to Cornwall to buy tin, and that Creegbraws—a mine still in existence—supplied the saint largely with that valuable mineral. Gwennap is regarded by Gwennap men as the centre of Christianity. This feeling has been kept alive by the annual meeting of the Wesleyan body in Gwennap Pit—an old mine-working—on Whitmonday. This high estate and privilege is due, says tradition, to the fact that St Paul himself preached in the parish.*

I have also been told that St Paul preached to the tinners on Dartmoor, and a certain cross on the road from Plympton to Princes-Town has been indicated as the spot upon which the saint stood to enlighten the benighted miners of this wild region. Of St Piran or Perran we have already spoken as the patron saint of the tinners, and of the discovery of tin a story has been told, (p. 21;) and we have already intimated that another saint, whose name alone is preserved, St Picrous, has his feast-day amongst the tinners of eastern Cornwall, on the second Thursday before Christmas.

Amidst the giant stories we have the very remarkable Jack the Tinker, who is clearly indicated as introducing the knowledge of tin, or of the dressing of tin, to the Cornish. This is another version of Wayland Smith, the blacksmith of Berkshire. The blacksmith of the Berkshire legend re-appears in a slightly altered character in Jack the Tinker. In Camden's "Britannia" we read, relative to Ashdown, in Berkshire :—

> "The burial-place of Baereg, the Danish chief, who was slain in this fight, (the fight between Alfred and the Danes,) is distinguished by a parcel of stones, less than a mile from the hill, set on edge, enclosing a piece of ground somewhat raised. On the east side of the southern extremity stand three squarish flat stones, of about four or five feet over either way, supporting a fourth, and now called by the vulgar, WAYLAND SMITH, from an idle tradition about an invisible smith replacing lost horse-shoes there."—*Gough's Camden.*

---

* Is this supported by the statement of Dr Stillingfleet, Bishop of Worcester, who says, "The Christian religion was planted in the Island of Great Britain during the time of the apostles, and probably by St Paul"?

See "Kenilworth," by Sir Walter Scott, who has appropriated Wayland Smith with excellent effect.

"The Berkshire legend of Wayland Smith ('Wayland Smith,' by W. S. Singer) is probably but a prototype of Dædalus, Tubal Cain, &c."—*Wilson's Prehistoric Annals of Scotland.*

See also Mr Thomas Wright's Essay on Wayland Smith.

The existence of the terms "Jews' houses," "Jews' tin," "Jews' leavings," or "atall," and "atall Saracen," prove the connexion of strangers with the Cornish tin mines. The inquiry is too large to be entered on here. I reserve it for another and more fitting place. I may, however, remark in passing, that I have no doubt the Romans were active miners during the period of their possession; and many relics which have been found and ascribed to the Britons are undoubtedly Roman. See further remarks on p. 118, "Who are the Knockers?"

Mr Edmonds supposes that he found in a bronze vessel discovered near Marazion a caldron in which tin was refined. In the first place, a bronze vessel would never have been used for that purpose—chemical laws are against it; and in the second place, it is more than doubtful if ever the "Jews' tin" was subjected to this process. In all probability, the bronze vessel discovered was a "Roman camp-kettle." A very full description of bronze caldrons of this description will be found in "The Archæology and Prehistoric Annals of Scotland," by Daniel Wilson, p. 274.

It may not be out of place to insert here the tradition of a very important application of this metal.

The use of tin as a mordant, for which very large quantities are now used, is said to have been thus discovered:—

Mr Crutchy, Bankside, married a Scotchwoman. This lady often told her husband that his scarlet was not equal to one she could dye. He set her to work. She dyed a skein of worsted in a saucepan, using the same material as her husband, but produced a better colour. She did not know this was owing to the saucepan's being tinned, but he detected the fact, and made his fortune as a dyer of scarlet and Turkey-red. The most important Turkey-red dye-works are even now in the neighbourhood of Lochlomond; therefore, this Scotchwoman may have been better acquainted with the process than the story tells.

THE TINNER OF CHYANNOR.

THE village of Trereen, near the Logan Stone, was at one time an important market-town. Here came all the tin-streamers who worked from Penberth to the hills, and to protect the place and the valuable property which was accumulated here, Castle Trereen was built. Here came—or rather into the cove near it came—the Tyrian merchants. They were not allowed to advance beyond the shores, lest they should discover the country from which the tin was brought. But it is not of them that we have now to tell, but of a knot of tinners who came from the low country between Chyannor and Trengothal. These were assembled round the Garrack Zans, which then stood in the centre of the market-place of Trereen. Times had been bad, and they were consulting together what they had better do. The "streams" had failed them, and they believed all the tin was worked out. Some of them had heard that there was tin in "the country a long way off," some miles beyond Market-Jew; but they had but a very dim idea of the place or of the people. One of them, who, though an old man, was more adventurous than any of his comrades, said he would travel there and see what could be done. It was then determined that Tom Trezidder should try his fortune, and the others would wait until he came home again, or sent for them to come to him. This was soon noised about, and all the women, old and young, came to say "Good-bye" to Tom. His parting with his wife was brief but bitter. He bore up well, and with a stout heart started on his adventure. Tom Trezidder arrived at length at a place not far from Goldsythney, and here he found one of the Jew merchants, who farmed the tin ground, and sold the tin at St Michael's Mount; and the Jew was very anxious to engage so experienced a "streamer" as Tom was. Tom, nothing loath, took service for a year. He was to have just enough to live on, and a share of profits at the year's end. Tom worked diligently, and plenty of tin was the result of his experienced labour. The year expired, and Tom looked for his share of the profits. The Jew contrived to put Tom off, and promised Tom great things if he would stop for another year, and persuaded him to send for some of his old comrades, clenching every argument which he employed with a small piece of advice, "Never leave an old road for a new one."

The other tinners were shy of venturing so far, so that two or three only could be persuaded to leave the West Country. With Tom and with his brethren the year passed by, and at the end he got no money, but only the same piece of advice, "Never leave an old road for a new one." This went on for a third year, when all of them, being naturally tired of this sort of thing, resolved to go home again.

Tom Trezidder was a favourite with his master, and was greatly esteemed for his honesty and industry by his mistress.

When they left she gave Tom a good currant cake to take home to his old woman, and told him to remember the advice, "Never leave an old road for a new one."

The tinners trudged on together until they were on the western side of Penzance. They were weary, and they found that since they had left home a new road had been made over the hills, which saved them a considerable distance—in fact it was a "short cut." On they went. "No," says Tom; "never leave an old road for a new one." They all laughed at him, and trudged on. But Tom kept in the old road along the valley round the hill. When Tom reached the other end of the "short cut" he thought he would rest a bit, and he sat down by the roadside and ate his *fuggan*. This his mistress had given him, that he might not break his cake until he got home.

He had not sat long when he heard a noise, and, looking up the hill, he saw his comrades, whom he thought were miles in advance of him, slowly and sorrowfully descending it. They came at last to where Tom was seated, and a sad tale had they to tell. They had scarcely got into the new road when they were set upon by robbers, who took from them "all their little bit of money," and then beat them because they had no more.

Tom, you may be sure, thought the piece of advice worth something now, as it had saved his bacon.

Tom arrived home at last, and glad was the old woman to see her old man once again; so she made him some "herby tea" at once. He shewed his wife the cake, and told her that all he had received for his share of profits was the piece of advice already given.

The ladies who read this story will understand how vexed was Tom's wife,—there are but few of them who would not have done as she did, that was to seize the cake from the table and fling it at her husband's head, calling him an old fool. Tom Trezidder stooped to avoid the blow. Slap against the corner of the dresser went the cake, breaking in pieces with the blow, and out on the lime-ash floor rolled a lot of gold coins.

This soon changed the aspect of things; the storm rolled back, and sunshine was once more in the cottage. The coins were all gathered up, and they found a scrap of paper, on which, when they got the priest to read it, they discovered was written an exact account of each year's profits, and Tom's share. The three years' shares had been duly hoarded for him by his master and mistress; and now this old couple found they had enough to make them comfortable for the rest of their days. Many were the prayers said by Tom and his wife for the happiness and health of the honest Jew tin merchant and his wife.

"WHO ARE THE KNOCKERS?"

CHARLES KINGSLEY in his "Yeast: a Problem," asks this question—Tregarra answers,—

"They are *the ghosts*, the miners hold, *of the old Jews that crucified our Lord, and were sent for slaves by the Roman emperors to work the mines:* and we find their old smelting-houses, which we call *Jews' houses*, and their blocks at the bottom of the great bogs, which we call *Jews' tin:* and then a town among us too, which we call *Market-Jew*, but the old name was Marazion, that means the bitterness of Zion, they tell me; and bitter work it was for them, no doubt, poor souls! We used to break into old shafts and adits which they had made, and find fine old stag's-horn pickaxes, that crumbled to pieces when we brought them to grass. And they say that if a man will listen of a still night about these shafts, he may hear the ghosts of them at work, knocking and picking, as clear as if there was a man at work in the next level."

In *Notes and Queries* will be found some learned discussions on the question of the Jews working the Cornish tin mines, as though it were merely one of tradition. That the Jews farmed the tin mines of Cornwall and Devonshire is an historical fact, of which we have evidence in charters granted by several of our kings, especially by King John, Carew in his "Survey of Cornwall" gives some account of their mode of dealing with the tinners. Hence the terms "Jews' houses," given to old and rude smelting-works,—many of which I have seen,—and hence the name of "Jews' tin," given to the old blocks of tin, specimens of which may be seen in the *Museum of Practical Geology*, and in the museum of the *Royal Institution of Cornwall*, at Truro. "*Atall Sarazin*" is another term applied to some of the old waste-heaps of the ancient tin mines.

"The Jews," says Whitaker, ("Origin of Arianism," p. 334,) "denominated themselves, and were denominated by the Britons of Cornwall, *Saracens*, as the geniune progeny of Sarah." Be this as it may, I have often heard in the mining villages —from twenty to thirty years since—a man coming from a distant parish, called "*a foreignerer;*" a man from a distant country, termed "*an outlandish man;*" and any one not British born, designated as "*a Saracen.*"

But this has led me away from the knockers, who are in some districts called also "*the buccas.*" Many a time have I been seriously informed by the miners themselves that these sprites have been heard working away in the remote parts of a lode, repeating the blows of the miner's pick or sledge with great precision. Generally speaking, the knockers work upon productive lodes only; and they have often kindly indicated to the trusting miner, where they might take good tribute pitches.

To Wesley, Cornwall owes a deep debt. He found the country steeped in the darkness of superstitious ignorance, and he opened a new light upon it. Associated with the spread of Wesleyan Methodism, has been the establishment of schools; and under the influence of religion and education, many of the superstitions have faded away. We rarely hear of the knockers now; but the following occurrence will shew that the knockers have not entirely left the land:—

One Saturday night I had retired to rest, having first seen that all the members of the household had gone to their bedrooms. These were my daughters, two female servants, and an old woman, named Mary, who was left, by the proprietor, in charge of the house which I occupied.

I had been some time in bed, when I distinctly heard a bedroom door open, and footsteps which, after moving about for some time in the passage or landing, from which the bedrooms opened, slowly and carefully descended the stairs. I heard a movement in the kitchen below, and the footsteps again ascended the stairs, and went into one of the bedrooms. This noise continued so long, and was so regularly repeated, that I began to fear lest one of the children were taken suddenly ill. Yet I felt assured, if it was so, one of the servants would call me. Therefore I lay still and listened until I fell asleep.

On the Sunday morning, when I descended to the breakfast-room, I asked the eldest of the two servants what had occasioned so much going up and down stairs in the night. She declared that no one had left their bedrooms after they had retired to them. I then inquired of the younger girl, and of each of my daughters as they made their appearance. No one had left their rooms—they had not heard any noises. My youngest daughter, who had been, after this inquiry of mine, for some minutes alone with the youngest servant, came laughing to me,—

"Papa, Nanny says the house is haunted, and that they have often heard strange noises in it."

So I called Nancy; but all I could learn from her was that noises, like that of men going up and down stairs,—of threshing corn, and of "beating the borer," (a mining operation,) were not uncommon.

We all laughed over papa's ghost during the breakfast, and by and by old Mary made her appearance.

"Yes," she said, "it is quite true, as Nanny as a told you. I have often heard all sorts of strange noises; but I b'lieve they all come from the lode of tin which runs under the house. *Wherever there is a lode of tin, you are sure to hear strange noises.*"

"What, Mary! was it the knockers I heard last night?"

"Yes; 'twas the knackers, down working upon the tin—no doubt of it."

This was followed by a long explanation, and numerous stories of mines in the Lelant and St Ives district, in which the knockers had been often heard.

After a little time, Mary, imagining, I suppose, that the young ladies might not like to sleep in a house beneath which the knockers were at work; again came with her usual low courtesy into the parlour.

"Beg pardon, sir," says she; "but none of the young ladies need be afraid. There are no spirits in the house; it is very nearly a new one, and no one has ever died in the house."

This makes a distinct difference between the ghost of the departed and those gnomes who are doomed to toil in the earth's dark recesses.* The Cornish knocker does not appear

* "Some are sent, like the spirit Gathon in Cornwall, to work the will of his master in the mines."—*Mrs Bray's Traditions of Devonshire.*

Who was the spirit Gathon?

"The miner starts as he hears the mischievous Gathon answering blow for blow the stroke of his pickaxe, or deluding him with false fires, noises, to be the "*cobal*" of German miners. The former are generally kindly, and often serve the industrious miner; the latter class are always malicious, and, I believe, are never heard but when mischief is near.

MINERS' SUPERSTITIONS.

MINERS say they often see little imps or demons underground. Their presence is considered favourable; they indicate the presence of lodes, about which they work during the absence of the miners. A miner told my informant that he had often seen them, sitting on pieces of timber, or tumbling about in curious attitudes, when he came to work.

and flames."—*A Guide to the Coasts of Devon and Cornwall. Mackenzie Walcott, M.A.*

Carne, in his "Tales of the West," alludes to this:—"The miners have their full share of the superstitious feelings of the country, and often hear with alarm the noises, as it were, of other miners at work deep underground, and at no great distance. The rolling of the barrows, the sound of the pickaxes, and the fall of the earth and stones, are distinctly heard through the night,—often, no doubt, the echo of their own labours; but sometimes continued long after that labour has ceased, and occasionally voices seem to mingle with them. Gilbert believed that he was peculiarly exposed to these visitations; he had an instinctive shrinking from the place where the accident had happened; and, when left alone there, it was in vain that he plied his toil with desperate energy to divert his thoughts. Another person appeared to work very near him: he stayed the lifted pick and listened. The blow of the other fell distinctly, and the rich ore followed it in a loud rolling; he checked the loaded barrow that he was wheeling; still that of the unknown workman went on, and came nearer and nearer, and then there followed a loud, faint cry, that thrilled through every nerve of the lonely man, for it seemed like the voice of his brother. These sounds all ceased on a sudden, and those which his own toil caused were the only ones heard, till, after an interval, without any warning, they began again, at times more near, and again passing away to a distance."—*The Tale of the Miner.*

Miners do not like the form of the cross being made underground. A friend of my informant, going through some "levels" or "adits," made a + by the side of one, to know his way back, as he would have to return by himself. He was compelled to alter it into another form.

If miners see a snail when going to "bal" in the morning, they always drop a piece of tallow from their candles by its side.

CHRISTMAS-EVE IN THE MINES.

ON Christmas-eve, in former days, the small people, or the spriggans, would meet at the bottom of the deepest mines, and have a midnight mass. Then those who were in the mine would hear voices melodious beyond all earthly voices, singing, "Now well! now well;"* and the strains of some deep-toned organ would shake the rocks. Of the grandeur of those meetings, old stories could not find words sufficiently sonorous to speak; it was therefore left to the imagination. But this was certain, the temple formed by the fairy bands in which to celebrate the eve of the birth of a Saviour, in whose mercy they all had hope, was of the most magnificent description.

Midsummer-eve and new-year's day and eve are holidays with the miners. It has been said they refuse to work on those days from superstitious reasons. I never heard of any.

* "Now well! now well! the angel did say
To certain poor shepherds in the fields who lay
Late in the night, folding their sheep;
A winter's night, both cold and deep.
Now well! now well! now well!
Born is the King of Israel!"

WARNINGS AND "TOKENS."

AMONGST the mining population there is a deeply-rooted belief in warnings. The following, related by a very respectable man, formerly a miner, well illustrates this:—

"My father, when a lad, worked with a companion (James or 'Jim,' as he was called) in Germo. They lived close by Old Wheal Grey in Breage. One evening, the daughter of the person with whom they lodged came in to her mother, crying, 'Billy and Jim ben out theer for more than a hour, and I ben chasin them among the Kilyur banks, and they waan't ler me catch them. As fast as I do go to one, they do go to another.' 'Hould your tongue, child,' said the mother; ''twas their forenoon core, and they both ben up in bed this hours.' 'I'm sure I ben chasin them,' said the girl. The mother then went upstairs and awoke the lads, telling them the story. One of them said, ''Tis a warning; somethin will happen in un old end, and I shan't go to mine this core.' 'Nonsense,' said the other; 'don't let us be so foolish; the child has been playing with some strangers, and it isn't worth while to be spaled for any such foolishness.' 'I tell you,' replied the other, 'I won't go.' As it was useless for one man to go alone, both remained away. In the course of the night, however, a run took place in the end they were working in, and tens of thousands of kibblefuls came away. Had they been at work, it was scarcely possible for them to have escaped."

At Wheal Vor it has always been and is now believed that a fatal accident in the mine is presaged by the appearance of a hare or white rabbit in one of the engine-houses. The men solemnly declare that they have chased these appearances till they were hemmed in apparently, without being able to catch them. The white rabbit on one occasion being *run into a "windbore"* lying on the ground, *and, though stopped in,* escaped.

In this mine there appears to be a general belief among the men in "tokens" and supernatural appearances. A few months since, a fine old man reported, on being relieved from his turn as watcher, that during the night he heard a loud sound like the emptying of a cartload of rubbish in front of the account-house, where he was staying. On going out, nothing was to be seen. The poor fellow, considering the strange sound as a "warning," pined away and died within a few weeks.

THE GHOST ON HORSEBACK.

BILLY —— and John ——, working at Wheal Vor, were in the habit, early in the morning, of calling out a dog or two, kept by the occupier of an adjoining farm, and with them hunt over the Godolphin warren adjoining. One morning, while thus engaged, one of them gave the alarm that a man on horseback was coming down the road. "'Tisn't possible," said the other; "no horse can ever come over that road." "There is a horse, and old Cap'n T. is upon it," replied the first. "Hold thy tongue," rejoined his comrade; "he's dead months ago." "I know that; but 'tis he, sure enough." Both crouched down behind a bush; and my informant, whose father was one of the parties, declared that the appearance of Capt. T., on a black horse, passed noiselessly down the road immediately before them, but without noticing their presence.

THE BLACK DOGS.

ABOUT thirty years since, a man and a lad were engaged in sinking a shaft at Wheal Vor Mine, when the lad, through carelessness or accident, missed in charging a hole, so that a necessity arose for the dangerous operation of picking out the charge. This they proceeded to do, the man severely reprimanding the carelessness of his assistant. Several other miners at the time being about to change their core, were on the plat above, calling down and conversing occasionally with man and boy. Suddenly the charge exploded, and the latter were seen to be thrown up in the midst of a volume of flame. As soon as help could be procured, a party descended, when the remains of the poor fellows were found to be shattered and scorched beyond recognition. When these were brought to the surface, the clothes and a mass of mangled flesh dropped from the bodies. A bystander, to spare the feelings of the relatives, hastily caught up the revolting mass in a shovel, and threw the whole into the blazing furnace of Woolf's engine, close at hand. From that time the enginemen declared that troops of little black dogs continually haunted the place, even when the doors were shut. Few of them liked to talk about it; but it was difficult to obtain the necessary attendance to work the machine.

PITMEN'S OMENS AND GOBLINS.

IT is curious to notice the correspondence between the superstitions of the coal-miner and those employed in the metalliferous mines. The following comes very opportunely to our hand:—

The superstitions of pitmen were once many and terrible; but so far from existing now-a-days, they are only matters of tradition among the old men. One class only of superstitions does exist among a few of the older and less-educated pitmen—namely, the class of omens, warnings, and signs. If one of these pitmen meet or see a woman, if he catch but a glimpse of her draperies, on his way, in the middle of the night to the pit, the probability is that he returns home and goes to bed again. The appearance of woman at this untimely hour has often materially impeded the day's winning, for the omen is held not to be personal to the individual perceiving it, but to bode general ill luck to all. The walk from home to pit mouth, always performed at dead of the night, was the period when omens were mostly to be looked for. The supernatural appearance of a little white animal like a rabbit, which was said to cross the miner's path, was another warning not to descend. Sometimes the omens were rather mental than visual. The pitmen in the midland counties have, or had, a belief, unknown in the north, in aerial whistlings, warning them against the pit. Who, or what the invisible musicians were, nobody pretended to know; but for all that, they must have been counted and found to consist of seven, as "The Seven Whistlers" is the name they bear to this day. Two goblins were believed to haunt the northern mines. One was a spiteful elf, who indicated his presence only by the mischief he perpetrated. He rejoiced in the name of "Cutty Soams," and appears to have employed himself only in the stupid device of severing the rope-traces or soams, by which an assistant-putter—honoured by the title of "the fool"—is yoked to the tub. The strands of hemp which were left all sound in the board at "kenner-time," were found next morning severed in twain. "Cutty Soams" has been at work, would the fool and his driver say, dolefully knotting the cord. The other goblin was altogether a more sensible, and, indeed, an honest and hard-working bogie, much akin to the Scotch brownie, or the hairy fiend, whom Milton rather scurvily apostrophises as a lubber. The supernatural personage in question was no other than a ghostly putter, and his name was "Bluecap." Sometimes the miners would perceive a light blue flame flicker through the air, and settle on a full coal-tub, which immediately moved towards the rolley-way, as though impelled by the sturdiest sinews in the working. Industrious Bluecap was at his vocation; but he required, and rightly, to be paid for his services, which he modestly rated as those of an ordinary average putter; therefore once a fortnight Bluecap's wages were left for him in a solitary corner of the mine. If they were a farthing below his due, the indignant Bluecap would not pocket a stiver; if they were a farthing above his due, indignant Bluecap left the surplus revenue where he found it. The writer asked his informant, a hewer, whether, if Bluecap's wages were now-a-days to be left for him, he thought they would be appropriated; the man shrewdly answered, he thought they would be taken by Bluecap, or by somebody else. Of the above notions it must be understood that the idea of omens is the only one still seriously entertained, and even its hold upon the popular mind, as has been before stated, is becoming weaker and weaker.—*Colliery Guardian, May* 23, 1863.

THE DEAD HAND.

"I'VE seen it—I've seen it!" exclaimed a young woman, pale with terror, approaching with much haste the door of a cottage, around which were gathered several of the miners' wives inhabiting the adjoining dwellings.

"God's mercy be with the chield!" replied the oldest woman of the group, with very great seriousness.

"Aunt Alice," asked one of the youngest women, "and do'e b'lieve any harm will come o' seeing it?"

"Mary Doble saw it and pined; Jinny Trestrail was never the same woman after she seed the hand in Wheal Jewel; and I knows ever so many more; but let us hope, by the blessing o' the Lord, no evil will come on Mary."

Mary was evidently impressed with a sense of some heavy trouble. She sighed deeply, and pressed her hand to her side, as if to still the beating of her heart. The thoughtless faith of the old woman promised to work out a fulfilment of her fears in producing mental distress and corporeal suffering in the younger one.

While this was passing in the little village, a group of men were gathered around a deserted shaft, which existed in too dangerous proximity with the abodes of the miners. They were earnestly discussing the question of the reality of the appearance of the *dead hand*—those who had not seen it expressing a doubt of its reality, while others declared most emphatically, "that in that very shaft they had seed un with a lighted candle in his hand, moving up and down upon the ladders, as though he was carried by a living man."

It appears that some time previously to the abandonment of the mine, an unfortunate miner was ascending from his subterranean labours, carrying his candle in his hand. He was probably seized with giddiness, but from that or some other cause, he fell away from the ladders, and was found by his comrades a bleeding corpse at the bottom. The character of this man was not of the best; and after his burial, it was stated by the people that *he had been seen.* From a vague rumour of his spectral appearance on the surface, the tale eventually settled itself into that of the dead hand moving up and down in the shaft.

By the spectral light of the candle, the hand had been distinctly visible to many, and the irregular motion of the light proved that the candle was held in the usual manner between the thumb and finger in its ball of clay, while the fingers were employed in grasping stave after stave of the ladder. The belief in the evil attendant on being unfortunate enough to see this spectral hand, prevailed very generally amongst the mining population about twenty years since. The dead hand was not, however, confined to one shaft or mine. Similar narrations have been met with in several districts.

DORCAS, THE SPIRIT OF POLBREEN MINE.

POLBREEN MINE is situated at the foot of the hill known as St Agnes Becon. In one of the small cottages which immediately adjoins the mine once lived a woman called Dorcas.

Beyond this we know little of her life; but we are concerned chiefly with her death, which we are told was suicidal.

From some cause, which is not related, Dorcas grew weary of life, and one unholy night she left her house and flung herself into one of the deep shafts of Polbreen Mine, at the bottom of which her dead and broken body was discovered. The remnant of humanity was brought to the surface; and after the laws of the time with regard to suicides had been fulfilled, the body of Dorcas was buried.

Her presence, however, still remained in the mine. She appears ordinarily to take a malicious delight in tormenting the industrious miner, calling him by name, and alluring him from his tasks. This was carried on by her to such an extent, that when a "tributer" had made a poor month, he was asked if he had "been chasing Dorcas." *

Dorcas was usually only a voice. It has been said by some that they have seen her in the mine, but this is doubted by the miners generally, who refer the spectral appearance to the fears of their "comrade."

But it is stated as an incontrovertible fact, that more than one man who has met the spirit in the levels of the mine has had his clothes torn off his back; whether in anger or in sport, is not clearly made out. On one occasion, and on one occasion only, Dorcas appears to have acted kindly. Two miners, who for distinction's sake we will call Martin and Jacky, were at work in their end, and at the time busily at work "beating the borer."

The name of Jacky was distinctly uttered between the blows. He stopped and listened—all was still. They proceed with their task: a blow on the iron rod.—"Jacky." Another blow.—"Jacky." They pause—all is silent. "Well, thee wert called, Jacky," said Martin, "go and see."

Jacky was, however, either afraid, or he thought himself the fool of his senses.

Work was resumed, and "Jacky! Jacky! Jacky!" was called more vehemently and distinctly than before.

Jacky threw down his heavy hammer, and went from his companion, resolved to satisfy himself as to the caller.

* A tributer is a man who agrees with the adventurers in a mine to receive a certain share of the profits on the ore raised by him in lieu of wages. This account is settled monthly or bi-monthly, which will explain the phrase a "poor month."

He had not proceeded many yards from the spot on which he had been standing at work, when a mass of rock fell from the roof of the level, weighing many tons, which would have crushed him to death. Martin had been stooping, holding the borer, and a projecting corner of rock just above him turned off the falling mass. He was securely enclosed, and they had to dig him out, but he escaped without injury. Jacky declared to his dying day that he owed his life to Dorcas.

Although Dorcas's shaft remains a part of Polbreen Mine, I am informed by the present agent that her presence has departed.

HINGSTON DOWNS.

> "Hengsten Down, well ywrought,
> Is worth London town dear vbought."
>
> CAREW—*Lord De Dunstanville's Edition.*

IT may be worthy of consideration whether we have not evidence in this distich of the extent to which mining operations were carried on over this moorland and the adjoining country by the ancient Cornish miners.

It is said that this moorland was originally Hengiston; and tradition affirms that the name preserves the memory of a severe contest, when the Welsh joined Egbright, a king of the West Saxons, and defeated the host of Danes, who had come over to "West Wales," meaning thereby Cornwall. On this waste Hengist had his fenced camp, and here the Cornish and the Welsh attacked and entirely overthrew him. It is evident, if tradition is to be believed, that the struggle was to gain possession of a valuable tin ground.

FISHERMEN AND SAILORS.

"I was saying to Jack, as we talk'd t' other day
  About lubbers and snivelling elves,
That if people in life did not steer the right way,
  They had nothing to thank but themselves.
Now, when a man 's caught by those mermaids the girls,
  With their flattering palaver and smiles;
He runs, while he 's list'ning to their fal de rals,
  Bump ashore on the Scilly Isles."

TOM DIBDIN.

ROMANCES OF FISHERMEN AND SAILORS.

THE PILOT'S GHOST STORY.

"On a sudden shrilly sounding,
Hideous yells and shrieks were heard;
Then each heart with fear confounding,
A sad troop of ghosts appear'd,
All in dreary hammocks shrouded,
Which for winding-sheets they wore."
Admiral Hosier's Ghost.

I PREFER giving this story in the words in which it was communicated. For its singular character, it is a ghost story well worth preserving :—

"Just seventeen years since, I went down on the wharf from my house one night about twelve and one in the morning, to see whether there was any 'hobble,' and found a sloop, the *Sally* of St Ives, (the *Sally* was wrecked at St Ives one Saturday afternoon in the spring of 1862,) in the bay, bound for Hayle. When I got by the White Hart public-house, I saw a man leaning against a post on the wharf,—I spoke to him, wished him good morning, and asked him what o'clock it was, but to no purpose. I was not to be easily frightened, for I didn't believe in ghosts; and finding I got no answer to my repeated inquiries, I approached close to him and said, 'Thee 'rt a queer sort of fellow, not to speak; I'd speak to the devil, if he were to speak to me. Who art a at all? thee 'st needn't think to frighten me; that thee wasn't do, if thou wert twice so ugly; who art a at all?' He turned his great ugly face on me, glared abroad his great eyes, opened his mouth, and it was a mouth sure nuff. Then I saw pieces of sea-weed and bits of sticks in his whiskers; the flesh of his face and hands were parboiled, just like a woman's hands after a good day's washing. Well, I did not like his looks a bit, and sheered off; but he followed close by my side, and I could hear the water squashing in his shoes every step he took. Well, I stopped a bit, and thought to be a little bit civil to him, and spoke to him again, but no answer. I then thought I would go to seek for another of our crew, and nock him up to get the vessel, and had got about fifty or sixty yards, when I turned to see if he was following me, but saw him where I left him. Fearing he would come after me, I ran for my life the few steps that I had to go. But when I got to the door, to my horror there stood the man in the door grinning horribly. I shook like as aspen-leaf; my hat lifted from my head; the sweat boiled out of me. What to do I didn't know, and in the house there was such a row, as if everybody was breaking up everything. After a bit I went in, for the door was 'on the latch,'—that is, not locked,—and called the captain of the boat, and got light, but everything was all right, nor had he heard any noise. We went out aboard of the *Sally*, and I put her into Hayle, but I felt ill enough to be in bed. I left the vessel to come home as soon as I could, but it took me four hours to walk two miles, and I had to lie down in the road, and was carried home to St Ives in a cart; as far as the Terrace from there I was carried home by my brothers, and put to bed. Three days afterwards all my hair fell off as if I had had my head shaved. The roots, and for about half an inch from the roots, being quite white.

I was ill six months, and the doctor's bill was £4, 17s. 6d. for attendance and medicine. So you see I have reason to believe in the existence of spirits as much as Mr Wesley had. My hair grew again, and twelve months after I had as good a head of dark-brown hair as ever."*

THE PHANTOM SHIP.

YEARS long ago, one night, a gig's crew was called to go off to a "hobble," to the westwards of St Ives Head. No sooner was one boat launched than several others were put off from the shore, and a stiff chase was maintained, each one being eager to get to the ship, as she had the appearance of a foreign trader. The hull was clearly visible, she was a schooner-rigged vessel, with a light over her bows.

Away they pulled, and the boat which had been first launched still kept ahead by dint of mechanical power and skill. All the men had thrown off their jackets to row with more freedom. At length the helmsman cried out, "Stand ready to board her." The sailor rowing the bow oar slipped it out of the row-lock, and stood on the forethought, taking his jacket on his arm, ready to spring aboard.

The vessel came so close to the boat that they could see the men, and the bow-oar man made a grasp at her bulwarks. His hand found nothing solid, and he fell, being caught by one of his mates, back into the boat, instead of into the water. Then ship and lights disappeared. The next morning the *Neptune* of London, Captain Richard Grant, was wrecked at Gwithian, and all perished. The captain's body was picked up after a few days, and that of his son also. They were both buried in Gwithian churchyard.

* "The man has still a good thick head of hair.—C. F. S."

JACK HARRY'S LIGHTS.

THE phantom lights are called, they tell me, "Jack Harry's lights," because he was the first man who was fooled by them. They are generally observed before a gale, and the ship seen is like the ship which is sure to be wrecked. The man who communicated this to me said, "What or how it is we can't tell, but the fact of its being seen is too plain."

The following is another version, which I received from an old pilot:—

"Some five years ago, on a Sunday night, the wind being strong, our crew heard of a large vessel in the offing, after we came out of chapel. We manned our big boat, the *Ark*,—she was nearly new then,—and away we went, under close-reefed foresail and little mizen, the sea going over us at a sweet rate. The vessel stood just off the head, the wind blowing W.N.W. We had gone off four or five miles, and we thought we were up alongside, when, lo! she slipped to windward a league or more. Well, off we went after her, and a good beating match we had, too; but the *Ark* was a safe craft, and we neared and neared till, as we thought, we got up close. Away she whizzed in a minute, in along to Godrevy, just over the course we sailed; so we gave it up for "Jack Harry's light," and, with wet jackets and disappointed hopes, we bore up for the harbour, prepared to hear of squalls, which came heavier than ever next day.

"Scores of pilots have seen and been led a nice chase after them. They are just the same as the *Flying Dutchman*, seen off the Cape of Good Hope."

Another man informed me that, once coming down channel, they had a phantom ship alongside of them for miles: it was a moonlight night, with a thin rain and mist. They could see several men aboard moving about. They hailed her several times, but could not get an answer, "and we didn't know what to think of her, when all at once she vanished."

THE PIRATE-WRECKER AND THE DEATH SHIP.

ONE lovely evening in the autumn, a strange ship was seen at a short distance from Cape Cornwall. The little wind there was blew from the land, but she did not avail herself of it. She was evidently permitted to drift with the tide, which was flowing southward, and curving in round Whitesand Bay towards the Land's-End. The vessel, from her peculiar rig, created no small amount of alarm amongst the fishermen, since it told them that she was manned by pirates; and a large body of men and women watched her movements from behind the rocks at Caraglose. At length, when within a couple of pistol-shots off the shore, a boat was lowered and manned. Then a man, whose limited movements shew him to be heavily ironed, was brought to the side of the ship and evidently forced,—for several pistols were held at his head,—into the boat, which then rowed rapidly to the shore in Priest's Cove. The waves of the Atlantic Ocean fell so gently on the strand, that there was no difficulty in beaching the boat. The prisoner was made to stand up, and his ponderous chains were removed from his arms and ankles. In a frenzy of passion he attacked the sailors, but they were too many and too strong for him, and the fight terminated by his being thrown into the water, and left to scramble up on the dry sands. They pushed the boat off with a wild shout, and this man stood uttering fearful imprecations on his former comrades.

It subsequently became known that this man was so monstrously wicked that even the pirates would no longer endure him, and hence they had recourse to this means of ridding themselves of him.

It is not necessary to tell how this wretch settled himself at Tregaseal, and lived by a system of wrecking, pursued with unheard-of cruelties and cunning. "It's too frightful to tell," says my correspondent, "what was said about his doings. We scarcely believed half of the vile things we heard, till we saw what took place at his death. But one can't say he died, because he was taken off bodily. We shall never know the scores, perhaps hundreds, of ships that old sinner has brought on the cliffs, by fastening his lantern to the neck of his horse, with its head tied close to the forefoot. The horse, when driven along the cliff, would, by its motion, cause the lantern to be taken for the stern-light of a ship; then the vessel would come right in on the rocks, since those on board would expect to find plenty of sea-room; and, if any of the poor sailors escaped a watery grave, the old wretch would give them a worse death, by knocking them on the head with his hatchet, or cutting off their hands as they tried to grasp the ledges of the rocks."

A life of extreme wickedness was at length closed with circumstances of unusual terror—so terrible, that the story is told with feelings of awe even at the present day. The old wretch fought lustily with death, but at length the time of his departure came. It was in the time of the barley-harvest. Two men were in a field on the cliff, a little below the house, mowing. A universal calm prevailed, and there was not a breath of wind to stir the corn. Suddenly a breeze passed by them, and they heard the words, "The time is come, but the man isn't come." These words appeared to float in the breeze from the sea, and consequently it attracted their attention. Looking out to sea, they saw a black, heavy, square-rigged ship, with all her sails set, coming in against wind and tide, and not a hand to be seen on board. The sky became black as night around the ship, and as she came under the cliff—and she came so close that the top of the masts could scarcely be perceived—the darkness resolved itself into a lurid storm-cloud, which extended high into the air. The sun shone brilliantly over the country, except on the house of the pirate at Tregaseal—that was wrapt in the deep shadow of the cloud.

The men, in terror, left their work; they found all the neighbours gathered around the door of the pirate's cottage, none of them daring to enter it. Parson —— had been sent for by the terrified peasants, this divine being celebrated for his power of driving away evil spirits.

The dying wrecker was in a state of agony, crying out, in tones of the most intense terror, "The devil is tearing at me with nails like the claws of a hawk! Put out the sailors with their bloody hands!" and using, in the paroxysms of pain, the most profane imprecations. The parson, the doctor, and two of the bravest of the fishermen, were the only persons in the room. They related that at one moment the room was as dark as the grave, and that at the next it was so light that every hair on the old man's head could be seen standing on end. The parson used all his influence to dispel the evil spirit. His powers were so potent that he reduced the devil to the size of a fly, but he could not put him out of the room. All this time the room appeared as if filled with the sea, with the waves surging violently to and fro, and one could hear the breakers roaring, as if standing on the edge of the cliff in a storm. At last there was a fearful crash of thunder, and a blaze of the intensest lightning. The house appeared on fire, and the ground shook, as if with an earthquake. All rushed in terror from the house, leaving the dying man to his fate.

The storm raged with fearful violence, but appeared to contract its dimensions. The black cloud, which was first seen to come in with the black ship, was moving, with a violent internal motion, over the wrecker's house. The cloud rolled together, smaller and smaller, and suddenly, with the blast of a whirlwind, it passed from Tregaseal to the ship, and she was impelled, amidst the flashes of lightning and roarings of thunder, away over the sea.

The dead body of the pirate-wrecker lay a ghastly spectacle, with eyes expanded and the mouth partly open, still retaining the aspect of his last mortal terror. As every one hated him, they all desired to remove his corpse as rapidly as possible from the sight of man. A rude coffin was rapidly prepared, and the body was carefully cased in its boards. They tell me the coffin was carried to the church-yard, but that it was too light to have contained the body, and that it was followed by a black pig, which joined the company forming the procession, nobody knew where, and disappeared nobody knew when. When they reached the church stile, a storm, similar in its character to that which heralded the wrecker's death, came on. The bearers of the coffin were obliged to leave it without the churchyard stile and rush into the church for safety. The storm lasted long and raged with violence, and all was as dark as night. A sudden blaze of light, more vivid than before, was seen, and those who had the hardihood to look out saw that the lightning had set fire to the coffin, and it was being borne away through the air, blazing and whirling wildly in the grasp of such a whirlwind as no man ever witnessed before or since.

THE SPECTRE SHIP OF PORTHCURNO.

PORTHCURNO Cove is situated a little to the west of the Logan Stone. There, as in nearly all the coves around the coast, once existed a small chapel * or oratory, which appears to have been dedicated to St Leven. There exists now a little square enclosure about the size of a (*bougie*) sheep's house, which is all that remains of this little holy place. Looking up the valley, (Bottom,) you may see a few trees, with the chimney-tops and part of the roof of an old-fashioned house. That place is Raftra, where they say St Leven Church was to have been built; but as fast as the stones were taken there by day, they were removed by night to the place of the present church. (These performances are usually the act of the devil, but I have no information as to the saint or sinner who did this work.) Raftra House, at the time it was built, was the largest mansion west of Penzance. It is said to have been erected by the Tresillians, and, ere it was finished, they appear to have been obliged to sell house and lands for less than it had cost them to build the house.

This valley is in every respect a melancholy spot, and during a period of storms, or at night, it is exactly the place which might well be haunted by demon revellers. In the days of the saint from whom the parish has its name—St Leven—he lived a long way up from the cove, at a place called Bodelan, and his influence made that, which is now so dreary, a garden. By his pure holiness he made the wilderness a garden of flowers, and spread gladness where now is desolation.

* I am informed that there are no less than four of these cliff chapels between St Leven and St Loy, which was a larger building, where mass was probably celebrated.

Few persons cared to cross that valley after nightfall; and it is not more than thirty years since that I had a narrative from an inhabitant of Penberth, that he himself had seen the spectre ship sailing over the land.

This strange apparition is said to have been observed frequently, coming in from sea about nightfall, when the mists were rising from the marshy ground in the Bottoms.

Onward came the ill-omened craft. It passed steadily through the breakers on the shore, glided up over the sands, and steadily pursued its course over the dry land, as if it had been water. She is described to have been a black, square-rigged, single-masted affair, usually, but not always, followed by a boat. No crew was ever seen. It is supposed they were below, and that the hatches were battened down. On it went to Bodelan, where St Leven formerly dwelt. It would then steer its course to Chygwiden, and there vanish like smoke.

Many of the old people have seen this ship, and no one ever saw it, upon whom some bad luck was not sure to fall.

This ship is somehow connected with a strange man who returned from sea, and went to live at Chygwiden. It may be five hundred years since—it may be but fifty.

He was accompanied by a servant of foreign and forbidding aspect, who continued to be his only attendant; and this servant was never known to speak to any one save his master. It is said by some they were pirates; others make them more familiar, by calling them privateers; while some insist upon it they were American bucaneers. Whatever they may have been, there was but little seen of them by any of their neighbours. They kept a boat at Portheurno Cove, and at daylight they would start for sea, never returning until night, and not unfrequently remaining out the whole of the night, especially if the weather was tempestuous. This kind of sea-life was varied by hunting. It mattered not to them whether it was day or night; when the storm was loudest, there was this strange man, accompanied either by his servant or by the devil, and the midnight cry of his dogs would disturb the country.

This mysterious being died, and then the servant sought the aid of a few of the peasantry to bear his coffin to the churchyard. The corpse was laid in the grave, around which the dogs were gathered, with the foreigner in their midst. As soon as the earth was thrown on the coffin, man and dogs disappeared, and, strange to say, the boat disappeared at the same moment from the cove. It has never since been seen; and from that day to this no one has been able to keep a boat in Porthcurno Cove.

THE LADY WITH THE LANTERN.

THE night was dark and the wind high. The heavy waves rolled round the point of "the Island" into St Ives Bay, as Atlantic waves only can roll. Everything bespoke a storm of no ordinary character. There were no ships in the bay—not a fishing-boat was afloat. The few small trading vessels had run into Hayle for shelter, or had nestled themselves within that very unquiet resting-place, St Ives pier. The fishing-boats were all high and dry on the sands.

Moving over the rocks which run out into the sea from the eastern side of "the Island," was seen a light. It passed over the most rugged ridges, formed by the intrusive Greenstone masses, and over the sharp edges of the upturned slate-rocks, with apparent ease. Forth and back—to and from—wandered the light.

"Ha!" said an old sailor with a sigh, as he looked out over

the sea; "a sad night! a sad night! The Lady and the Lantern is out."

"The Lady and the Lantern," repeated I; "what do you mean?"

"The light out yonder"——

"Is from the lantern of some fisherman looking for something he has lost," interrupted I.

"Never a fisherman nor a 'salt' either would venture there to-night," said the sailor.

"What is it, then?" I curiously inquired.

"Ha'ast never heard of the Lady and the Lantern?" asked a woman who was standing by.

"Never."

Without any preface, she began at once to enlighten me. I am compelled, however, to reduce her rambling story to something like order, and to make her long-drawn tale as concise as possible.

In the year —— there were many wrecks around the coast. It was a melancholy time. For more than a month there had been a succession of storms, each one more severe than the preceding one. At length, one evening, just about dusk, a large ship came suddenly out of the mist. Her position, it was at once discovered, equally by those on board and by the people on the shore, was perilous beyond hope. The sailors, as soon as they saw how near they were to the shore, made every effort to save the ship, and then to prepare for saving themselves. The tempest raged with such fury from the west, that the ship parted her anchors at the moment her strain came upon them, and she swang round,—her only sail flying into ribbons in the gale—rushing, as it were, eagerly upon her fate. Presently she struck violently upon a sunken rock, and her masts went by the board, the waves sweeping over her, and clearing her decks. Many perished at once, and, as each successive wave urged her onward, others of the hardy and daring seamen were swept into the angry sea.

Notwithstanding the severity of the storm, a boat was manned by the St Ives fishermen, and launched from within the pier. Their perfect knowledge of their work enabled them, by the efforts of willing hearts, anxiously desiring to succour the distressed, to round the pier-head, and to row towards the ship.

These fishermen brought their boat near to the ship. It was impossible to get close to her, and they called to the sailors on board to throw them ropes. This they were enabled to do, and some two or three of the sailors lowered themselves by their aid, and were hauled into the boat.

Then a group appeared on the deck, surrounding and supporting a lady, who held a child in her arms. They were imploring her to give her charge into the strong arms of a man ere they endeavoured to pass her from the ship to the boat.

The lady could not be prevailed on to part with the infant. The ship was fast breaking up, not a moment could be lost. So the lady, holding her child, was lowered into the sea, and eagerly the fishermen drew her through the waves towards the boat.

In her passage the lady had fainted, and she was taken into the boat without the infant. The child had fallen from her arms, and was lost in the boiling waters.

Many of the crew were saved by these adventurous men, and taken safely into St Ives. Before morning the shore was strewed with fragments of wreck, and the mighty ship had disappeared.

Life returned to the lady; but, finding that her child was

gone, it returned without hope, and she speedily closed her eyes in death. In the churchyard they buried her; but, shortly after her burial, a lady was seen to pass over the wall of the churchyard, on to the beach, and walk towards the Island. There she spent hours amidst the rocks, looking for her child, and not finding it, she would sigh deeply and return to her grave. When the nights were tempestuous or very dark, she carried a lantern; but on fine nights she made her search without a light. The Lady and the Lantern have ever been regarded as predictors of disaster on this shore.

May not the Lady Sibella, or Sibbets, mentioned by Mr Blight as passing from the shore to a rock off Morva, be but another version of this story?

THE DROWNED "HAILING THEIR NAMES."

THE fishermen dread to walk at night near those parts of the shore where there may have been wrecks. The souls of the drowned sailors appear to haunt those spots, and the "calling of the dead" has frequently been heard. I have been told that, under certain circumstances, especially before the coming of storms, or at certain seasons, but always at night, these callings are common. Many a fisherman has declared he has heard the voices of dead sailors "hailing their own names."

THE VOICE FROM THE SEA.

A FISHERMAN or a pilot was walking one night on the sands at Porth-Towan, when all was still save the monotonous fall of the light waves upon the sand.

He distinctly heard a voice from the sea exclaiming,—

"The hour is come, but not the man."

This was repeated three times when a black figure, like that of a man, appeared on the top of the hill. It paused for a moment, then rushed impetuously down the steep incline, over the sands, and was lost in the sea.

In different forms this story is told all around the Cornish coast.

THE SMUGGLER'S TOKEN.

UNTIL about the time of the close of the last French war, a large portion of the inhabitants of the south-west coast of Cornwall were in some way or other connected with the practice of smuggling. The traffic with the opposite coast was carried on principally in boats or undecked vessels. The risks encountered by their crews produced a race of hardy, fearless men, a few of whom are still living, and it has been said that the Government of those days winked at the infraction of the law, from an unwillingness to destroy so excellent a school for seamen. Recently the demand for ardent spirits has so fallen off that there is no longer an inducement to smuggle; still it is sometimes exultingly rumoured that, the "Coast Guard having been cleverly put off the scent, a cargo has been successfully run." The little coves in the Lizard promontory formed the principal trading places, the goods being taken as soon as landed to various places of concealment, whence they were withdrawn as required for disposal. About eighty years since, a boat, laden with "ankers" of spirits, was about, with its crew, to leave Mullion Cove for Newlyn. One of the farmers concerned in the venture, members of whose family are still living, was persuaded to accompany them, and entered the boat for the purpose, but, recollecting he had business at Helston, got out again, and the boat left without him. On his return from Helston, late in the evening, he sat down, exclaiming, "The boat and all on board are lost! I met the men as I passed the top of Halzaphron, (a very high cliff on the road,) with their hair and clothes dripping wet!" In spite of the arguments of his friends, he persisted in his statement. The boat and crew were never more heard of, and the farmer was so affected by the circumstance, that he pined and died shortly after.

THE HOOPER, OR THE HOOTER, OF SENNEN COVE.

THIS was supposed to be a spirit which took the form of a band of misty vapour, stretching across the bay, so opaque that nothing could be seen through it. It was regarded as a kindly interposition of some ministering spirit, to warn the fishermen against venturing to sea. This appearance was always followed, and often suddenly, by a severe storm. It is seldom or ever seen now. One profane old fisherman would not be warned by the bank of fog. The weather was fine on the shore, and the waves fell tranquilly on the sands; and this aged sinner, declaring he would not be made a fool of, persuaded some young men to join him. They manned a boat, and the aged leader, having with him a threshing-flail, blasphemously declared that he would drive the spirit away; and he vigorously beat the fog with the "threshel"—so the flail is called.

The boat passed through the fog, and went to sea. A severe storm came on. No one ever saw the boat or the men again; and since that time the Hooper has been rarely seen.

HOW TO EAT PILCHARDS.

IT is unlucky to commence eating pilchards, or, indeed, any kind of fish, from the head downwards. I have often heard persons rebuked for committing such a grievous sin, which is "sure to turn the heads of the fish away from the coasts."

The legitimate process—mark this, all fish-eaters—*is to eat the fish from the tail towards the head.* This brings the fish to our shores, and secures good luck to the fishermen.

PILCHARDS CRYING FOR MORE.

WHEN there is a large catch of fish, (pilchards,) they are preserved,—put in bulk, as the phrase is,—by being rubbed with salt, and placed in regular order, one on the other, head and tails alternately, forming regular walls of fish.

The fish often, when so placed, make a squeaking noise; this is called "crying for more," and is regarded as a most favourable sign. More fish may soon be expected to be brought to the same cellar.

The noise which is heard is really produced by the bursting of the air-bladders; and when many break together, which, when hundreds of thousands are piled in a mass, is not unusual, the sound is a loud one.

THE PRESSING-STONES.

THOSE who are not familiar with the process of "curing," (salting) pilchards for the Italian markets, will require a little explanation to understand the accompanying story.

The pilchards being caught in vast quantities, often amounting to many thousand hogsheads at a time, in an enclosing net called a "seine," are taken out of it—the larger net—in a smaller net, called the "tuck net," and from it loaded into boats and taken to the shore. They are quickly transferred to the fish-sellers, and "put in bulk"—that is, they are well rubbed with salt, and carefully packed up—all interstitial spaces being filled with salt—in a pile several feet in height and depth. They remain in this condition for about six weeks, when they are removed from "the bulk," washed, and put into barrels in very regular order. The barrels being filled with pilchards, pressing-stones,—round masses of granite, weighing about a hundredweight,—with an iron hook fixed into them for the convenience of moving, are placed on the fish. By this they are much compressed, and a considerable quantity of oil is squeezed out of them. This process being completed, the cask is "headed," marked, and is ready for exportation.

Jem Tregose and his old woman, with two sons and a daughter, lived over one of the fish-cellars in St Ives. For many years there had been a great scarcity of fish;* their cellar had been empty; Jem and his boys were fishermen, and it had long been hard times with them. It is true they went out "hook-and-line" fishing now and then, and got a little money. They had gone over to Ireland on the herring-fishing, but very little luck attended them.

Summer had passed away, and the early autumn was upon them. The seine-boats were out day after day, but no "signs of fish." One evening, when the boys came home, Ann Jenny Tregose had an unusual smile upon her face, and her daughter Janniper, who had long suffered from the "megrims," was in capital spirits.

* Pilchards are called *par excellence* "fish."

"Well, mother," says one of the sons, "and what ails thee a'?"

"The press-stones a bin rolling."

"Haas they, sure enuff," says the old man.

"Ees! ees!" exclaims Janniper; "they has been making a skimmage!"

"Hark ye," cries the old woman, "there they go again."

And sure enough there was a heavy rolling of the stones in the cellar below them. It did not require much imagination to image these round granite pebbles sliding themselves down on the "couse," or stone flooring, and dividing themselves up into sets, as if for a dance,—a regular "cows' courant," or game of romps.

"Fish to-morrow!" exclaimed the old woman. The ejaculations of each one of the party shewed their perfect faith in the belief, that the stones rolling down from the heap, in which they had been useless for some time, was a certain indication that pilchards were approaching the coast.

Early on the morrow the old man and his sons were on their "stem;" and shortly after daylight the cry of "Heva! heva!" * was heard from the hills; the seine was shot, and ere night a large quantity of fish might be seen in the cellar, and every one joyous.

* Heva is shouted from the hills, upon which a watch is kept for the approach of pilchards by the "huer," who telegraphs to the boats by means of bushes covered with white cloth, or, in modern days, with wire frames so covered. These signals are well understood, and the men in the seine and the other boats act according to the huer's directions. The following song contains all the terms employed in this fishery; many of them, especially *Could Roos*, do not appear to have any definite meaning attached to them.

The song is by the late C. Taylor Stevens of St Ives, who was for some time the rural postman to Zennor. I employed Mr Taylor Stevens for some time collecting all that remains of legendary tales and supersti-

WHIPPING THE HAKE.

IT is not improbable that the saying applied to the people of one of the Cornish fishing-towns, of "Who whipped the hake?" may be explained by the following:—

"Lastly, they are persecuted by the hakes, who (not long

tions in Zennor and Morva. The net is spelled sometimes *Seine* at others *Sean*.

"MERRY SEAN LADS.

"With a cold north wind and a cockled sea,
Or an autumn's cloudless day,
At the huer's bid, to stem we row,
Or upon our paddles play.
All the signs, 'East, West, and Quiet,
Could Roos,' too well we know;
We can bend a stop, secure a cross,
For brave sean lads are we!
Chorus—We can bend a stop, secure a cross,
For brave sean lads are we!

"If we have first stem when heva comes,
We'll the huer's bushes watch;
We will row right off or quiet lie,
Flying summer sculls to catch.
And when he winds the towboat round,
We will all ready be,
When he gives Could Roos, we'll shout hurrah!
Merry sean lads are we!
Chorus—When he gives Could Roos, we'll shout hurrah!
Merry sean lads are we!

"When the sean we've shot, upon the tow,
We will heave with all our might,
With a heave! heave O! and rouse! rouse O!
Till the huer cries, 'All right.'
Then on the bunt place kegs and weights,
And next to tuck go we.
We'll dip, and trip, with a 'Hip hurrah!'
Merry sean lads are we!
Chorus—We'll dip, and trip, with a 'Hip hurrah!'
Merry sean lads are we!"

sithence) haunted the coast in great abundance; but now being deprived of their wonted bait, are much diminished, verifying the proverb, '*What we lose in hake we shall have in herring.*'"—*Carew, Survey,* p. 34.

Annoyed with the hakes, the seiners may, in their ignorance, have actually served one of those fish as indicated.

DEATH SUPERSTITIONS.

"Continually at my bed's head
A hearse doth hang, which doth me tell
That I ere morning may be dead,
Though now I feel myself full well."

ROBERT SOUTHWELL.

DEATH TOKENS AND SUPERSTITIONS.

THE DEATH-TOKEN OF THE VINGOES.

> "The messenger of God
> With golden trumpe I see,
> With many other angels more,
> Which sound and call for me.
> Instead of musicke sweet,
> Go toll my passing bell."
>
> *The Bride's Burial.*

WHEN you cross the brook which divides St Leven from Sennen, you are on the estate of Treville.

Tradition tells us that this estate was given to an old family who came with the Conqueror to this country. This ancestor is said to have been the Duke of Normandy's wine-taster, and that he belonged to the ancient counts of Treville, hence the name of the estate. Certain it is the property has ever been held without poll deeds. For many generations the family has been declining, and the race is now nearly, if not quite, extinct.

Through all time a peculiar token has marked the coming death of a Vingoe. Above the deep caverns in the Treville cliff rises a carn. On this, chains of fire were seen ascending and descending, and often accompanied by loud and frightful noises.

It is said that these tokens have not been seen since the last male of the family came to a violent end.

THE DEATH FETCH OF WILLIAM RUFUS.

ROBERT, Earl of Moreton, in Normandy,—who always carried the standard of St Michael before him in battle,—was made Earl of Cornwall by William the Conqueror. He was remarkable for his valour and for his virtue, for the exercise of his power, and his benevolence to the priests. This was the Earl of Cornwall who gave the Mount in Cornwall to the monks of Mont St Michel in Normandy. He seized upon the priory of St Petroc at Bodmin, and converted all the lands to his own use.

This Earl of Cornwall was an especial friend of William Rufus. It happened that Robert, the earl, was hunting in the extensive woods around Bodmin—of which some remains are still to be found in the Glyn Valley. The chase had been a severe one; a fine old red deer had baffled the huntsmen, and they were dispersed through the intricacies of the forest, the Earl of Cornwall being left alone. He advanced beyond the shades of the woods on to the moors above them, and he was surprised to see a very large black goat advancing over the plain. As it approached him, which it did rapidly, he saw that it bore on its back "King Rufus," all black and naked, and wounded through in the midst of his breast. Robert adjured the goat, in the name of the Holy Trinity, to tell what it was he carried so strangely. He answered, "I am carrying your king to judgment; yea, that tyrant William Rufus, for I am an evil spirit, and the revenger of his malice which he bore to the Church of God. It was I that did cause this slaughter; the protomartyr of England, St Albyn, commanding me so to do, who complained to God of him, for his grievous oppression in this Isle of Britain, which he first hallowed." Having so spoken, the spectre vanished. Robert, the earl, related the circumstance to his followers, and they shortly after learned that at that very hour William Rufus had been slain in the New Forest by the arrow of Walter Tirell.

SIR JOHN ARUNDELL.

IN the first year of the reign of Edward IV., the brave Sir John Arundell dwelt on the north coast of Cornwall, at a place called Efford, on the coast near Stratton. He was a magistrate, and greatly esteemed amongst men for his honourable conduct. He had, however, in his official capacity, given offence to a wild shepherd, who had by some means acquired considerable influence over the minds of the people, under the impression of his possessing some supernatural powers. This man had been imprisoned by Arundell, and on his return home he constantly waylaid the knight, and, always looking threateningly at him, slowly muttered,—

> "When upon the yellow sand,
> Thou shalt die by human hand."

Notwithstanding the bravery of Sir John Arundell, he was not free from the superstitions of the period. He might, indeed, have been impressed with the idea that this man intended to murder him. It is, however, certain that he removed from Efford on the sands, to the wood-clad hills of Trerice, and here he lived for some years without the annoyance of meeting his old enemy. In the tenth year of Edward IV., Richard de Vere, earl of Oxford, seized St Michael's Mount. Sir John Arundell, then sheriff of Cornwall, gathered together his own retainers and a large host of volunteers, and led them to the attack on St Michael's Mount. The retainers of the Earl of Oxford, on one occasion, left the castle, and made a sudden rush upon Arundell's followers, who were encamped on the sands near Marazion. Arundell then received his death-wound. Although he left Efford "to counteract the will of fate," the prophecy was fulfilled; and in his dying moments, it is said his old enemy appeared, singing joyously,—

> "When upon the yellow sand,
> Thou shalt die by human hand."

PHANTOMS OF THE DYING.

A GAY party were assembled one afternoon, in the latter days of January, in the best parlour of a farmhouse near the Land's-End. The inhabitants of this district were, in many respects, peculiar. Nearly all the land was divided up between, comparatively, a few owners, and every owner lived on and farmed his own land.

This circumstance, amongst others, led to a certain amount of style in many of the old farmhouses of the Land's-End district; and even now, in some of them, from which, alas! the glory has departed, may be seen the evidences of taste beyond that which might have been expected in so remote a district.

The "best parlour" was frequently panelled with carved oak, and the ceiling, often highly, though it must be admitted, heavily decorated. In such a room, in the declining light of a January afternoon, were some ten or a dozen farmers' daughters, all of them unmarried, and many of them having an eye on the farmer's eldest son, a fine young man about twenty years of age, called Joseph.

This farmer and his wife, at the time of which we speak, had three sons and two daughters. The eldest son was an excellent and amiable young man, possessed of many personal attractions, and especially fond of the society of his sisters and their friends. The next son was of a very different stamp, and was more frequently found in the inn at Churchtown than in his father's house; the younger son was an apprentice at Penzance. The two daughters, Mary and Honour, had coaxed their mother into "a tea and heavy cake" party, and Joseph was especially retained, to be, as every one said he was, "the life of the company."

In those days, when, especially in those parts, every one took dinner at noon, and tea not much after four o'clock, the party had assembled early.

There had been the usual preliminary gossip amongst the young people, when they began to talk about the wreck of a fruit-ship which had occurred but a few days before, off the Land's-End, and it was said that considerable quantities of oranges were washing into Nangissell Cove. Upon this, Joseph said he would take one of the men from the farm, and go down to the cove—which was not far off—and see if they could not find some oranges for the ladies.

The day had faded into twilight, the western sky was still bright with the light of the setting sun, and the illuminated clouds shed a certain portion of their splendour into the room in which the party were assembled. The girls were divided up into groups, having their own pretty little bits of gossip, often truly delightful from its entire freedom and its innocence; and the mother of Joseph was seated near the fireplace, looking with some anxiety through the windows, from which you commanded a view of the Atlantic Ocean. The old lady was restless; sometimes she had to whisper something to Mary, and then some other thing to Honour. Her anxiety, at length, was expressed in her wondering where Joseph could be tarrying so long. All the young ladies sought to ease her mind by saying that there were no doubt so many orange-gatherers in the Cove, that Joseph and the man could not get so much fruit as he desired.

Joseph was the favourite son of his mother, and her anxiety evidently increased. Eventually, starting from her chair, the old lady exclaimed, "Oh, here he is; now I'll see about the tea."

With a pleased smile on her face, she left the room, to return, however, to it in deeper sorrow.

The mother expected to meet her son at the door—he came not. Thinking that he might possibly have been wetted by the sea, and that he had gone round the house to nother door leading directly into the kitchen, for the purpose of drying himself, or of changing his boots, she went into the dairy to fetch the basin of clotted cream,—which had been "taken up" with unusual care,—to see if the junket was properly set, and to spread the flaky cream thickly upon its surface.

Strange,—as the old lady subsequently related,—all the pans of milk were agitated—"the milk rising up and down like the waves of the sea."

The anxious mother returned to the parlour with her basin of cream, but with an indescribable feeling of an unknown terror. She commanded herself, and, in her usual quiet way, asked if Joseph had been in. When they answered her "No," she sighed heavily, and sank senseless into a chair.

Neither Joseph nor the servant ever returned alive. They were seen standing together upon a rock, stooping to gather oranges as they came with each wave up to their feet, when one of the heavy swells—the lingering undulations of a tempest, so well known on this coast—came sweeping onward, and carried them both away in its cave of waters, as the wave curved to ingulf them.

The undertow of the tidal current was so strong that, though powerful men and good swimmers, they were carried at once beyond all human aid, and speedily perished.

The house of joy became a house of mourning, and sadness rested on it for years. Day after day passed by, and, although a constant watch was kept along the coast, it was not until the fated ninth day that the bodies were discovered, and they were then found in a sadly mutilated state.

Often after long years, and when the consolations derivable from pure religious feeling had brought that tranquillity upon the mind of this loving mother,—which so much resembles the poetical repose of an autumnal evening,—has she repeated to me the sad tale.

Again and again have I heard her declare that she saw Joseph, her son, as distinctly as ever she saw him in her life, and that, as he passed the parlour windows, he looked in upon her and smiled.

This is not given as a superstition belonging in any peculiar way to Cornwall. In every part of the British Isles it exists; but I have never met with any people who so firmly believed in the appearance of the phantoms of the dying to those upon whom the last thoughts are centred, as the Cornish did.

Another case is within my knowledge.

A lady, the wife of an officer in the navy, had been with her husband's sister, on a summer evening, to church. The husband was in the Mediterranean, and there was no reason to expect his return for many months.

These two ladies returned home, and the wife, ascending the stairs before her sister-in-law, went into the drawing-room—her intention being to close the windows, which, as the weather had been warm and fine, had been thrown open.

She had proceeded about half way across the room, when

she shrieked, ran back, and fell into her sister-in-law's arms. Upon recovery, she stated that a figure, like that of her husband, enveloped in a mist, appeared to her to fill one of the windows.

By her friends, the wife's fancies were laughed at; and, if not forgotten, the circumstance was no longer spoken of.

Month after month glided by, without intelligence of the ship to which that officer belonged. At length the Government became anxious, and searching inquiries were made. Some time still elapsed, but eventually it was ascertained that this sloop of war had perished in a white squall, in which she became involved, near the Island of Mitylene, in the Grecian Archipelago, on the Sunday evening when the widow fancied she saw her husband.

THE WHITE HARE.

IT is a very popular fancy that when a maiden, who has loved not wisely but too well, dies forsaken and broken-hearted, that she comes back to haunt her deceiver in the shape of a white hare.

This phantom follows the false one everywhere, mostly invisible to all but him. It sometimes saves him from danger, but invariably the white hare causes the death of the betrayer in the end.

The following story of the white hare is a modification of several tales of the same kind which have been told me. Many, many years have passed away, and all who were in any way connected with my story have slept for generations in the quiet churchyard of ——.

A large landed proprietor engaged a fine, handsome young fellow to manage his farm, which was a very extensive as well as a high-class one. When the young farmer was duly settled in his new farmhouse, there came to live with him, to take the management of the dairy, a peasant's daughter. She was very handsome, and of a singularly fine figure, but entirely without education.

The farmer became desperately in love with this young creature, and eventually their love passed all the bounds of discretion. It became the policy of the young farmer's family to put down this unfortunate passion, by substituting a more legitimate and endearing object.

After a long trial, they thought they were successful, and the young farmer was married.

Many months had not passed away when the discharged dairy-maid was observed to suffer from illness, which, however, she constantly spoke of as nothing; but knowing dames saw too clearly the truth. One morning there was found in a field a newly-born babe strangled. The unfortunate girl was at once suspected as being the parent, and the evidence was soon sufficient to charge her with the murder. She was tried, and, chiefly by the evidence of the young farmer and his family, convicted of, and executed for, the murder.

Everything now went wrong in the farm, and the young man suddenly left it and went into another part of the country.

Still nothing prospered, and gradually he took to drink to drown some secret sorrow. He was more frequently on the road by night than by day; and, go where he would, a white hare was constantly crossing his path. The white hare was often seen by others, almost always under the feet of his horse; and the poor terrified animal would go like the wind to avoid the strange apparition.

One morning the young farmer was found drowned in a forsaken mine; and the horse, which had evidently suffered extreme terror, was grazing near the corpse. Beyond all doubt the white hare, which is known to hunt the perjured and the false-hearted to death, had terrified the horse to such a degree, that eventually the rider was thrown into the mine-waste in which the body was found.

THE HAND OF A SUICIDE.

PLACING the hand of a man who has died by his own act is a cure for many diseases.

The following is given me by a thinking man, living in one of the towns in the west of Cornwall:—

"There is a young man in this town who had been afflicted with running tumours from his birth. When about seventeen years of age he had the hand of a man who had hanged himself passed over the wounds on his back, and, strange to say, he recovered from that time, and is now comparatively robust and hearty. This incident is true; I was present when the charm was performed. It should be observed that the notion appears to be that the 'touch' is only effectual on the opposite sex; but in this case they were both, the suicide and the afflicted one, of the same sex."

This is only a modified form of the superstition that a wen, or any strumous swelling, can be cured by touching it with the dead hand of a man who has just been publicly hanged.

I once saw a young woman led on to the scaffold, in the Old Bailey, for the purpose of having a wen touched with the hand of a man who had just been executed.

THE NORTH SIDE OF A CHURCH.

A STRONG prejudice has long existed against burying on the northern side of the church. In many church-yards the southern side will be found full of graves, with scarcely any on the northern side.

I have sought to discover, if possible, the origin of this prejudice, but I have not been able to trace it to any well-defined feeling. I have been answered, "Oh, we like to bury a corpse where the sun will shine on the grave;" and, "The northern graveyard is in the shadow, and cold;" but beyond this I have not advanced.

We may infer that this desire to place the remains of our friends in earth on which the sun shines, is born of that love which, forgetting mortality, lives on the pleasant memories of the past, hoping for that meeting beyond the grave which shall know no shadow. The act of planting flowers, of nurturing an evergreen tree, of hanging "eternals" on the tomb, is only another form of the same sacred feeling.

POPULAR SUPERSTITIONS.

IT is, or rather was, believed, in nearly every part of the West of England, that death is retarded, and the dying kept in a state of suffering, by having any lock closed, or any bolt shot, in the dwelling of the dying person.

A man cannot die easy on a bed made of fowls' feathers, or the feathers of wild birds.

Never carry a corpse to church by a new road.

Whenever a guttering candle folds over its cooling grease, it is watched with much anxiety. If it curls upon itself it is said to form the "handle of a coffin," and the person towards whom it is directed will be in danger of death.

Bituminous coal not unfrequently swells into bubbles, these bubbles of coal containing carburetted hydrogen gas.

When the pressure becomes great they burst, and often throw off the upper section with some explosive force. According to the shape of the piece thrown off, so is it named. If it proves round it is a purse of money; if oblong, it is a coffin, and the group towards which it flew will be in danger.

If a cock crows at midnight, the angel of death is passing over the house; and if he delays to strike, the delay is only for a short season.

The howling of a dog is a sad sign. If repeated for three nights, the house against which it howled will soon be in mourning.

A raven croaking over a cottage fills its inmates with gloom.

There are many other superstitions and tokens connected with life and death, but those given shew the general character of those feelings which I may, I think, venture to call the "inner life" of the Cornish people. It will be understood by all who have studied the peculiarities of any Celtic race, that they have ever been a peculiarly impressible people. They have ever observed the phenomena of nature; and they have interpreted them with hopeful feelings, or despondent anxiety, according as they have been surrounded by cheerful or by sorrow-inducing circumstances. That melancholy state of mind, which is so well expressed by the word "whisht," leads the sufferer to find a "sign" or a "token" in the trembling of a leaf, or in the lowering of the tempest-clouds. A collection of the almost infinite variety of these "signs and tokens" which still exist, would form a curious subject for an essay. Yet this could only now be done by a person who would skilfully win the confidence of the miner or the peasant. They feel that they might subject themselves to ridicule by an indiscreet disclosure of the religion of their souls. When, if ever, such a collection is made, it will be found that these superstitions have their origin in the purest feelings of the heart—that they are the shadowings forth of love, tinctured with the melancholy dyes of that fear which is born of mystery.

One would desire that even those old superstitions should be preserved. They illustrate a state of society, in the past, which will never again return. There are but few reflecting minds which do not occasionally feel a lingering regret that times should pass away during which life was not a reflection of cold reason.

But these things must fade as a knowledge of nature's laws is disseminated amongst the people. Yet there is—

> The lonely mountains o'er,
> And the resounding shore,
>   A voice of weeping heard, and loud lament;
> From haunted spring and dale,
> Edged with poplar pale,
>   The parting genius is, with sighing sent.

OLD USAGES.

" The king was to his palace, though the service was ydo,
Yled with his meinie, and the queen to her also;
For she held *the old usages.*"

Robert of Gloucester.

CUSTOMS OF ANCIENT DAYS.

SANDING THE STEP ON NEW YEAR'S-DAY.

"They say, miracles are past, and we have our philosophical persons, to make modern and familiar things supernatural and causeless. Hence is it that we make trifles of terrors, ensconcing ourselves into seeming knowledge."—*All's Well that Ends Well*—SHAKESPEARE.

IN the rural districts of Cornwall, it is thought to be unlucky if a female is the first to enter the house on new-year's morning. To insure the contrary, it was customary to give boys some small reward for placing sand on the door-steps and in the passage.

In many places, not many years since, droves of boys would march through the towns and villages, collecting their fees for "sanding your step for good luck."

This custom prevails over most parts of England. I know a lady who, at the commencement of the present year, sent a cabman into her house before her, upon promise of giving him a glass of spirits, so that she might insure the good luck which depends upon "a man's taking the new year in."

MAY-DAY.

THE first of May is inaugurated with much uproar. As soon as the clock has told of midnight, a loud blast on tin trumpets proclaims the advent of May. This is long continued. At daybreak, with their "tintarrems," they proceed to the country, and strip the sycamore-trees (called May-trees) of all their young branches, to make whistles. With these shrill musical instruments they return home. Young men and women devote May-day to junketing and pic-nics.

It was a custom at Penzance, and probably at many other Cornish towns, when the author was a boy, for a number of young people to sit up until twelve o'clock, and then to march round the town with violins and fifes, and summon their friends to the Maying.

When all were gathered, they went into the country, and were welcomed at the farmhouses at which they called, with some refreshment in the shape of rum and milk, junket, or something of that sort.

They then gathered the "May," which included the young branches of any tree in blossom or fresh leaf. The branches of the sycamore were especially cut for the purpose of making the "May music." This was done by cutting a circle through the bark to the wood a few inches from the end of the branch. The bark was wetted and carefully beaten until it was loosened and could be slid off from the wood. The wood was cut angularly at the end, so as to form a mouth-piece, and a slit was made in both the bark and the wood, so that when the bark was replaced a whistle was formed. Prepared with a sufficient number of May whistles, all the party returned to the town, the band playing, whistles blowing, and the young people singing some appropriate song.

SHROVE TUESDAY AT ST IVES.

FORMERLY it was customary for the boys to tie stones to cords, and with these parade the town, slinging these stones against the doors, shouting aloud,—

"Give me a pancake, now—now—now,
Or I'll souse in your door with a row—tow—tow."

A genteel correspondent assures me "this is observed now in the lower parts of the town only."

"THE FURRY"—HELSTONE.

THIS ancient custom, which consists in dancing through the streets of the town, and entering the houses of rich and poor alike, is thus well described :—

"On the 8th of May, at Helstone, in Cornwall, is held what is called 'the Furry.' The word is supposed by Mr Polwhele to have been derived from the old Cornish word *fer*, a fair or jubilee. The morning is ushered in by the music of drums and kettles, and other accompaniments of a song, a great part of which is inserted in Mr Polwhele's history, where this circumstance is noticed. So strict is the observance of this day as a general holiday, that should any person be found at work, he is instantly seized, set astride on a pole, and hurried on men's shoulders to the river, where he is sentenced to leap over a wide place, which he, of course, fails in attempting, and leaps into the water. A small contribution towards the good cheer of the day easily compounds for the leap. About nine o'clock the revellers appear before the grammar-school, and demand a holiday for the schoolboys, after which they collect contributions from houses. They then *fade* into the country, (fade being an old English word for *go*,) and, about the middle of the day, return with flowers and oak-branches in their hats and caps. From this time they dance hand in hand through the streets, to the sound of the fiddle, playing a particular tune, running into every house they pass without opposition. In the afternoon a select party of the ladies and gentlemen make a progress through the street, and very late in the evening repair to the ball-room. A stranger visiting the town on the eighth of May would really think the people mad, so apparently wild and thoughtless is the merriment of the day. There is no doubt of 'the Furry' originating from the 'Floralia,' anciently observed by the Romans on the fourth of the calends of May."—*Every-Day Book.*

MIDSUMMER SUPERSTITIOUS CUSTOMS.

IF on midsummer-eve a young woman takes off the shift which she has been wearing, and, having washed it, turns it wrong side out, and hangs it in silence over the back of a chair, near the fire, she will see, about midnight, her future husband, who deliberately turns the garment.

If a young lady will, on midsummer-eve, walk backwards into the garden and gather a rose, she has the means of knowing who is to be her husband. The rose must be cautiously sewn up in a paper bag, and put aside in a dark drawer, there to remain until Christmas-day.

On the morning of the Nativity the bag must be carefully opened in silence, and the rose placed by the lady in her bosom. Thus she must wear it to church. Some young man will either ask for the rose, or take it from her without asking. That young man is destined to become eventually the lady's husband.

> "At eve last midsummer no sleep I sought,
> But to the field a bag of hemp-seed brought;
> I scatter'd round the seed on every side,
> And three times in a trembling accent cried,—
> 'This hemp-seed with my virgin hand I sow,
> Who shall my true love be, the crop shall mow.'
> I straight look'd back, and, if my eyes speak truth,
> With his keen scythe behind me came the youth."
>
> *Gay's Pastorals.*

The practice of sowing hemp-seed on midsummer-eve is not especially a Cornish superstition, yet it was at one time a favourite practice with young women to try the experiment. Many a strange story have I been told as to the result of the sowing, and many a trick could I tell of, which has been played off by young men who had become acquainted with the secret intention of some maidens. I believe there is but little difference in the rude rhyme used on the occasion,—

> "Hemp-seed I sow,
> Hemp-seed I hoe,"

(the action of sowing the seed and of hoeing it in, must be deliberately gone through ;)—

> "And he
> Who will my true love be,
> Come after me and mow."

A phantom of the true lover will now appear, and of course the maid or maidens retire in wild affright.

If a young unmarried woman stands at midnight on midsummer-eve in the porch of the parish church, she will see, passing by in procession, every one who will die in the parish during the year. This is so serious an affair that it is not, I believe, often tried. I have, however, heard of young women who have made the experiment. But every one of the stories relate that, coming last in the procession, they have seen shadows of themselves; that from that day forward they have pined, and ere midsummer has again come round, that they have been laid to rest in the village graveyard.

CRYING THE NECK.

OWING to the uncertain character of the climate of Cornwall, the farmers have adopted the plan of gathering the sheaves of wheat, as speedily as possible, into "arish-mows." These are solid cones from ten to twelve feet high, the heads of the stalks turned inwards, and the whole capped with a sheaf of corn inverted. Whence the term, I know not; but "arish" is commonly applied to a field of corn recently cut, as, "Turn the geese in upon the 'arish'"—that is, the short stubble left in the ground.

After the wheat is all cut, on most farms in Cornwall and Devon, the harvest people have a custom of "crying the neck." I believe that this practice is seldom omitted on any large farm in these counties. It is done in this way. An old man, or some one else well acquainted with the ceremonies used on the occasion, (when the labourers are reaping the last field of wheat,) goes round to the shocks and sheaves, and picks out a little bundle of all the best ears he can find; this bundle he ties up very neat and trim, and plats and arranges the straws very tastefully. This is called "the neck" of wheat, or wheaten-ears. After the field is cut out, and the pitcher once more circulated, the reapers, binders, and the women stand round in a circle. The person with "the neck" stands in the centre, grasping it with both his hands. He first stoops and holds it near the ground, and all the men forming the ring take off their hats, stooping and holding them with both hands towards the ground. They then all begin at once, in a very prolonged and harmonious tone, to cry, "The neck!" at the same time slowly raising themselves upright, and elevating their arms and hats above their heads; the person with the neck also raising it on high. This is done three times. They then change their cry to "We yen! we yen!" which they sound in the same prolonged and slow manner as before, with singular harmony and effect, three times. This last cry is accompanied by the same movements of the body and arms as in crying "the neck." I know nothing of vocal music, but I think I may convey some idea of the sound by giving you the following notes in gamut:—

Let these notes be played on a flute with perfect *crescendoes*

and *diminuendoes*, and perhaps some notion of this wild-sounding cry may be formed. Well, after this they all burst out into a kind of loud joyous laugh, flinging up their hats and caps into the air, capering about, and perhaps kissing the girls. One of them then gets "the neck," and runs as hard as he can down to the farmhouse, where the dairy-maid, or one of the young female domestics, stands at the door prepared with a pail of water. If he who holds "the neck" can manage to get into the house in any way unseen, or openly by any other way than the door at which the girl stands with the pail of water, then he may lawfully kiss her; but, if otherwise, he is regularly soused with the contents of the bucket. I think this practice is beginning to decline of late, and many farmers and their men do not care about keeping up this old custom. The object of crying "the neck" is to give notice to the surrounding country of the *end* of the harvest, and the meaning of "we yen" is "*we have ended.*" It may probably mean "we end," which the uncouth and provincial pronunciation has corrupted into "we yen." The "neck" is generally hung up in the farm-house, where it often remains for three or four years.

DRINKING TO THE APPLE-TREES ON TWELFTH NIGHT EVE.

IN the eastern part of Cornwall, and in western Devonshire, it was the custom to take a milk-panful of cider, into which roasted apples had been broken, into the orchard. This was placed as near the centre of the orchard as possible, and each person, taking a "clomben" cup of the drink, goes to different apple-trees, and addresses them as follows:—

> "Health to the good apple-tree;
> Well to bear, pocketfuls, hatfuls,
> Peckfuls, bushel-bagfuls."

Drinking part of the contents of the cup, the remainder,

with the fragments of the roasted apples, is thrown at the tree, all the company shouting aloud. Another account tells us, "In certain parts of Devonshire, the farmer, attended by his workmen, goes to the orchard this evening; and there, encircling one of the best bearing trees, they drink the following toast three times:—

> 'Here 's to thee, old apple-tree;
> Hence thou mayst bud, and whence thou mayst blow,
> And whence thou mayst bear apples enow!
> Hats full! caps full!
> Bushel, bushel-sacks full!
> And my pockets full, too! Huzza!'

This done, they return to the house, the doors of which they are sure to find bolted by the females, who, be the weather what it may, are inexorable to all entreaties to open them, till some one has guessed what is on the spit, which is generally some nice little thing difficult to be hit on, and is the reward of him who first names it. The doors are then thrown open, and the lucky clodpole receives the tit-bit as his recompense. Some are so superstitious as to believe that if they neglect this custom, the trees will bear no apples that year."*

Christmas-eve was selected in some parts of England as the occasion for wishing health to the apple-tree. Apples were roasted on a string until they fell into a pan of spiced ale, placed to receive them. This drink was called *lamb's-wool*, and with it the trees were wassailed, as in Devonshire and Cornwall.

Herrick alludes to the custom:—

> "Wassaile the trees, that they may beare
> You many a plum, and many a peare;
> For more or lesse fruits they will bring,
> And you do give them wassailing."

* Hone's "Every-Day Book."

May not Shakespeare refer to this?—

> "Sometimes lurk I in a gossip's bowl,
> In very likeness of a roasted crab;
> And when she drinks, against her lips I bob,
> And on her wither'd dew-lap pour the ale."
>
> *Midsummer Night's Dream.*

In some localities apples are blessed on St James's-day, July 25.

ALLHALLOWS-EVE AT ST IVES.

THE ancient custom of providing children with a large apple on Allhallows-eve is still observed, to a great extent, at St Ives. "Allan-day," as it is called, is the day of days to hundreds of children, who would deem it a great misfortune were they to go to bed on "Allan-night" without the time-honoured Allan apple to hide beneath their pillows. A quantity of large apples are thus disposed of, the sale of which is dignified by the term Allan Market.

THE TWELFTH CAKE.

THE custom, apparently a very ancient one, of putting certain articles into a rich cake, is still preserved in many districts. Usually, sixpence, a wedding-ring, and a silver thimble are employed. These are mixed up with the dough, and baked in the cake. At night the cake is divided. The person who secures the sixpence will not want money for that year; the one who has the ring will be the first married; and the possessor of the thimble will die an old maid.

> "Then also every householder,
> To his abilitie
> Doth make a mighty cake, that may
> Suffice his companie:
> Herein a pennie doth he put,
> Before it come to fire;

This he divides according as
  His household doth require,
And every peece distributeth
  As round about they stand,
Which in their names unto the poor
  Is given out of hand.
But who so chanceth on the peece
  Wherein the money lies,
Is counted king amongst them all ;
  And is with shoutes and cries
Exalted to the heavens up."

Naogeorgus's Popish Kingdom.

OXEN PRAY ON CHRISTMAS EVE.

I REMEMBER, when a child, being told that all the oxen and cows kept at a farm, in the parish of St Germans, at which I was visiting with my aunt, would be found on their knees when the clock struck twelve. This is the only case within my own knowledge of this wide-spread superstition existing in Cornwall. Brand says, "A superstitious notion prevails in the western parts of Devonshire, that at twelve o'clock at night on Christmas-eve, the oxen in their stalls are always found on their knees, as in an attitude of devotion ; and that, (which is still more singular,) since the alteration of the style, they continue to do this only on the eve of old Christmas-day. An honest countryman, living on the edge of St Stephen's Down, near Launceston, Cornwall, informed me, October 28, 1790, that he once, with some others, made a trial of the truth of the above, and, watching several oxen in their stalls at the above time,—at twelve o'clock at night,—they observed the two oldest oxen only, fall upon their knees and, as he expressed it in the idiom of the country, make 'a cruel moan, like Christian creatures.' I could not, but with great difficulty, keep my countenance : he saw, and seemed angry, that I gave so little credit to his tale ;

and, walking off in a pettish humour, seemed to 'marvel at my unbelief.' There is an old print of the Nativity, in which the oxen in the stable, near the Virgin and the Child, are represented upon their knees, as in a suppliant posture. This graphic representation has probably given rise to the above superstitious notion on this head."

"ST GEORGE"—THE CHRISTMAS PLAYS.

THE Christmas play is a very ancient institution in Cornwall. At one time religious subjects were chosen, but those gave way to romantic plays. The arrangements were tolerably complete, and sometimes a considerable amount of dramatic skill was displayed.

"ST GEORGE, and the other tragic performers, are dressed out somewhat in the style of morris-dancers, in their shirt sleeves and white trousers, much decorated with ribbons and handkerchiefs, each carrying a drawn sword in his hand, if they can be procured, otherwise a cudgel. They wear high caps of pasteboard, adorned with beads, small pieces of looking-glass, coloured paper, &c.; several long strips of pith generally hang down from the top, with small pieces of different coloured cloth strung on them: the whole has a very smart effect.

Father Christmas is personified in a grotesque manner, as an ancient man, wearing a large mask and wig, and a huge club, wherewith he keeps the bystanders in order.

The *Doctor*, who is generally the merry-andrew of the piece, is dressed in any ridiculous way, with a wig, three-cornered hat, and painted face.

The other comic characters are dressed according to fancy.

The *female*, where there is one, is usually in the dress worn half a century ago.

The *hobby-horse*, which is a character sometimes introduced, wears a representation of a horse's-hide.

Beside the regular drama of "St George," many parties of mummers go about in fancy dresses of every sort, most commonly the males in female attire, and *vice versâ*.

Battle of St George.

[*One of the party steps in, crying out,*—

Room, a room, brave gallant, room,
Within this court

I do resort,
To shew some sport
And pastime,
Gentlemen and ladies, in the Christmas time.

[*After this note of preparation, Old Father Christmas capers into the room, saying,—*

Here comes I, Old Father Christmas,
Welcome or welcome not;
I hope Old Father Christmas
Will never be forgot.

I was born in a rocky country, where there was no wood to make me a cradle; I was rocked in a stouring-bowl, which made me round shouldered then, and I am round shouldered still.

[*He then frisks about the room, until he thinks he has sufficiently amused the spectators, when he makes his exit, with this speech :—*

Who went to the orchard to steal apples to make gooseberry pies against Christmas?

[*These prose speeches, you may suppose, depend much upon the imagination of the actor.*

Enter Turkish Knight.

Here comes I, a Turkish knight,
Come from the Turkish land to fight;
And if St George do meet me here,
I'll try his courage without fear.

Enter St George.

Here come I, St George,
That worthy champion bold;
And, with my sword and spear,
I won three crowns of gold.
I fought the dragon bold,
And brought him to the slaughter;
By that I gain'd fair Sabra,
The King of Egypt's daughter.

T. K. St George, I pray, be not too bold;
If thy blood is hot, I'll soon make it cold.

St G. Thou Turkish knight, I pray, forbear;
I'll make thee dread my sword and spear.

[*They fight until the Turkish Knight falls.*

St G. I have a little bottle, which goes by the name of Elicumpane;
If the man is alive, let him rise and fight again.

[*The Knight here rises on one knee, and endeavours to continue the fight, but is again struck down.*

T. K. Oh, pardon me, St George; oh, pardon me, I crave;
Oh, pardon me this once, and I will be thy slave.
St G. I'll never pardon a Turkish knight;
Therefore arise, and try thy might.
[*The Knight gets up, and they again fight, till the Knight receives a heavy blow and then drops on the ground as dead.*
St G. Is there a doctor to be found,
To cure a deep and deadly wound?

Enter Doctor.

Oh yes, there is a doctor to be found,
To cure a deep and deadly wound.
St G. What can you cure?
Doctor. I can cure the itch, the palsy, and gout:
If the devil's in him, I'll pull him out.
[*The Doctor here performs the cure with sundry grimaces, and St George and the Knight again fight, when the latter is knocked down, and left for dead.*
[*Then another performer enters, and, on seeing the dead body, says,*—
Ashes to ashes, dust to dust;
If Uncle Tom Pearce won't have him, Aunt Molly must.
[*The hobby-horse here capers in, and takes off the body.*

Enter Old Squire.

Here comes I, old, Old Squire,
As black as any friar,
As ragged as a colt,
To leave fine clothes for malt.

Enter Hub Bub.

Here comes I, old Hub Bub Bub Bub;
Upon my shoulders I carries a club,
And in my hand a frying-pan,
So am I not a valiant man?
[*These characters serve as a sort of burlesque on St George and the other hero, and may be regarded in the light of an anti-masque.*

Enter the Box-holder.

Here comes I, great head and little wit;
Put your hand in your pocket, and give what you think fit.
Gentlemen and ladies, sitting down at your ease,
Put your hands in your pockets, and give me what you please.
St G. Gentlemen and ladies, the sport is almost ended;
Come pay to the box, it is highly commended.
The box it would speak, if it had but a tongue;
Come throw in your money, and think it no wrong.

The characters now generally finish with a dance, or sometimes a song or two is introduced. In some of the performances, two or three other tragic heroes are brought forward, as the King of Egypt and his son, &c.; but they are all of them much in the style of that I have just described, varying somewhat in length and number of characters."—*The Every-Day Book.*

Of the Cornish mystery plays which were once acted in the famous "Rounds," it is not necessary, in this place, to say anything. The translations by Mr Norris preserve their characteristics, which indeed differ in few respects from the mystery plays of other parts.

The "Perran Round" is fortunately preserved by the proprietor in its original state. Every one must regret the indifference of the wealthy inhabitants of St Just to their "Round," which is now a wretched ruin.

GEESE-DANCING—PLOUGH MONDAY.

THE first Monday after Twelfth-day is Plough Monday, and it is the ploughman's holiday.

At this season, in the Islands of Scilly, at St Ives, Penzance, and other places, the young people exercise a sort of gallantry called "geese-dancing." The maidens are dressed up for young men, and the young men for maidens; and, thus disguised, they visit their neighbours in companies, where they dance, and make jokes upon what has happened during the year, and every one is humorously "told their own," without offence being taken. By this sort of sport, according to yearly custom and toleration, there is a spirit of wit and drollery kept up among the people. The music and dancing done, they are treated with liquor, and then they go to the next house, and carry on the same sport. A correspondent, writing to the "Table-Book," insists on calling these revels "goose-dancing." The true Cornishman never uses the term, which is, as I have elsewhere shewn, derived from *dance deguiser*,—hence guise-dancing, or geese-dancing, by corruption.

CHRISTMAS AT ST IVES.

"THE GUISE-DANCING."

"WE doubt if there is a spot in 'merrie England' where Christmas receives so hearty a welcome, and is 'made so much of,' as in the old-fashioned 'antient borough of beloved St Ives.' It is often said that 'extremes meet;' but as well might we expect the extremities of Britain—John o'Groat's and Cape Cornwall—to meet, as that the frolic-loving descendants of Albion will ever imitate the cold, mountain-nurtured Caledonians in their observance of Christmas time. For months previous to the merry-making time, preparations are made for the approaching 'carnival;' we can assure our readers that never were the real 'carnivals' ushered in with greater festivities at Rome or Venice, in the zenith of their glory, than is observed here at Christmas. Were many of the denizens of our large towns to witness the making up of the scores of 'sugar-loaf,' 'three-cocked,' and indescribable-shaped hats, caps, bonnets, bloomer skirts, leggings, jackets, &c., numberless *et ceteras* of the most grotesque and pantomimic character, colour, and shape, which goes on in October and November, they would imagine there was to be a *bal masque* on a large scale, or a pantomime at 'the theatre,' of metropolitan proportions. But not so, for there is not even a singing class in the town, if we except the choirs of the various congregations, and all 'this wilful waste' of long cloth, scarlet, ringstraked, and speckled, is to do honour to King Christmas during the twelve nights which intervene 'twixt the birth of Christmas common and Christmas proper, which said outward manifestations of honour are known in the neighbourhood as 'Christmas geezze-daancing,' or guise-dancing; but of this presently. Not only are the 'lovers of pleasure' on the alert, but the choirs of the different places of worship strive to 'get up' a piece or two to tickle the ears of their hearers on Christmas-night, and the house that boasts the best 'singing seat' is sure to be crammed by persons attracted by the twofold advantage of a short sermon and a good lively tune. A pretty brisk trade is carried on by children in the retailing unquenched lime, in small quantities to suit the convenience of purchasers; and few are the domiciles but have had a lick of the lime brush, either on the wall, window-sill, door-post, or chimney. 'A slut, indeed,' is she declared who refuses to have a thorough clean out before Christmas. New shoes and clothes are worn for the first time on the great holiday; and woe betide the unlucky Crispin who, by some unaccountable oversight, has neglected to make Jennifer's bran new shoes, for her to go and see how smart the church is on Christmas-day. As in other parts of England, a pretty large sum is spent in evergreens, such as holly, or, as it is called here, 'prickly Christmas,' bays, and laurels. Of mistletoe and cypress there is very little in the neighbourhood, and the windows of shops and private dwellings, as well as the parish church, are profusely and tastefully decorated. As to provisions there is no lack. Many a flock of geese has been bespoken, and set apart for private customers; whilst the ears of the grocers, who generally do a supplementary trade in swine's flesh, are so accustomed to receive a month's notice for 'a nice bit of flea (spare) rib,' that they are loth to engage any of the porcine fraternity that are not all rib. The Christmas market is not a mean affair at St Ives; if the butchers cannot boast of many prize oxen or 'South Downs,' they generally manage to make the best of their 'home-raised' and well-fed cattle, and the stalls are 'titivated off' nicely too. This year, however, the inspector of nuisances, who is also market-toll collector and police constable, sergeant, and inspector, actually refused to clean, or allow to be cleaned, the St Ives market on Tuesday for the Christmas-eve market, because there was no extra tolls payable for the Christmas markets, and, as may be expected, the epithets bestowed on him were by no means flattering or complimentary—we did hear of a suggestion to put the 'gentleman' policeman in an aldermanic stall on the 5th of next November, or maybe during the guise-dancing. Tradesmen have for the most part 'cacht their jobs,' and the good housewife 'done her churs in season' on Christmas-eve. In many families, a crock of 'fish and tatees' is discussed in West-Cornwall style before the 'singers' commence their time-honoured carol, 'While Shepherds,' which is invariably sung to 'the same old tune,' struck by some novice in *u* flat. There is usually a host of young men and maidens to accompany the 'singers;' these are composed of the choirs of two or three dissenting bodies, who chiefly select the members of their respective congregations for the honour of being disturbed from a sound nap on the eventful morning. The last two or three years the choirs have done their carolling amongst the most respectable of the inhabitants on the evening of Christmas-day, after divine service.

"On Christmas-day the mayor, aldermen, and councillors walk in procession to church from the house of the mayor for the time being. The church is, as we have before remarked, gaily decked with evergreens. Two or three days after the singers make a call 'for something for singing,' the proceeds, which are pretty handsome, being spent in a substantial supper for the choir.

"But of the 'guise-dancing,' which has found a last retreat at St Ives,—this is the only town in the country where the old Cornish Christmas revelry is kept up with spirit. The guise-dancing time is the twelve nights after Christmas, *i.e.*, from Christmas-day to Twelfth-day. Guise-dancing at St Ives is no more nor less than a pantomimic representation or *bal masque* on an extensive scale, the performers out-numbering the audience, who in this case take their stand at the corners of the streets, which are but badly lighted with gas, and rendered still more dismal of late years by the closing of the tradesmen's shops after sunset during this season, on account of the noise and uproar occasioned, the town being literally given up to a lawless mob, who go about yelling and hooting in an unearthly manner, in a tone between a screech and a howl, so as to render their voices as undistinguishable as their buffoon-looking dresses. Here a Chinese is exhibiting 'vite mishe' and 'Dutch dops;' there a turbaned Indian asks you if you 'vant a silver vatch.' A little further on you meet with a Highlander with 'dops to cure the gout.' The home-impoverishing packman, or duffer, has also his representative, urging to be allowed just to leave 'a common low-price dress at an uncommon high price, and a quartern of his 6s. sloe-leaves, of the best quality.' Faithless swains not unfrequently get served out by the friends of the discarded one at this time, whilst every little peccadillo meets with a just rebuke and exposure. About eighteen years ago, a party of youngsters, to give more variety to the sports, constructed a few nice representations of elephants, horses, and—start not gentle reader—lifelike facsimiles of that proverbially stupid brute, the ass. For several seasons it was quite a treat to witness the antics of the self-constituted elephants, horses, and asses, in the thoroughfares of this little town. On the whole, the character of the guise-dancing has degenerated very much this last twenty years. It was formerly the custom for parties to get up a little play, and go from house to house to recite their droll oddities, and levy contributions on their hearers in the form of cake or plum-pudding. Wassailing, as far as I can learn, never obtained much in this neighbourhood. Old Father Christmas and bold King George were favourite characters. It is not uncommon to see a most odiously-disguised person with a bedroom utensil, asking the blushing bystanders if there is 'any need of me.' Some of the dresses are, indeed, very smart, and even costly; but for the most part they consist of old clothes, arranged in the oddest manner, even frightfully ugly. It is dangerous for children, and aged or infirm persons, to venture out after dark, as the roughs generally are armed with a sweeping brush or a shillaly. The uproar at times is so tremendous as to be only equalled in a 'rale Irish row.' As may be anticipated, these annual diversions have a very demoralising influence on the young, on account of the licentious nature of the conversation indulged in, though we really wonder that there are not many more instances of annoyance and insult than now take place, when we consider that but for such times as Christmas and St Ives feast, the inhabitants have no place of amusement, recreation, or public instruction; there being no library, reading-room, institution, literary or scientific, or evening class; and unless there is one at the National School-room, not a night school or even a working-men's institution is in the town.

"We should not omit that one of the old customs still observed is the giving apprentices three clear holidays (not including Sunday) after Christmas-day, though we hear of attempts being made to lessen this treat to the youngsters. If we don't wish success to these efforts, we do desire those should succeed who will endeavour to impart to our rising population a thorough contempt for guise-dancing and all such unmeaning buffoonery. There is one thing which must not be overlooked—viz., the few drunken brawls that occur at such times. Cases of drunkenness certainly occur, but these are far below the average of towns of its size, the population being in 1861 (parliamentary limits) 10,354."—*St Ives Correspondent.*

LADY LOVELL'S COURTSHIP.

BY the especial kindness of one who has a more abundant store of old Cornish stories than any man whom I have ever met, I am enabled to give some portion of one of the old Cornish plays, or guise-dances. Many parts are omitted, as they would, in our refined days, be considered coarse; but as preserving a true picture of a peculiar people, as they were a century and a half or two centuries since, I almost regret the omissions.

SCENE 1.—*The Squire's Kitchen—Duffy sitting on the chimney-stool—Jane, the housekeeper, half drunk, holding fast by the table.*

Jane. Oh, I am very bad, I must go to bed with the wind in my stomach. You can bake the pie, Duffy, and give the Squire his supper. Keep a good waking fire on the pie for an hour or more. Turn the glass again; when the sand is half down, take the fire from the kettle. Mind to have a good blazing fire in the hall, for the Squire will be as wet as a shag. The old fool, to stay out hunting with this flood of rain! Now, I'll take a cup of still waters, and crawl away to bed.

Duffy. Never fear, I'll bake the pie as well as if you were under the kettle along with it; so go to bed, Jane.

[*As soon as Jane turns her back, Huey Lenine (Lanyon) comes in with,—*

Huey. What cheer, Duffy, my dear? how dost aw get on, then?

Duffy. Never the better for thee, I bla, Huey. What do bring thee here this time of night?

Huey. Why, thee art never the worse, nan, I'm sure. Nor thee cussent say that the lanes are longer than the love neither, when I'm come a-courting to *thee* with this rainy weather.

[*Huey places himself on the chimney-stool, at a good distance from Duffy.*

D. Why doesn't aw come a little nearer then, Huey?

H. Near enuff, I bla.

D. Nearer the fire, I mean. Why doesn't aw speak to me then, Huey?

H. What shall I say, nan?

D. Why, say thee dost love me, to be sure.

H. So I do.

D. That's a dear. Fine pretty waistcoat on to you, man, Huey.

H. Cost pretty money too.

D. What did it cost, man?

H. Two-and-twenty pence, buttons and all.

D. Take good care of en, man.

H. So I will.

D. That's a dear.

[*The Squire is heard calling the dogs.*

D. Dost aw hear? there's the Squire close to the door. Where shall I put thee? Oh, I'm in such a fright. Wouldn't for the world that he found thee here this time of night. Get in the wood-corner, quick, out of sight, and I'll cover thee up with the furze.

H. No.

D. Then jump into the oven. A little more baking will make thee no worse.

[*Duffy pushes Huey back into the oven with the fire-prong, till he gets out of sight, when the Squire comes in, calling,—*

Squire. Jane, take the hares and rabbits; be sure hang them out of the way of the dogs.

D. Give them to me, master; Jane is gone to bed. The wind from her stomach is got up in her head, at least so she said.

S. Why, who is here, then? I heard thee speaking to some one as I opened the door.

D. I was driving away a great owl, master, that fell out of the ivy-bush on the top of the chimney, and came tumbling down through the smoke, perched hisself there on the end of the chimney-stack; there he kept blinking and peeping, like a thing neither waking nor sleeping, till he heard the dogs barking, when he stopped his winking, cried out, "Hoo! hoo!" flapped his wings, and fled up the chimney the same way he came down.

D. Now, master, you had better go up in the hall; you will find there a good blazing fire.

[*The Squire examines his legs by the fire-light.*

S. Well, I declare, these are the very best stockings I ever had in my life. I've been hunting, since the break of day, through the bogs and the brambles, the furze and the thorns, in all sorts of weather; and my legs,—look, Duffy, look—are still as dry and sound as if they had been bound up in leather.

D. Then take good care of them, master; for I shall soon have a man of my own to knit for. Huey and I are thinking to get married before the next turfey season.

S. You think of having a man! a young girl like you! If I but catch the boy Huey Lenine here, I'll break his neck I declare. I can never wear old Jane's stockings any more. Why, thee dust ought to be proud to know that the people from all over the parish, who were never to church before in their lives, come, and from parishes round, that they may see my fine stockings. And don't I stop outside the church door—ay, sometimes two hours or more—that the women may see thy fine work? Haven't I stopped at the cross till the parson came out to call the people in, because he and the clerk, he said, wanted to begin?

[*The Squire places himself beside Duffy on the chimney-stool. The devil comes out of the wood-corner, and ranges himself behind them. Whenever the Squire is backward, the devil tickles him behind the ear or under the ribs. His infernal highness is supposed to be invisible throughout. Huey shews a wry face now and then, with clenched fist, through the oven door.*

The following portion, which is the Squire's courtship of Duffy with the help of the devil, is a sort of duet in the old play. I don't remember the whole, yet sufficient, I think, to give some idea of the way it is intended to be carried out:—

S. No; I'll marry thee myself, rather than Huey Lenine
Shall ever wear stockings the equal of mine.
Thou shall have the silk gowns, all broider'd in gold,
In the old oak chest; besides jewels and rings,
With such other fine things,
In the old oak chest, as thee didst never behold.

D. I'd rather work all the day by any young man's side,
Than sit in the bower, and be an old man's bride.

S. Thou shalt have silver and gold, and riches untold.

D. I'll buy my true love his shirt, rather than your silver and gold,
With one like yourself, both feeble and old.

S. You must say I'm old; though I'm near sixty,
I'm stronger still than many a man of twenty.
Thou shalt ride to church behind me, upon a new pillion,
As grand as Madam Noy, or Madam Trezillian.

D. O master, hold your flattering tongue;
I'm very foolish, and very young.
But ——

[*Here the devil tickles the Squire sharply under the ribs, when the Squire attempts to hug and kiss Duffy, who takes the fire-prong and brandishes it in the Squire's face. The devil tickles them both.*

Stand off, keep your distance, and none of your hugging;
No man shall kiss me till he takes me to church;
I'll never cry at Michaelmas for Christmas laughing,
Like the poor maid left in the lurch.

Look, the sand is all down, the pie is burn'd black,
And the crust is too hard for your colt's teeth to crack;
Up to the hall now, and take your supper.

[*Here Duffy pushes the Squire off the stool. The Squire jumps up and begins to dance, singing the old dancing tune, "Here's to the devil, with his wooden pick," &c. Duffy and the devil soon join in the dance, and cut all sorts of capers, till the Squire dances off to the hall, followed by the devil; when Huey crawls out of the oven, Duffy opens the kitchen, drives Huey out, saying,—*

Now take thyself outside the door,
And never shew thy face here any more;
Don't think I'd have a poor pityack like thee,
When I may marry a squire of high degree.

[*Then takes up the pie, and dances away. During the old pitch-and-pass dance, they beat time with the fire-prong and hunting-staff.*

SCENE 2.—*The first appearance of Lady Lovell (Duffy) after the wedding. She is seen walking up and down the hall dressed in all sorts of ill-assorted, old-fashioned finery, that might have been forgotten in the old oak chest for many generations of Lovells. The high-heeled shoes, train, fan, ruff, high tete. All sorts of rings on her fingers, and in her ears are* de rijeur. *Then she sings something like the following:—*

Now I have servants to come at my call,
As I walk in grand state in the hall,
Deck'd in silks and satins fine;
But I grieve all the day, and fret the long night away,
To think of my true love, young Huey Lenine.

Many a weary long hour I sit all alone in my bower,
Where I do nothing but pine,
Whilst I grieve all the day, and fret the night away,
To think of my true love, young Huey Lenine.

Would the devil but come at my call, and take the old Squire, silks, satins, [and all,
With jewels and rings so fine;

Then merry and gay I'd work all the day, and pass the night away,
Kissing my true love, young Huey Lenine.

Another Cornish "Droll" is preserved, in part, as an example of the kind of doggerel verse in which many of those stories were told.

Bet of the Mill tells the Squire and company that, one Christmas night, all the inmates of Trevider House were gone off to a guise-dance, except Madam Pender and herself, and that they agree to spin for pastime:—

"One Christmas night, from Trevider Hall,
They were off in a guise-dance, big and small;
Nobody home but Madam Pender and I.
So to pass away time we agreed to try
Which would spin the finest yarn,
The length of the hall,
While the holly and bays
Deck'd window and wall.

"We took the rushes up from the floor,
From up by the chimney down to the door.
When we had the wool carded, ready to spin,
It came into our heads, before we'd begin,
We'd have a jug of hot-spiced beer,
To put life in our heels, our hearts to cheer.
So we drank to the healths of one and all,
While the holly and bays
Look'd bright on the wall.

"The night was dark, the wind roar'd without,
And whirl'd the cold snow about and about.
But the best part of that night,
By the bright fire-light,
While the Christmas stock did burn,
We danced forth and back as light as a feather,
Spinning and keeping good time together,
To the music of the 'turn.' *
And we never felt weary that night at all,
While the holly and bays
Hung so gay on the wall.

* Spinning-wheel.

"We pull'd out the yarn as even and fine,
As a spinner can spin the best of twine:
All the length of the hall,
From window to wall,
From up by the chimney
Down to the door,—
Full a dozen good paces and more;
And never felt weary at all,
While the holly and bays
Were so green on the wall.
At the turn of the night,
Old Nick, out of spite,
To see the log burn,
And to hear the gay 'turn,'
Made my yarn to crack;
And I fell on my back,
Down the steps of the door.
I thought I was dead, or, twice as bad,
Should never be good any more.
If I had broken my bones on the cursed hard stones,
'Twas no wonder.
But, worst of all, with the force of the fall,
My twadling-string burst asunder.

. . . .

Old madam was seized with frights and fears,—
She thought the house falling about her ears;
And, to save herself, she tore up-stairs,
Where they found her next morning under the bed,
With the brandy-bottle close to her head."

Bet is found in a similar plight, and all is attributed to spinning; however, the Squire orders that Madam Pender shall spin no more,—

"And dance, one and all,
With the holly and bays so bright on the wall."

THE GAME OF HURLING.

THE game of "Hurling" was, until a recent period, played in the parishes to the west of Penzance on the Sunday afternoon. The game was usually between two parishes, sometimes between Burian and Sancreed, or against St Leven and Sennen, or the higher side of the parish played against the lower side.

The run was from Burian Cross in the Church-town, to the Pipers in Boloeit. All the gentry from the surrounding parishes would meet at Boloeit to see the ball brought in.

"Hurling matches" are peculiar to Cornwall. They are trials of skill between two parties, consisting of a considerable number of men, forty to sixty a side, and often between two parishes. These exercises have their name from "hurling" a wooden ball, about three inches in diameter, covered with a plate of silver, which is sometimes gilt, and has commonly a motto, "Gware wheag yeo gware teag," "Fair play is good play." The success depends on catching the ball dexterously when thrown up, or *dealt*, and carrying it off expeditiously, in spite of all opposition from the adverse party; or, if that be impossible, throwing it into the hands of a partner, who, in his turn, exerts his efforts to convey it to his own goal, which is often three or four miles' distance. This sport, therefore, requires a nimble hand, a quick eye, a swift foot, and skill in wrestling; as well as strength, good wind, and lungs. Formerly it was practised annually by those who attended corporate bodies in surveying the bounds of parishes; but from the many accidents that usually attended that game, it is now scarcely ever practised. Silver prizes used to be awarded to the victor in the games. A correspondent at St Ives, writes:—

Hurling the Silver Ball.—This old custom is still observed at St Ives. The custom is also kept up at St Columb and St Blazey, on the anniversary of the dedication of the church. St Ives' feast is governed by the Candlemas-day, it being the nearest Sunday next before that day. On the Monday after, the inhabitants assemble on the beach, when the ball, which is left in the custody of the mayor for the time being, is thrown from the churchyard to the crowd. The sides are formed in this way,—

> Toms, Wills, and Jans,
> Take off all 's on the san's—

that is, all those of the name of Thomas, John, or William are ranged on one side, those of any other *Christian* name on the other ; of late years the odd names outnumber the Toms, Wills, and Jans. There is a pole erected on the beach, and each side strives to get the oftenest at the "goold," *i.e.*, the pole ; the other side as manfully striving to keep them out, and to send their opponents as great a distance from the pole as possible. The tradition is, that the contest used to be between the parishes of Ludgvan, Lelant, and St Ives,—St Ives then being part of the *living* of Ludgvan,—and that they used to have a friendly hurling at Ludgvan, and that afterwards the contest was between Lelant and St Ives. A stone near to Captain Perry's house is shewn, where the two parishes used to meet at the feast, and the struggle was to throw the ball into the parish church, the successful party keeping the ball, the unsuccessful buying a new one. St Ives is said to have outnumbered the Lelant folks, so that they gave up the contest, and the ball was left with St Ives. Thus much is certain—that the feasts of St Ives, Lelant, and Ludgvan fall properly on one Sunday, though a misunderstanding has arisen, Lelant claiming to be governed by the day before Candlemas-day, which will alter the three every seven years.

The game of hurling is now but rarely played, and the Sabbath is never broken by that or by any other game.

SHAM MAYORS.

I.—THE MAYOR OF MYLOR.

THERE was a curious custom in the town of Penryn in Cornwall, which long outlived all modern innovations. On some particular day in September or October, (I forget the exact date,) about when the hazel-nuts are ripe, the festival of nutting-day is kept. The rabble of the town go into the country to gather nuts, returning in the evening with boughs of hazel in their hands, shouting and making a great noise. In the meantime the journeymen tailors of the town have proceeded to the adjoining village of Mylor, and elected one of their number "Mayor of Mylor," taking care the selection falls on the wittiest. Seated in a chair shaded with green boughs, and borne on the shoulders of four stalwart men, the worthy mayor proceeds from his "good town of Mylor" to his "ancient borough of Penryn," the van being led by the "body-guard" of stout fellows well armed with cudgels,—which they do not fail to use should their path be obstructed,—torch-bearers, and two "town serjeants," clad in official gowns and cocked hats, and carrying each a monstrous cabbage on his shoulder in lieu of a mace. The rear is brought up by the rabble of the "nutters." About midday a band of music meets them, and plays them to Penryn, where they are received by the entire population. The procession proceeds to the town-hall, in front of which the mayor delivers a speech, declaratory of his intended improvements, &c., for the coming year, being generally an excellent sarcastic burlesque on the speeches of parliamentary candidates. The procession then moves on to each public-house door, where the mayor, his council, and officers are liberally supplied with liquor, and the speech is repeated with variations. They then adjourn to the "council-chamber," in some public-house, and devote the night to drinking. At night the streets are filled with people bearing torches, throwing fireballs, and discharging rockets ; and huge bon-fires are kindled on the "Green," and "Old Wall." The legal mayor once made an effort to put a stop to this Saturnalia, but his new-made brother issued prompt orders to his body-guards, and the *posse comitatus* had to fly.

The popular opinion is, that there is a clause in the borough charter compelling the legitimate mayor to surrender his power to the "Mayor of Mylor" on the night in question, and to lend the town sergeants' paraphernalia to the gentlemen of the shears.

II.—THE MAYOR OF ST GERMANS.

One of the first objects that attracts attention on entering the village of St Germans is the large walnut-tree, at the foot of what is called Nut-Tree Hill. In the early part of the present century there was a very ancient dwelling a few yards south-east of this tree, which was supposed to have been the residence of some ecclesiastic of former times. Many a gay May fair has been witnessed by the old tree; in the morning of the 28th of the month splendid fat cattle, from some of the largest and best farms in the county, quietly chewed the cud around its trunk ; in the afternoon the basket-swing dangled from its branches, filled with merry laughing boys and girls from every part of the parish. On the following day, the mock mayor, who had been chosen with many formalities, remarkable only for their rude and rough nature, starting from some "bush-house," where he had been supping too freely of the fair ale, was mounted on wain or cart, and drawn around it, to claim his pretended jurisdiction over the ancient borough, until his successor was chosen at the following fair. Leaving the old nut-tree, which is a real ornament to the town, we pass by a stream of water running into a large trough, in which many a country lad has been drenched for daring to enter the town on the 29th of May without the leaf or branch of oak in his hat.

III.—THE MAYOR OF HALGAVER MOOR.

The people of Bodmin had an old custom of assembling in large numbers on Halgaver Moor in the month of July, and electing a "Mayor of Misrule," for the punishment of petty offenders. Our old historian gives a quaint description. "The youthlyer sort of Bodmin townsmen use sometimes to sport themselves by playing the box with strangers, whom they summon to Halgaver; the name signifieth the Goats' Moore, and such a place it is, lying a little without the town, and very full of quagmires. When these mates meet with any raw serving-man or other young master, who may serve and deserve to make pastime, they cause him to be solemnly arrested for his appearance before the Mayor of Halgaver, where he is charged with wearing one spur, or wanting a girdle, or some such like felony, and after he hath been arraigned and tried with all requisite circumstances, judgment is given in formal terms, and executed in some one ungracious prank or other, more to the scorn than hurt of the party condemned. Hence is sprung the proverb, when we see one slovenly apparelled, to say, 'He shall be presented in Halgaver Court.'"

THE FACTION FIGHT AT CURY GREAT TREE.

ON a green knoll in the centre of the intersection of the roads from Helston to the Lizard, and Mawgan to Cury, flourished an ash-tree of magnificent dimensions. The peculiarity of its position, together with its unusual size, in the midst of a district singularly destitute of trees, rendered it famous throughout the surrounding neighbourhood; and in designating a special locality, reference was, and still continues to be, made to "Cury Great Tree," as a position generally known. During the last fifty years the tree has been gradually decaying, and at present only a portion of the hollow trunk remains, which is rapidly disappearing. It stands about half way up a gentle rise facing the north; and in passing over the road, the country people speak of a dim tradition of a time when the "road ran with blood." The occasion of this, which is almost forgotten, was a faction fight, on a large scale, between the men of the parishes of Wendron and Breage, happening about a hundred years since. A wreck took place near the Lizard, and the Wendron-men being nearest, were soon upon the spot to appropriate whatever flotsam and jetsam might come in their way. Returning laden with their spoils, they were encountered at the Great Tree by the Wendron-men bound on a similar errand, and a fight, as a matter of course, ensued, which was prolonged till the following day. The contest is said to have been a most terrible one, each party being armed with staves. The savage nature of the fight may be inferred from the following fact:—A Wendron-man named Gluyas, having been disabled, was put upon the top of the roadside hedge, out of the *mêlée*, when he was seen by a Breage termagant known as "Prudy the Wicked," and by her quickly dragged into the road, "Prudy" exclaiming, "Ef thee artn't ded, I make thee," suiting the action to the word by striking Gluyas with her patten iron until he was dead. There is some account of Prudy's having been taken before the "Justice," but she does not appear to have been punished. These fights between parishes were so common in those days that any death occurring in the fray was quietly passed over as a thing of course, and soon forgotten. "So late as thirty years since it was unsafe to venture alone through the streets of the lower part of this town (Helston) after nightfall on a market-day, owing to the frays of the Breage, Wendron, and Sithney men." So writes a friend residing in Helston.

TOWEDNACK CUCKOO FEAST.

THE parish feast takes place on the nearest Sunday to the 28th of April.

It happened in very early times, when winters extended further into the spring than they now do, that one of the old inhabitants resolved to be jovial notwithstanding the inclemency of the season; so he invited all his neighbours, and to warm his house he placed on the burning faggots the stump of a tree. It began to blaze, and, inspired by the warmth and light, they began to sing and drink; when, lo, with a whiz and a whir, out flew a bird from a hollow in the stump, crying, Cuckoo! cuckoo! The bird was caught and kept by the farmer, and he and his friends resolved to renew the festal meeting every year at this date, and to call it their "cuckoo feast." Previous to this event Towednack had no "feasten Sunday," which made this parish a singular exception to the rule in Cornwall.

This feast is sometimes called "crowder" feast, because the fiddler formed a procession at the church door, and led the people through the village to some tune on his "crowd."

THE DUKE OF RESTORMEL.

A VERY singular custom formerly prevailed at Lostwithiel, in Cornwall, on Easter Sunday. The freeholders of the town and manor having assembled together, either in person or by their deputies, one among them, each in his turn, gaily attired and gallantly mounted, with a sceptre in his hand, a crown on his head, and a sword borne before him, and respectfully attended by all the rest on horseback, rode through the principal street in solemn state to the church. At the church-yard stile, the curate, or other minister, approached to meet him in reverential pomp, and then conducted him to church to hear divine service. On leaving the church, he repaired, with the same pomp and retinue, to a house previously prepared for his reception. Here a feast, suited to the dignity he had assumed, awaited him and his suite; and, being placed at the head of the table, he was served, kneeling, with all the rites and ceremonies that a real prince might expect. This ceremony ended with the dinner; the prince being voluntarily disrobed, and descending from his momentary exaltation, to mix with common mortals. On the origin of this custom but one opinion can be reasonably entertained, though it may be difficult to trace the precise period of its commencement. It seems to have originated in the actual appearance of the prince, who resided at Restormel Castle in former ages; but, on the removal of royalty, this mimic grandeur stepped forth as its shadowy representative, and continued for many generations as a memorial to posterity of the princely magnificence with which Lostwithiel had formerly been honoured.*

This custom is now almost forgotten, and Lostwithiel has little to disturb its quiet.

* Every-Day Book.

POPULAR SUPERSTITIONS.

"The carrion crow, that loathsome beast,
  Which cries against the rain,
Both for her hue, and for the rest,
  The devil resembleth plain.
And as with guns we kill the crow
  For spoiling our relief,
The devil so must we o'erthrow
  With gunshot of belief."

GEORGE GASCOIGNE.

CHARMING, PROPHETIC POWER, ETC.

CHARMING, AND PROPHETIC POWER.

"Late, late yestreen I saw the new moone
Wi' the auld moone in her arme;
And I feir, I feir, my dear master,
That we will com to harme."

SIR PATRICK SPENCE.

I CANNOT more appropriately preface this section, than by quoting the remarks of a medical gentleman in large practice, on the subject of charms:—"In common with most of the lower classes of the West of England, the miner is not free from many absurd superstitions, (though I am glad to observe, even in the last few years, a great change has taken place, and such follies are gradually declining.) Some think themselves endowed with a species of supernatural agency, and, like the Egyptian alluded to by Othello, call themselves charmers, and profess to stop the flowing of blood, (no matter from what cause—a divided artery even,) to remove specks from the cornea, (which, in the dialect of the country, are called canons!) and cure erysipelas, by charming. But I have never been able to ascertain by what means the charm is supposed to work. I only know that it is an every-day occurrence for mothers to bring children to the surgery, afflicted with either of the diseases mentioned, and say that they have had them charmed; but they were no better, such want of improvement having obviously excited the greatest feelings of astonishment. I knew a person connected with the mines, who felt himself endowed with prophetic powers; and in his case the divination was not confined to events momentous and terrible, but extended to the most trifling minutiæ of life.

"He with grave simplicity told me one day, by way of exemplifying the proper estimation in which his prophetic powers were held by his wife, that on one occasion, his pig having wandered from his sty, she came to him to ascertain in what direction it was to be sought for; and on his professing utter ignorance of the animal's peregrinations, she exclaimed, in reproachful tones, '*Ah, you are not so pious as you used to be. I remember the time when you could have told me in an instant the exact spot to have found it.*'"*

FORTUNE-TELLING, CHARMS, ETC.

IN relation to this subject, and confirming an opinion already expressed in the existence still of a belief in magic and charms, I print the following communication from a lady of considerable literary ability:—

"Every country, it may be safely inferred, has its own individual, perhaps characteristic, Charm-record; and inquiry into it would more than probably recompense the labour, by the light it would let in on the still but little investigated philosophy of the human mind, and the growth of popular superstitions. The portion of our country best known to the writer of these remarks is Cornwall, remarkable for the picturesque wildness of its scenery, and not less so for its numerous superstitions. The Rev. Charles Kingsley, in his

* On the Diseases of Cornish Miners. By William Wale Tayler, F.R.C.S.

'Yeast,' has availed himself, with his usual tact and power, of one of the most striking of these, having reference to the cruel treatment of the Jews, who were sold as slaves to work in the mines; the evil treatment they experienced being avenged on modern miners, by the terrors the souls of the departed Hebrews inflicted, in returning to the scene of their former compulsory toil, and echoing the sounds of the workmen now labouring in flesh and blood. But this is a digression from the main object of this article—viz., the belief in charms. Several years ago, while residing at Falmouth, I remember to have heard of a man in humble life, named Thomas Martin, whose abode was said to be at a village in the neighbourhood of Redruth, and who accomplished wonderful cures of children subject to fits, or personally injured by any deformity, by his power of charming. This man also practised soothsaying to a considerable extent, and revealed, with unquestionable accuracy, where articles mysteriously abstracted were concealed. If a cow suddenly lost her milk, whether witchcraft had exerted its malignant influence on the non-producing animal or no, such a personage could not but exercise an important power over the rustic population of the neighbourhood. But belief in the mysterious intelligence of Martin was by no means confined to the peasant class. A highly-respected and even ladylike person told the writer, with all the gravity becoming such a communication, that she had once made an appointment with Thomas Martin to meet him at a certain stile, for the purpose of receiving from him the prediction of her future lot,—in other words, having her fortune told; and hastening thither at the time appointed, was horrified to find the stile occupied by a large black snake. As Martin did not make his appearance, she inferred that he had assumed the serpent form, and not being disposed to hold any intercourse with a being of such questionable exterior, she hastened away, determined never more to risk the attainment of the knowledge she coveted through a probably diabolic channel.

"This anecdote is given as veritable experience of the belief which may prevail in a mind fairly intelligent, and generally rational in conducting the ordinary business of life.

"Martin's reputation was disputed by no one, and that it continued unimpaired to the close of his life reflects no inconsiderable credit on the shrewdness and sagacity of his mind and his power of guessing.

"In the town where the writer has been residing for the last four months, there is a female, advanced in years and of good character, who, according to the report of many persons,—one a relative of her own,—is peculiarly endowed with the power of charming away the disease called the "kennel," an affection of the eye, which causes extreme pain. A young lady's father was one evening suffering severe pain in the right eye, and after trying various remedies without effect, (the agony having greatly increased,) in her despair she sought an occasion to leave the house, and hastened at once to the abode of the charmer. She told her errand to the woman, who said that many had come to her for the purpose of ridiculing her, and she did not like to say anything about charming—she did not wish to be laughed at. On this the young lady assured her that her object in true faith was to obtain relief for her suffering father, and by no means to indulge the spirit of ridicule. On this representation she was satisfied, and desired to know the *kind* of kennel which affected the gentleman's eye. This information the daughter was unable to give her, being unacquainted with their peculiarities; 'because,' said the charmer, 'there are nine kinds of kennels,' intimating at the same time that a different charm might be said or applied to each,—so that, to avoid omitting any, she must say the charms for all, in order that the one especially affecting the diseased eye should be certainly included in the charm. She went up-stairs, and remained about half an hour. On her return she addressed the young lady, and told her she might go home, where she would learn whether the eye had been relieved. She took no money for her incantation. Any little present might be offered at a subsequent visit, but no direct payment was ever requested, and indeed would have been declined. The amazement and pleasure of the anxious daughter, on her arrival at home, will be imagined, on learning from her father that the intense pain in the eye had ceased during her absence, though he had not been made acquainted with her errand. The influence of the faith of another, in this case, on the relief of the afflicted person, has no verisimilitude save with that of the father of the demoniac in the gospel, or the removal of the son's fever in consequence of the faith of the father. I have no reason whatever to question the truth of this story, which was confirmed by the wife of the gentleman thus relieved.

"A still more curious instance of the effect of charm, though quite of another character, was related to me by the same party. The gentleman referred to being much afflicted with cramp, his wife was earnestly advised, by a country woman to whom she mentioned the circumstance, to request her husband to place his slippers, with the toes turned upward, at the foot of the bed. Half smiling at the wise counsel, yet perhaps not altogether incredulous, he followed the good woman's advice, and to his great comfort found himself unaffected by his dreaded enemy throughout the night. His faith being thus established in the *anti-cramp* influence of upturned slippers, he took care to place them, or to have them placed, in the prescribed attitude on several successive nights. One night, however, he was again seized with some appalling twinges, and bethinking himself of the cause, suddenly recollected that in hastening into bed he had not observed the important rule; instantly he had the slippers restored to their proper position, and, to his astonishment and delight, the pain ceased, and visited him no more. After this experience of the wonderful effects that followed so simple a specific, it may be easily imagined that he did not again risk the return of the cramp from neglecting it. Such phenomena seem beyond the power of explanation on any known medical principles. If any one more than usually versed in the subtle power exercised on the body by the mind, can throw light on the *slipper* cure of the cramp, he will deserve much at the hands of physiological and mental science."

S. E. M.

THE ZENNOR CHARMERS.

BOTH men and women in this parish possessed this power to a remarkable degree. They could stop blood, however freely it might be flowing. "Even should a pig be sticked in the very place, if a charmer was present, and *thought* of his charm at the time, the pig would not bleed." This statement, made by a Zennor-man, shews a tolerably large amount of faith in their power. The charmers are very cautious about communicating their charms. A man would not on any account tell his charm to a woman, or a woman communicate hers to a man. People will travel many miles to have themselves or their children charmed for "wildfires," (erysipelas,) ringworms, pains in the limbs or teeth, "kennels" on the eyes, (ulcerations.) A correspondent writes me: —"Near this lives a lady charmer, on whom I called. I found her to be a really clever, sensible woman. She was reading a learned treatise on ancient history. She told me there were but three charmers left in the west,—one at New Mill, one in Morva, and herself." Their charm for stopping blood is but another version of one given on another page.

> "Christ was born in Bethlehem;
> Baptized in the river Jordan.
> The river stood,—
> So shall thy blood,
> *Mary Jane Polgrain,* [*or whatever the person may be called,*]
> In the name of the Father," &c.

J—— H——, THE CONJURER OF ST COLOMB.

THIS old man was successful in persuading his dupes that he owed his powers over evil spirits to his superior learning and his unblemished life. This assumption of piety was well preserved, and to the outside world his sanctity was undoubted. The only practice which can be named as peculiar to H—— was that of lighting scores of candles and placing them around the meadow near his house. Of course such a display would attract much attention; and J—— succeeded in conveying an impression to the minds of the country people that this process was required to counteract the spells of the witches. When this old fellow has been summoned, as he often was, to the houses supposed to be under the influence of evil, or to be bewitched, his practice was not a little original, though wanting in all that dignifies the office of an exorcist. When he arrived at the house, before speaking to any one, he would commence operations by beating with a heavy stick on the wooden partitions, screens, or pieces of furniture, so as to make the greatest possible noise, shouting loudly all the time, "Out! out! out!—Away! away! away!—to the Red Sea—to the Red Sea—to the Red Sea." Frequently he would add, with violent enunciation and much action, a torrent of incoherent and often incomprehensible words, (locally, "*gibberish.*") The proceeding being brought to a close, and the spirits of evil flown, every part of the house was ordered to be well cleansed, and the walls and ceilings to be thoroughly lime-washed,—certainly the only sensible part of the whole operation. When J—— H—— was applied to respecting stolen property, his usual practice was to shew the face of the thief in a tub of water. J—— drove a considerable trade in selling powders to throw over bewitched cattle.*

CURES FOR WARTS.

I.

THE vicar of Bodmin found, not long since, a bottle full of pins laid in a newly-made grave. I have heard of this as an unfailing remedy; each wart was touched with a new pin, and the pin then dropped into the bottle. I am not quite certain that it was necessary that the bottle should be placed in a newly-made grave; in many cases burying it in the earth, and especially at a "four cross-roads," was quite sufficient. As the pins rust, the warts decay.

II.

A piece of string should be taken, and as many knots tied on it as there are warts on the body; each wart being carefully touched with the knot dedicated to it. The string is then to be buried, and the warts fade away as it decays. A

* When cattle or human beings have been bewitched, it was very commonly thought that if a bottle of urine from the diseased beast or person was obtained, then corked very tight and buried mouth downwards, that the witch would be afflicted with strangury, and in her suffering confess her crime and beg forgiveness.

few years since a shipwright in Devonport dockyard professed to cure warts by merely receiving from an indifferent person a knotted string,—the knots of which had been tied by the afflicted. What he did with the string I know not.

III.

To touch each wart with a pebble, place the pebbles in a bag, and to lose the bag on the way to church, was for many years a very favourite remedy; but the unfortunate person who found the bag received the warts. A lady once told me that she picked up such a bag, when a child, and out of curiosity, and in ignorance, examined the contents. The result was that she had, in a short time, as many warts as there were stones in the bag.

IV.

Another remedy was to *steal* a piece of meat from a butcher's stall in the public market, and with this to touch the warts, and bury it. As the meat putrefied the warts decayed.

V.

I remember, when quite a child, having a very large "seedy wart" on one of my fingers. I was taken by a distant relation, an elderly lady, residing in Gwinear, to some old woman, for the purpose of having this wart charmed. I well remember that two charred sticks were taken from the fire on the hearth, and carefully crossed over the fleshy excrescence, while some words were muttered by the charmer. I know not how long it was before the wart disappeared, but certainly, at some time, it did so.

A CURE FOR PARALYSIS.

MARGERY PENWARNE, a paralysed woman, about fifty years of age, though from her affliction looking some ten years older, sat in the church porch of St ——, and presented her outstretched withered arm and open palm to the congregation as they left the house of God after the morning service.

Penny after penny fell into her hand, though Margery never opened her lips. All appeared to know the purpose, and thirty pennies were speedily collected. Presently the parson came with his family, and then she spoke for the first time, soliciting the priest to change the copper coins into one silver one. This wish was readily acceded to, and the paralytic woman hobbled into the church, and up the aisle to the altar rails. A few words passed between her and the clerk; she was admitted within the rails, and the clerk moved the communion-table from against the wall, that she might walk round it, which she did three times.

"Now," said Margery, "with God's blessing, I shall be cured; my blessed bit of silver must be made into a ring," (this was addressed to the clerk, half aside;) "and within three weeks after it is on my finger I shall get the use of my limbs again."

This charm is common throughout the three western counties for the cure of rheumatism,—the Devonshire halt,—or for any contraction of the limbs.

A CURE FOR RHEUMATISM.

CRAWL under a bramble which has formed a second root in the ground. Or get a woman who has been delivered of a child, feet foremost, to tread the patient.

SUNDRY CHARMS.

THE vicar of a large parish church informs me that a woman came to him some time since for water from the font after a christening; she required it to undo some spell. The vicar states, that all the fonts in the country were formerly locked, to prevent people from stealing the "holy water," as they called it.

CURE FOR COLIC IN TOWEDNACK.

To stand on one's head for a quarter of an hour.

FOR A SCALD OR BURN.

"There came three angels out of the East,
One brought fire and two brought frost;
Out fire and in frost,
In the name of the Father, Son, and Holy Ghost.
Amen!"

Bramble-leaves, or sometimes the leaves of the common dock, wetted with spring water, are employed in this charm, as also in the following one.

CHARMS FOR INFLAMMATORY DISEASES.

A similar incantation to that practised for a burn is used. Three angels are invoked to come from the East, and this form of words is repeated three times to each one of nine bramble-leaves immersed in spring water, making passes with the leaves *from* the diseased part.

CHARMS FOR THE PRICK OF A THORN.

I.

"Christ was of a virgin born,
And He was prick'd by a thorn,
And it did never bell* nor swell,
As I trust in Jesus this never will."

* Throb.

II.

"Christ was crown'd with thorns
The thorns did bleed, but did not rot,
No more shall thy finger.
In the name,"* &c.

CHARMS FOR STANCHING OF BLOOD.

"Sanguis mane in te,
Sicut Christus fuit in se;
Sanguis mane in tuâ venâ,
Sicut Christus in suâ penâ;
Sanguis mane fixus,
Sicut Christus quando crucifixus."

As this is repeated by ignorant old men or women, it becomes a confused jargon of unmeaning words, but it impresses the still more ignorant sufferer with awe, approaching to fear. The following is more common:—

"Christ was born in Bethlehem,
Baptized in the river Jordan;
There He digg'd a well,
And turn'd the water against the hill,
So shall thy blood stand still.
In the name," &c.

CHARM FOR A TETTER.

"Tetter, tetter, thou hast nine brothers.
God bless the flesh and preserve the bone;
Perish, thou tetter, and be thou gone.
In the name," &c.

"Tetter, tetter, thou hast eight brothers.
God bless the flesh and preserve the bone;
Perish, thou tetter, and be thou gone.
In the name," &c.

"Tetter, tetter, thou hast seven brothers."
&c., &c.

Thus the verses are continued until tetter, having "no brother," is imperatively ordered to begone.

* The invocation of the "Father, Son, and Holy Ghost," invariably accompanies every form of charm.

CHARM FOR THE STING OF A NETTLE.

Many a time do I remember, when a child playing in the fields, having suffered from the stings of the nettle, and constantly seeking for the advantages of the charm of the dock-leaf. The cold leaf was placed on the inflamed spot, and the well-known rhyme three times repeated:—

"Out nettle,
In dock;
Dock shall have
A new smock."

CHARM FOR TOOTHACHE.

"Christ pass'd by His brother's door,
Saw His brother lying on the floor.
'What aileth thee, brother?
Pain in the teeth?—
Thy teeth shall pain thee no more.
In the name,'" &c.

CHARM FOR SERPENTS.

The body of a dead serpent bruised on the wound it has occasioned, is said to be an infallible remedy for its bite. Common report is sufficient to warrant a poetical allusion:—

"The beauteous adder hath a sting,
Yet bears a balsam too."

Polwheel's Sketches.

THE CURE OF BOILS.

The sufferer is to pass nine times against the sun, under a bramble-bush growing at both ends. This is the same as the cure prescribed for rheumatism.

RICKETS, OR A CRICK IN THE BACK.

The holed stone—Mên-an-tol—in Lanyon, is commonly called by the peasantry the crick-stone. Through this the sufferer was drawn nine times against the sun—or, if a man, he was to crawl through the hole nine times.

Strumous children were not unfrequently treated after another fashion.

A young ash-tree was cleft vertically, and the parts being drawn forcibly asunder, the child was passed "three times three times" against the sun through the tree. This ceremony having been performed, the tree was carefully bound together: if the bark grew together and the tree survived, the child would grow healthy and strong; if the tree died, the death of the child, it was believed, would surely follow.

THE CLUB-MOSS,

(LYCOPODIUM INUNDATUM.)

IF this moss is properly gathered, it is "good against all diseases of the eyes."

The gathering is regarded as a mystery not to be lightly told; and if any man ventures to write the secret, the virtues of the moss avail him no more. I hope, therefore, my readers will fully value the sacrifice I make in giving them the formula by which they may be guided.

On the third day of the moon—when the thin crescent is seen for the first time—shew it the knife with which the moss is to be cut, and repeat,—

> "As Christ heal'd the issue of blood,
> Do thou cut, what thou cuttest, for good!"

At sun-down, having carefully washed the hands, the club-moss is to be cut kneeling. It is to be carefully wrapped in a white cloth, and subsequently boiled in some water taken from the spring nearest to its place of growth. This may be used as a fomentation. Or the club-moss may be made into an ointment, with butter made from the milk of a new cow.

MOON SUPERSTITIONS.

THE following superstitions are still prevalent on the north coast of Cornwall:—

"This root, (the sea-poppy,) so much valued for removing all pains in the breast, stomach, and intestines, is good also for disordered lungs, and is so much better here than in other places, that the apothecaries of Cornwall send hither for it; and some people plant them in their gardens in Cornwall, and will not part with them under sixpence a root. A very simple notion they have with regard to this root, which falls not much short of the Druids' superstition in gathering and preparing their selago and samolus. This root, you must know, is accounted very good both as an emetic and cathartic. If, therefore, they design that it shall operate as the former, their constant opinion is that it should be scraped and sliced upwards—that is, beginning from the root, the knife is to ascend towards the leaf;—but if that it is intended to operate as a cathartic, they must scrape the root downwards. The *senecio* also, or groundsel, they strip upwards for an emetic and downwards for a cathartic. In Cornwall they have several such groundless opinions with regard to plants, and they gather all the medicinal ones when the moon is just such an age; which, with many other such whims, must be considered as the reliques of the Druid superstition." *

They, the Druids, likewise used great ceremonies in gathering an herb called *samolus*, marsh-wort, or fen-berries, which consisted in a previous fast, in not looking back during the time of their plucking it, and, lastly, in using their left hand only; from this last ceremony, perhaps, the herb took the name of *samol*, which, in the Phœnician tongue, means the

* Borlase's Observations on the Ancient and Present State of the Island of Scilly.—"Notes and Queries," vol. x. p. 181. 1854.

left hand. This herb was considered to be particularly efficacious in curing the diseases incident to swine and cattle.—(*C. S. Gilbert.*)

CURES FOR WHOOPING-COUGH.

I.

GATHER nine spar stones from a running stream, taking care not to interrupt the free passage of the water in doing so. Then dip a quart of water from the stream, which must be taken in the direction in which the stream runs;—by no means must the vessel be dipped against the stream.

Then make the nine stones red hot, and throw them into the quart of water. Bottle the prepared water, and give the afflicted child a wine-glass of this water for nine mornings following. If this will not cure the whooping-cough, nothing else can, says the believer.

II.

A female donkey of three years old was taken, and the child was drawn naked nine times over its back and under its belly. Then three spoonfuls of milk were drawn from the teats of the animal, and three hairs cut from the back and three hairs cut from the belly were placed in it. This was to stand for three hours to acquire the proper virtue, and then the child drank it in three doses.

This ceremony was repeated three mornings running, and my informant said the child was always cured. I knew of several children who were treated in this manner in one of the small villages between Penzance and Madron Church-town, some twenty or thirty years since. There were some doggerel lines connected with the ceremony, which have escaped my memory, and I have endeavoured, in vain, to find any one remembering them. They were to the effect that, as Christ placed the cross on the ass's back when He rode into Jerusalem, and so rendered the animal holy, if the child touched where Jesus sat, it should cough no more.

CURE OF TOOTHACHE.

ONE good man informed me that, though he had no faith in charming, yet this he knew, that he was underground one day, and had the toothache "awful bad, sure enough; and Uncle John ax'd me, 'What's the matter?' says he. 'The toothache,' says I. 'Shall I charm it?' says he. 'Ees,' says I. 'Very well,' says he; and off he went to work in the next pitch. Ho! dedn't my tooth ache, Lor' bless ee; a just ded ye knaw; just as if the charm were tugging my very life out. At last Uncle John comed down to the soller, and sing'd out, 'Alloa! how's your tooth in there?' says he. 'Very bad,' says I. 'How's a feeling?' says he. 'Pulling away like an ould hoss with the "skwitches,"' says I. 'Hal drag my jaw off directly,' says I. 'Ees the charm working?' says he. 'Es, a shure enuf,' says I. 'Es,' says he, 'al be better d'rectly.' 'Hope a will,' says I. Goodness gracious! dedn't a ache; I believe a did you; then a stopped most to once. 'Es better,' says I. 'I thought so,' says he; 'and you waan't have un no more for a long time,' says he. 'Thank ee, Uncle John,' says I; 'I'll give ee a pint o' beer pay-day,' and so I ded; an' I haben't had the toothache ever since. Now, if he dedn't charm un, how ded a stop? and if he dedn't knaw a would be better a long time, how ded he say so? No, nor I haven't had un never since. So that's a plain proof as he knaw'd all about it, waden't a you?"

I nodded assent, convinced it was useless to argue against such reasoning as that.

THE CONVALESCENT'S WALK.

IF an invalid goes out for the first time and makes a circuit, this circuit must be with the sun; if against the sun, there will be a relapse.

ADDERS, AND THE MILPREVE.

THE country people around the Land's-End say that in old times no one could live in the low grounds, which were then covered with thickets, and these swarming with adders. Even at a much later period, in the summer-time, it was not safe to venture amongst the furze on the Downs without a *milpreve*. (I have never seen a milpreve; but it is described to me as being about the size of a pigeon's egg, and I am told that it is made by the adders when they get together in great numbers. Is it not probable that the milpreve may be one of the madrepore corals—*millepore*—found sometimes on the beaches around Land's-End?)

A friend writes me:—"I was once shewn a milpreve; it was nothing more than a beautiful ball of coralline limestone, the section of the coral being thought to be entangled young snakes."

When some old men were streaming the "Bottoms" up near Partimey, they were often obliged to leave work on account of the number of adders that would get together as if by agreement, and advance upon them.

One day one of the tin streamers chanced to leave his pot of milk, uncovered, out of the moor-house, when an adder got into it. The man cut a turf and put over the pot to prevent the reptile from escaping. In a few minutes the tinners saw "the ugly things crawling and leaping from all quarters towards the pot." The streamers were obliged to run, and take which way they would ; the adders seemed to be coming from every direction, further and further off.

At last "they formed a heap round the pot as large as a pook [cock] of hay." Towards night all the reptiles were quite still, then the men gathered together, around the mass of adders, a great quantity of furze, (being summer, there was plenty cut and dry close at hand,) and piled it up like sheaves to make a mow, laying a circle of well-dried turf without it. They then fired the turf on every side, and when it was well ignited, they fired the furze. "Oh, it was a sight to see the adders when they felt the smoke and the flame ! they began to boil, as it were, all in a heap, and fell back into the flaming furze ; those which leaped through perishing on the brilliant ring of burning peat. Thus were killed thousands upon thousands of adders, and the moors were clear for a long, long period."

This is related nearly as the story was told ; but it appears necessary to make some allowance for that spirit of exaggeration which is a characteristic of all Celtic people, ere they have been tutored to know the dignity of truth.

"The country people retaine a conceite, that the snakes, by their breathing upon a hazel-wand, doe make a stone ring of blew colour, in which there appeareth the yellow figure of a snake, and that beasts which are stung, being given to drink of the water wherein this stone hath bene socked, will there-through recover." *

This was clearly one of the so-called "Druidic rings,"—examples of which may be seen in our museums,—which have been found in England and in Ireland. It is curious that at the glassworks of Murano, near Venice, they still make rings, or beads, precisely resembling the ancient ones, and these are used largely as money in Africa.

* The Survey of Cornwall. By Richard Carew.

Snakes were formerly held in great reverence; and Camden asserts that one of the prevailing superstitions concerning them was that, about midsummer-eve, they all met together in companies, and, joining their heads, began a general hiss, which they continued until a kind of bubble was formed, which immediately hardened, and gave to the finder prosperity in all his undertakings.*

Lhuyd, in a letter written in 1701, gives a curious account of the then superstitious character of the people in this district. "The Cornish retain variety of charms, and have still towards the Land's-End the amulets of *Maen Magal* and *Glain-neider*, which latter they call a *Melprer*, a thousand worms, and have a charm for the snake to make it, when they have found one asleep, and struck a hazel-wand in the centre of its *spiræ*." Camden mentions the use of snake-stones as a Cornish superstition.

"The very same story, in fact, is told of the *Adder-stane* in the popular legends of the Scottish Lowlands, as Pliny records of the origin of the *Ovum Anguinum*. The various names by which these relics are designated all point to their estimation as amulets or superstitious charms; and the fact of their occurrence, most frequently singly, in the sepulchral cist or urn, seems to prove that it was as such, and not merely as personal ornaments, that they were deposited with the ashes of the dead. They are variously known as adder-beads, serpent-stones, Druidical beads; and, amongst the Welsh and Irish, by the synonymous terms of *Gleini na Droedh* and *Glaine nan Druidhe*, signifying the magician's or Druid's glass."—*Wilson's Archæology and Prehistoric Annals of Scotland*, p. 304.

* Draw and Hitchin's Cornwall.

SNAKES AVOID THE ASH-TREE.

IT is said that no kind of snake is ever found near the "ashen-tree," and that a branch of the ash-tree will prevent a snake from coming near a person.

A child, who was in the habit of receiving its portion of bread and milk at the cottage door, was found to be in the habit of sharing its food with one of the poisonous adders. The reptile came regularly every morning, and the child, pleased with the beauty of his companion, encouraged the visits. The babe and adder were close friends.

Eventually this became known to the mother, and, finding it to be a matter of difficulty to keep the snake from the child whenever it was left alone,—and she was frequently, being a labourer in the fields, compelled to leave her child to shift for itself,—she adopted the precaution of binding an "ashen-twig" about its body.

The adder no longer came near the child; but from that day forward the child pined, and eventually died, as all around said, through grief at having lost the companion by whom it had been fascinated.

TO CHARM A SNAKE.

WHEN an adder or snake is seen, a circle is to be rapidly drawn around it, and the sign of the cross made within it, while the two first verses of the 68th Psalm are repeated :—

> "Let God arise, let his enemies be scattered : let them also that hate him flee before him.
>
> "As smoke is driven away, so drive them away : as wax melteth before the fire, so let the wicked perish at the presence of God."

When a child, I well remember being shewn a snake, not

yet dead, within a circle of this kind; the gardener who drew my attention to the reptile informing me that he had charmed it in the manner related.

THE ASH-TREE.*

WEAKLY children—"children that wouldn't goode," or thrive—were sometimes drawn through the cleft ash-tree. I have seen the ceremony performed but in one case.

The tree was young, and it was taken by the two forks,—bifurcation having taken place,—and by force rended longitudinally. The cleft was kept open, and the child, quite naked, was passed head first through the tree nine times. The tree was then closed and carefully tied together. If the severed parts reunited, the child and the tree recovered together; if the cleft gaped in any part, the operation was certain to prove ineffectual.

I quote another example. A large knife was inserted into the trunk of the young tree, about a foot from the ground, and a vertical rending made for about three feet. Two men then forcibly pulled the parts asunder, and held them so, whilst the mother passed the child through it three times. This "passing" alone was not considered effective; it was necessary that the child should be washed for three successive mornings in the dew from the leaves of the "charmed ash."

In the *Athenæum* for September 1846, Ambrose Merton—Mr Thoms—has some interesting notices of the wide-spread belief in, and the antiquity of, this superstition.

* See also p. 216.

RHYME ON THE EVEN ASH.

"EVEN ash, I thee do pluck;
Hoping thus to meet good luck.
If no luck I get from thee,
I shall wish thee on the tree."

A TEST OF INNOCENCY.

A FARMER in Towednack having been robbed of some property of no great value, was resolved, nevertheless, to employ a test which he had heard the "old people" resorted to for the purpose of catching the thief. He invited all his neighbours into his cottage, and when they were assembled, he placed a cock under the "brandice," (an iron vessel formerly much employed by the peasantry in baking, when this process was carried out on the hearth, the fuel being furze and ferns.) Every one was directed to touch the brandice with his, or her, third finger, and say, "In the name of the Father, Son, and Holy Ghost, speak." Every one did as they were directed, and no sound came from beneath the brandice. The last person was a woman, who occasionally laboured for the farmer in his fields. She hung back, hoping to pass unobserved amidst the crowd. But her very anxiety made her a suspected person. She was forced forward, and most unwillingly she touched the brandice, when, before she could utter the words prescribed, the cock crew. The woman fell faint on the floor, and, when she recovered, she confessed herself to be the thief, restored the stolen property, and became, it is said, "a changed character from that day."

THE BONFIRE TEST.

A BONFIRE is formed of faggots of furze, ferns, and the like. Men and maidens by locking hands form a circle, and commence a dance to some wild native song. At length, as the dancers become excited, they pull each other from side to side across the fire. If they succeed in treading out the fire without breaking the chain, none of the party will die during the year. If, however, the ring is broken before the fire is extinguished, "bad luck to the weak hands," as my informant said.

LIGHTS SEEN BY THE CONVERTED.

THERE is, in many parts of the county, a belief, derived no doubt from the recollection of St Paul's conversion, that, when sinners are converted, they see shining lights about themselves. I have many times heard this, but every one seems to have his own particular mode of describing the phenomenon,—where they can be prevailed on to describe it at all,—and usually that is derived from some picture which has made an impression on their minds: such as, "exactly like the light shining round the angel appearing to St Peter, in fayther's Bible."

THE MIGRATORY BIRDS.

I FIND a belief still prevalent amongst the people in the outlying districts of Cornwall, that such birds as the cuckoo and the swallow remain through the winter in deep caves, cracks in the earth, and in hollow trees; and instances have been cited of these birds having been found in a torpid state in the mines, and in hollow pieces of wood. This belief appears to be of some antiquity, for Carew writes in his "Survey of Cornwall" as follows:—

"In the west parts of Cornwall, during the winter season, swallows are found sitting in old deep tynne-works, and holes in the sea cliffes: but touching their lurking-places, *Olaus Magnus* maketh a far stranger report. For he saith that in the north parts of the world, as summer weareth out, they clap mouth to mouth, wing to wing, and legge to legge, and so, after a sweet singing, fall downe into certain lakes or pools amongst the caves, from whence at the next spring they receive a new resurrection; and he addeth, for proofe thereof, that the fishermen who make holes in the ice, to dip up such fish in their nets as resort thither for breathing, doe sometimes light on these swallows congealled in clods, of a slymie substance, and that, carrying them home to their stoves, the warmth restored them to life and flight."

A man employed in the granite quarries near Penryn, informed me that he found such a "slymie substance" in one of the pools in the quarry where he was working, that he took it home, warmth proved it to be a bird, but when it began to move it was seized by the cat, who ran out on the downs and devoured it.

SHOOTING STARS.

A MUCILAGINOUS substance is found on the damp ground near the granite quarries of Penryn, this is often very phosphorescent at night. The country people regard this as the substance of shooting stars. A tradesman of Penryn once brought me a bottle full of this substance for analysis, informing me that the men employed at the quarries, whenever they observed a shooting star, went to the spot near which they supposed it to fall, and they generally found a hat full of this mucus. It is curious that the Belgian peasants also call it "the substance of shooting stars," ("Phosphorescence," p. 109. By T. L. Phipson.) This author says, "I have sketched the history of this curious substance in the *Journal de Médecine et de Pharmacologie* of Bruxelles, for 1855. It was analysed chemically by Mulder, and anatomically by Carus, and from their observations appears to be the peculiar mucus which envelops the eggs of the frog. It swells to an enormous volume when it has free access to water. As seen upon the damp ground in spring, it was often mistaken for some species of fungus; it is, however, simply the spawn of frogs, which has been swallowed by some large crows or other birds, and afterwards vomited, from its peculiar property of swelling to an immense size in their bodies."

In Mulder's account of its chemical composition, given by Berselius in his *Rapport Annual,* he distinguishes it by designation of *mucilage atmosphérique.*

THE SUN NEVER SHINES ON THE PERJURED.

THERE appears to exist a very old superstition, to the effect that when a man has deeply perjured himself,—especially if by his perjury he has sacrificed the life of a friend,—he not merely loses the enjoyment of the sunshine, but he actually loses all consciousness of its light or its warmth. Howsoever bright the sun may shine, the weather appears to him gloomy, dark, and cold.

I have recently been told of a man living in the western part of Cornwall, who is said to have sworn away the life of an innocent person. "The face of this false witness is the colour of one long in the tomb; and he has never, since the death of the victim of his forswearing, seen the sun." It must be remembered the perjured man is not blind. All things around him are seen as by other men, but the sense of vision is so dulled that the world is for ever to him in a dark, vapoury cloud.

CHARACTERISTICS.

AN esteemed and learned correspondent, himself a Cornishman, writing to me on the Cornish character, says :—

"There are some adages in which beadledom receives various hard knocks—that abstraction mostly taking the shape of some unlucky mayor; and I have heard in Cornwall, but never elsewhere, that the greatest fool in the place for the time being is always made the mayor.

"There is an adage of the Mayor of Calenich, (and yet I doubt if ever that hamlet had such an officer.) Calenich is one mile from Truro, and the mayor's hackney was pastured two miles from home; so, as his worship would by no means compromise his dignity by walking to Truro, he invariably walked to his horse to ride there, so that it was said of any one who would keep up appearances at great trouble, that he was '*like the Mayor of Calenich, who walked two miles to ride one.*'

"The class who never know on which side their bread is buttered, are said to be '*like the Mayor of Market-Jew, sitting in their own light;*' and the stupid man whose moods, whether of sadness or merriment, are inopportune, is, as may be, said to be '*like the Mayor of Falmouth, who thanked God when the town-jail was enlarged.*'

"Many persons are chronicled in the same manner.

"'*Like Nicholas Kemp, he 's got occasion for all.*' Nicholas was said to be a voter in a Cornish borough, who was told to help himself (so that no one should have given him a bribe,) from a table covered with gold, in the election committee-room. Taking off his hat, he swept the whole mass into it, saying, 'I 've occasion for all.'

"'*Like Uncle Acky Stoddern, the picture of ill luck.*' This was always applied to a once well-known Gwennap-man.

"When a boy is asked what he will be, it is sometimes answered on his behalf, '*I'll be like Knuckey, be as I am.*'

"'*Like Nanny Painter's hens, very high upon the legs,*' is applied to a starveling or threadpaper.

"'*Like Malachi's cheeld, choke-full of sense,*' applied derisively to any one boasting of himself or of his children. This is, I believe, purely Cornish.

"'*Like a toad under a harrow, I don't know whichee corse to steer.*' The first division of this adage is common property, the last is confined to Cornwall.

"'*He's coming home with Penny Liggan,*' sometimes 'Peter Lacken,' signifies the return of a pennyless scapegrace. The term was probably 'penny lacking' originally.

"Are the Cornish folk given to making 'bulls,' like the Irish?" asks my correspondent. "I have heard of one or two curious inversions of speech.

"Once upon a time a little boy having vainly importuned his seniors for a penny to go and buy sweets, being determined not to be disappointed, went off, exclaiming, 'I don't care; I'll go and *trust* Betty Rule,' (the sweetmeat vendor.) This is native and genuine Gwennapian.

"The common people are fond of figures of speech. Port-wine negus was christened by the miners 'black wine toddy.' They go on Midsummer-day to Falmouth or Penzance, to get '*a pen'ord o' say*'—that is, they go out in a boat on payment of a penny.

"With them, when their health is inquired after, every man is '*brave,*' and every woman '*charming;*' and friendship takes dear household names into its mouth for more expressiveness.

"'Well, Billy, my son, how's faether?'

"'Brave, thank ee.'

"'How are you, Coden [Cousin] Jaan, and how's Betty?'

"'She's charming, thank ee.'

"*Trade* is a word of special application, '*a pa'cel o' trade.*'

"A precious mess is '*a brave shape.*'

"Of an undecided person it is said, '*He is neither Nim nor Doll.*' Does this mean he is neither Nimrod nor Dorothy?

"A phrase descriptive of vacuity of expression is, '*He looks like anybody that has neither got nor lost.*'"

Years since it was a common custom to assign some ridiculous action to the people of a small town or village. For example, the people of one place were called "Buccas," "because some one of them was frightened at his shadow."

Those of another town were named "Gulls," "because two of the townsmen threw a gull over a cliff to break its neck."

The men of a fishing-village were nicknamed "Congers," "because they threw a conger overboard to drown it."

"Who whipped the hake?" was applied to the inhabitants of another town, because hake, it is said, being excessively plenty, the fishermen flogged one of those fish, and flung it back into the sea; upon which all the hakes left that coast, and kept away for years.*

"Who drowned the man in a dry ditch?" belongs especially to another place.

Certain Cornishmen built a wall around the cuckoo, to prevent that bird from leaving the county, and thus to insure an early spring. When built, the bird flew out, crying

* In Hugh Miller's "Scenes and Legends of the North of Scotland," edit. 1858, pp. 256, 257, will be found some stories of the flight of the "herring drove" from the coast of Cromarty, which are analogous to this.

"Cuckoo! cuckoo!" "If we had put one course more on the wall we should a' kept 'n in," said they.

Camborne is so called from *Camburne*, a *crooked well-pit* of water. This crooked well was at one time far famed for the cure of many diseases.

The persons who washed in this well were called *Merrasicke.* I know not the meaning of the word. According to an old Cornish custom of fixing nicknames on people, the inhabitants of Camborne are called *Mearageeks*, signifying perverse, or obstinate.—(*Lanyon.*)

The Church was anciently called *Mariadoci.* I therefore suspect that the above terms have some connexion with this name. By an easy corruption, and the addition of *geeks*, or *gawks*, (meaning awkward,) either word can be produced.

Of the Gorran men it is asked, "Who tried to throw the moon over the cliffs?"

THE MUTTON FEAST.

AN old tradition—the particulars of which I have failed to recover—says that a flock of sheep were blown from the Gwithian Sands over into St Ives Bay, and that the St Ives fishermen caught them,—believing them to be a new variety of fish,—either in their nets, or with hook and line, and brought them ashore as their night's catch.

I learn that Mr Fortescue Hitchins, some fifty or sixty years since, wrote a "copy of verses" on this tradition, but I have never seen this production.

THE FLOATING GRINDSTONE.

I HAVE already told of St Piran and his grindstone. I have, however, another and a more modern story, which is told with great glee at some of the social meetings of the fishermen. This is given merely to indicate the simplicity of this honest race.

A party was got together on a promontory at the extremity of the bay which enclosed a fishing-town. They were gathered to see a wonder, a *floating grindstone.* Seeing that grindstones were grindstones in those days, and worth many pounds sterling, a boat was manned, and away they went, the mover of the expedition being in the bow of the boat.

As they approached the grindstone, this man planted his foot on the gunwale, ready for a spring. They were close aboard the circular mass,—"All my own, and none for nobody," he cries, and sprang off, as he fancied, on to the grindstone. Lo! to his great surprise, he sank under water, presently popping up again within his charmed circle, to be greeted with roars of laughter. He had leaped into a sheet of "salt sea foam" which had gathered, and was confined within a large hoop.

CELTS—FLINT ARROW-HEADS, ETC.

THE common people believe these to be produced by thunder, and thrown down from the clouds, and that they shew what weather will ensue by changing their colour.

I have also found a belief prevailing in many districts, that Celts impart a virtue to water in which they have been soaked, and that diseases have been cured by drinking it.

HORNS ON THE CHURCH TOWER.

WHEN the masons were building the tower of Towednack Church, the devil came every night and carried off the pinnacles and battlements. Again and again this work was renewed during the day, and as often was it removed during the night, until at length the builders gave up the work in despair, feeling that it was of no use to contend with the evil one.

Thus it is that Towednack Church stands lonely, with its squat and odd-looking tower, a mark of the power of evil to the present day. Associated with this tower is a proverb: "There are no cuckolds in Towednack, because there are no horns on the church tower."

TEA-STALKS AND SMUT.

STEMS of tea floating in that beverage indicate strangers. Flakes of smut hanging loose to the fire-bars do the same thing.

The time of the stranger's arrival may be known by placing the stem on the back of one hand, and smacking it with the other; the number of blows given before it is removed indicates the number of days before his arrival.

The flake of carbon is blown upon, and according as it is removed by the first, second, or third blow, so is the time at the end of which the visitor may be expected.

AN OLD CORNISH RHYME.

"WHEN the corn is in the shock,
Then the fish are on the rock."

The pilchard visits this coast in the early autumn. These are the "fish" *par excellence* of the Cornish, and they are thus distinguished.

TO CHOOSE A WIFE.

ASCERTAIN the day of the young woman's birth, and refer to the last chapter of Proverbs. Each verse from the 1st to the 31st is supposed to indicate, either directly or indirectly, the character, and to guide the searcher—the verse corresponding with her age indicating the woman's character.

THE ROBIN AND THE WREN.

"THOSE who kill a robin or a wran,
Will never prosper, boy or man."

This feeling is deeply impressed on every young mind; there are few, therefore, who would injure either of those birds.

I remember that a boy in Redruth killed a robin: the dead robin was tied round his neck, and he was marched by the other boys through the town, all of them singing the above lines.

TO SECURE GOOD LUCK FOR A CHILD.

GIVE the first person whom you meet between your own house and the church to which you are taking the infant to be christened, a piecc of bread and salt.

INNOCENCY.

TO wash the hands is an attestation of innocency. To call a man "dirty fingers," is to accuse him of some foul or unjust deed.

RAIN AT BRIDAL OR BURIAL.

"BLESSED is the bride
Whom the sun shines on,
Blessed is the dead
Whom the rain rains on."

If it rains while a wedding party are on their way to the

church, or on returning from it, it betokens a life of bickering and unhappiness.

If the rain falls on a coffin, it is supposed to indicate that the soul of the departed has "arrived safe."

CROWING HENS, ETC.

A WHISTLING maid and a crowing hen in one house, is a certain sign of a downfall to some one in it. I have known hens killed for crowing by night.

The braying of an ass is a sign of fair weather; so is also the crowing of a cock. The quacking of ducks foretells rain.

THE NEW MOON.

TO see the new moon for the first time, through glass, is unlucky; you may be certain that you will break glass before that moon is out. I have known persons whose attention has been called to a clear new moon, hesitate. "Hev I seed her out a' doors afore?" if not, they will go into the open air, and if possible shew the moon "a piece of gold," or, at all events, turn their money.

LOOKING-GLASSES.

BREAKING a looking-glass is certain to insure seven years of misfortune.

THE MAGPIE.

"ONE is a sign of anger,
Two is a sign of mirth,
Three is a sign of a wedding,
Four is a sign of a { birth. / death."

A scolding woman is called a magpie. Whenever you see

a magpie, take off your hat to it; this will turn away the anger.

THE MONTH OF MAY UNLUCKY.

MAY is regarded by many as an unhealthy and unlucky month.

Children born in the month of May are called "May chets," and kittens cast in May are invariably destroyed, for—

> "May chets
> Bad luck begets."

Another rhyme is—,

> "A hot May,
> Fat church hay,"

meaning that funerals will be plenty.

ON THE BIRTHS OF CHILDREN.

> "SUNDAY'S child is full of grace,
> Monday's child is full in the face,
> Tuesday's child is solemn and sad,
> Wednesday's child is merry and glad,
> Thursday's child is inclined to thieving,
> Friday's child is free in giving,
> Saturday's child works hard for his living."

ON WASHING LINEN.

> "THEY that wash Monday got all the week to dry,
> They that wash Tuesday are pretty near by,
> They that wash Wednesday make a good housewife,
> They that wash Thursday must wash for their life,
> They that wash Friday must wash in need,
> They that wash Saturday are sluts indeed".

ITCHING EARS.

WHEN the ears are red and itch, it is a sign that some one is talking of the suffering individual. If it is the left ear, they are being scandalised; if the right ear, they are being praised.

Often have I heard, when the lower and middle class people have been indulging in some gossip of their neighbours or friends, "I 'll bet how their ears do itch."

THE SPARK ON THE CANDLE.

A BRIGHT spark on the candle-wick indicates a letter coming to the house. The person towards whom it shines will receive it. The time of its arrival is determined by striking the bottom of the candlestick on the table. If the spark comes off on the first blow, it will be received to-morrow; if two blows are required, on the second day, and so on.

THE BLUE VEIN.

A FOND mother was paying more than ordinary attention to a fine healthy-looking child, a boy about three years old. The poor woman's breast was heaving with emotion, and she struggled to repress her sighs. Upon inquiring if anything was really wrong, she said "the old lady of the house had just told her that the child could not live long, because *he had a blue vein across his nose.*"

THE CROAKING OF THE RAVEN.

THERE is a common feeling that the croaking of a raven over the house bodes evil to some member of the family. The following incident, given to me by a really intelligent man, illustrates the feeling: *—

"One day our family were much annoyed by the continued croaking of a raven over our house. Some of us believed it to be a token; others derided the idea; but one good lady,

* "See "Death Tokens."

our next-door neighbour, said, 'Just mark the day, and see if something does not come of it.' The day and hour were carefully noted. Months passed away, and unbelievers were loud in their boastings and inquiries after the token.

"The fifth month arrived, and with it a black-edged letter from Australia, announcing the death of one of the members of the family in that country. On comparing the dates of the death and the raven's croak, they were found to have occurred on the same day."

WHISTLING.

TO whistle by night is one of the unpardonable sins amongst the fishermen of St Ives. My correspondent says, "I would no more dare go among a party of fishermen at night whistling a popular air than into a den of untamed tigers."

No miner will allow of whistling underground. I could never learn from the miners whether they regarded it as unlucky or not. I rather think they feel that whistling indicates thoughtlessness, and they know their labour is one of danger, requiring serious attention.

MEETING ON THE STAIRS.

IT is considered unlucky to meet on the stairs, and often one will retire to his or her room rather than run the risk of giving or receiving ill luck.

I find this superstition prevails also in the Midland counties.

TREADING ON GRAVES.

"TO see a man tread over graves,
I hold it no good mark;
'Tis wicked in the sun and moon,
And bad luck in the dark!"

So sings Coleridge in his ballad of "The Three Graves."

Whenever a person shivers from a sensation of cold down the spine, it is said some one is walking over his or her grave.

Persons believing this will give directions that they may be buried in some secluded corner of the churchyard, so that their corpse may not be disturbed by unholy footsteps.

A LOOSE GARTER.

IF an unmarried woman's garter loosens when she is walking, her sweetheart is thinking of her.

TO CURE THE HICCOUGH.

WET the forefinger of the right hand with spittle, and cross the front of the left shoe or boot three times, repeating the Lord's Prayer backwards.

THE SLEEPING FOOT.

THIS irregularity in the circulation is at once removed by crossing the foot with saliva.

THE HORSE-SHOE.

TO nail a horse-shoe, which has been cast on the road, over the door of any house, barn, or stable, is an effectual means of preventing the entrance of witches.

THE BLACK CAT'S TAIL.

THOSE little gatherings which occur on the eye-lids of children, locally called "wilks," are cured by passing a black cat's tail nine times over the place. If a ram cat, the cure is more certain.

UNLUCKY THINGS.

TO put the loaf on the table upside down—to cut the butter at both ends—to place the bellows on the table —to upset the salt—to cross your knife and fork—to pour gravy out of a spoon backwards, (or back-handed,) is each unlucky, and leads to quarrels. To borrow or lend a bellows is most unlucky, and many would rather give than lend one.

If you are going on an errand, never turn back to your house, it presages ill luck to do so. If, however, you are compelled to it, fail not to sit down. By doing this, some mischief may be avoided.

THE LIMP CORPSE.

IF a corpse stiffens shortly after death, all is thought to proceed naturally; but if the limbs remain flexible, some one of the family is shortly to follow. If the eyes of a corpse are difficult to close, it is said "they are looking after a follower."

To find a louse on one's linen, is a sign of sickness. To find two, indicates a severe illness. If three lice are so found within a month, it is a "token to prepare."

Talking backwards, or putting one word incorrectly before another,—"the cart before the horse,"—is considered to foretell that you will shortly see a stranger.

If two young people, in conversation, happen to think of the same thing at the same time, and one of them utters the thought before the other, that one is certain to be married first.

"BY HOOK OR BY CROOK."

IN the parish of Egles-Hayle are two crosses, known as "Peverell's Crosses;" and near Mount Charles, also in this parish, is another "moorstone" cross, called the Prior's Cross, whereon is cut the figure of a hook and a crook, in memory of the privileges granted by a prior, belonging to the family of the Peverells, who are said to have possessed lands in this parish since the time of Richard II.

The poor of Bodmin were greatly distressed through the scarcity of fuel, the "turf," or peat of the moors being insufficient to supply their wants. The prior gave "privilege and freedom" to the poor of Bodmin for gathering, for "fire-boote and house-boote," such boughs and branches of oak-trees in his woods of Dunmear, as they could reach to, or come at, with a "hook and a crook," without further damage to the trees.

Hence the proverb concerning filching, "that they will have it by hook or by crook."

WEATHER SIGNS.

THE WEATHER DOG.—It frequently happens in unsettled weather that banks of rain-cloud gather around the horizon, and that, over isolated tracts, the rain falls. If these depositions from this low stratum of clouds occur opposite to the sun, the lower limb of a bow is formed, often appearing like a pillar of decomposed light; and sometimes two of these coloured bands will be seen, forming indeed the two extremities of the arch. These are "weather dogs," and they are regarded as certain prognostications of showery or stormy weather.*

* "There appeared in the north-east the frustrum of a large rainbow; all the colours were lively and distinct, and it was three times as wide as the

The usual proverb with regard to the full bow, which prevails generally, is common in Cornwall,—

> "The rainbow in the morning
> Is the shepherd's warning;
> The rainbow at night
> Is the shepherd's delight."

But, as far as I know, the "weather dog" is peculiarly Cornish.

WEATHER AT LISKEARD.

> "THE south wind always brings wet weather;
> The north wind, wet and cold together.
> The west wind always brings us rain;
> The east wind blows it back again.
> If the sun in red should set,
> The next day surely will be wet;
> If the sun should set in gray,
> The next will be a rainy day."
>
> *Bond's Looe.*

THE FIRST BUTTERFLY.

"ONE of the superstitions prevailing in Devonshire is, that any individual neglecting to kill the first butterfly he may see for the season, will have ill luck throughout the year."* The following recent example is given by a young lady:—"The other Sunday, as we were walking to church, we met a man running at full speed, with his hat in one hand, and a stick in the other. As he passed us he exclaimed, 'I shan't hat 'en now, I b'lieve.' He did not give us time to inquire what he was so eagerly pursuing; but we presently overtook an old man, whom we knew to be his father, and who, being very infirm, and upwards of seventy, generally

---

arch of an ordinary complete rainbow, but no higher than it was wide. They call it here, in Cornwall, *a weather dog;* but in the Cornish language, *Lagas-auel,*—that is, the weather's eye,—and pronounce it a certain sign of hard rain."—*Borlase's Natural History of Cornwall.*

* Hone's Table-Book.

hobbled about by the aid of two sticks. Addressing me, he observed, 'My *zin* a took away wan a my sticks, miss; wan't be ebble to kill 'n now though, I b'lieve.' 'Kill what?' said I. 'Why, 'tis a butterfly, miss,—the *furst* hee'th a zeed for the year; and they zay that a body will have cruel bad luck if a ditn'en kill a *furst* a zeeth.'"

I have found this belief prevailing in the east, but never in the west, of Cornwall.

PECULIAR WORDS AND PHRASES.

"THE people in the west," writes a correspondent, "have adopted many words from the Danish invaders." Tradition assures us that the sea-rovers of the North frequently landed at Witsand Bay, burned and pillaged the villages of Escols and Mayon, sometimes took off the women, but never made a settlement. Certain red-haired families are often referred to as Danes, and the dark-haired people will not marry with "a red-haired Dane." He continues:—'If you were in Buryan Church-town this evening, you might probably hear Betty Trenoweth say, 'I'll take off my *touser*, [toute serve,] and run up to Janey Angwins to *cousey* [causer] a spell; there's a lot of boys gone in there, so there'll be a grand *courant*, [de courir,] I expect.' In a short time Betty may come back disappointed, saying, ''Twas a mere *cow's courant* after all, cheld vean—all hammer and tongs.'"

The *touser* is a large apron or wrapper to come quite round and keep the under garments clean. By a *courant* with the boys, they mean a game of running romps. It is not at all uncommon in other parts of the country to hear the people say, "It was a fine *courant*," "We've had a good *courant*," when they intend to express the enjoyment of some pleasure party. These are, however, probably more nearly allied to Norman-French.

There are some proverbial expressions peculiar to the west:—

"Sow barley in dree, and wheat in pul."*

"To make an old nail good, right it on wood."

"Fill the sack, then it can stand."

The last meaning that neither man nor beast can work on an empty stomach.

The following are a few of less common expressions, preserving remarkable words:—

'Tis not *bezibd*—It is not allotted me.

He will never *scrip* it—He will never escape it.

He is nothing *pridy*—He is not handsome.

Give her *dule*—Give her some comfort or consolation.

Hark to his *lidden*—Listen to his word or talk.

It was *twenty* or *some*—It was about twenty.

The wind brings the *pilme*—The wind raises the dust.

How thick the *brusse* lies—How thick the dust lies.

He is *throyting*—He is cutting chips from sticks.

He came of a good *havage*—He belongs to a good or respectable family.

Hame—a straw collar with wooden collar-trees, to which are fastened the rope traces.

Scalpions (*buckthorn*, or rather *buckhorn*)—salt dried fish, usually the whiting.

"Eating fair maids, or fermades—(*fumadoes*)—[pilchards,] and drinking mahogany, [gin and treacle.]"

* In pul; meaning in mud.

MISCELLANEOUS STORIES.

"Farewell, rewards and fairies,
  Good housewives now may say;
For now foul sluts in dairies
  Do fare as well as they.

. . . . . .

"A tell-tale in their company
  They never could endure;
And who kept not secretly
  Their mirth, was punish'd sure."

Farewell to the Fairies—RICHARD CORBET.

VARIOUS ROMANCES & SUPERSTITIONS.

THE BELLS OF FORRABURY CHURCH.

"The Cornish drolls are dead, each one;
The fairies from their haunts have gone:
There's scarce a witch in all the land,
The world has grown so learn'd and grand."

HENRY QUICK, *the Zennor Poet.*

TO this day the tower of Forrabury Church, or, as it is called by Mr Hawker, "the silent tower of Bottreaux," remains without bells. "At Forrabury the chimes have never sounded for a marriage, the knell has never been heard for a funeral."—*Collins.*

In days long ago, the inhabitants of the parish of Forrabury—which does not cover a square mile, but which now includes the chief part of the town of Boscastle and its harbour—resolved to have a peal of bells which should rival those of the neighbouring church of Tintagel, which are said to have rung merrily at the marriage, and tolled solemnly at the death, of Arthur.

The bells were cast; the bells were blessed; and the bells were shipped for Forrabury. Few voyages were more favourable; and the ship glided, with a fair wind, along the northern shores of Cornwall, waiting for the tide to carry her safely into the harbour of Bottreaux.

The vesper bells rang out at Tintagel, and the pilot, when he heard the blessed sound, devoutly crossed himself, and bending his knee, thanked God for the safe and quick voyage which they had made.

The captain laughed at the superstition of the pilot, as he called it, and swore that they had only to thank themselves for the speedy voyage, and that, with his arm at the helm, and his judgment to guide them, they should soon have a happy landing. The pilot checked this profane speech; but the wicked captain—and he swore more impiously than ever that all was due to himself and his men—laughed to scorn the pilot's prayer. "May God forgive you!" was the pilot's reply.

Those who are familiar with the northern shores of Cornwall will know that sometimes a huge wave, generated by some mysterious power in the wide Atlantic, will roll on, overpowering everything by its weight and force.

While yet the captain's oaths were heard, and while the inhabitants on the shore were looking out from the cliffs, expecting, within an hour, to see the vessel, charged with their bells, safe in their harbour, one of these vast swellings of the ocean was seen. Onward came the grand billow in all the terror of its might. The ship rose not upon the waters as it came onward. She was overwhelmed, and sank in an instant close to the land.

As the vessel sank, the bells were heard tolling with a muffled sound, as if ringing the death-knell of the ship and sailors, of whom the good pilot alone escaped with life.

When storms are coming, and only then, the bells of Forrabury, with their dull, muffled sound, are heard from beneath the heaving sea, a warning to the wicked; and the tower has remained to this day silent.

THE TOWER OF MINSTER CHURCH.

"The Minster of the Trees! a lonely dell,
Deep with old oaks, and 'mid their quiet shade,
Gray with the moss of years, yon antique cell!
Sad are those walls: the cloister lowly laid,
Where pacing monks at solemn evening made
Their chanted orisons: and as the breeze
Came up the vale, by rock and tree delay'd,
They heard the awful voice of many seas
Blend with thy pausing hymn, thou Minster of the Trees!"

HAWKER.

ON a visit to this old church, which is allowed to perish under the influences of damp and the accompanying vegetable growth, in a way which is but little creditable to the parishioners, I was struck at the evidence that the tower had either been taken down or that it had fallen. Amidst the long grass of the churchyard I found many remains of carved stones, which clearly belonged at one time to the tower. I sought for some information, but I could obtain none. The officiating clergyman, and several gentlemen of Boscastle, were alike ignorant of any tradition connected with the tower—the prevalent idea being that it was left unfinished.

At length, the ostler at the inn informed me that the story of the destruction of the tower ran thus:—

The tower of the church of the ancient abbey was seen through the gorge which now forms the harbour of Boscastle, far out at sea. The monks were in the habit of placing a light in one of the windows of the tower to guide the worshippers, at night, to the minster.

Frequently sailors mistook this, by day for some landmark, and at night for a beacon, and were thus led into a trap from which they could not easily extricate themselves, and within which they often perished. This accident occurred so frequently that the sailors began at last to declare their belief that the monks purposely beguiled them to their fate, hinting, indeed, that plunder was their object. Eventually, a band of daring men, who had been thus lured into Boscastle, went to the abbey, and, in spite of the exertions made by the monks, they pulled down the tower, since which time it has never been rebuilt.

TEMPLE MOORS.

THE parish of Temple in 1851 had a population of 24. Yet once the Knights Templars built a church here; and with the purpose of civilising the inhabitants of the moors in the midst of which it was founded, they secured for their temple some special privileges. "Many a bad marriage bargain," says Tonkin, "is there yearly slubbered up, and grass widows with their fatlings put to lie-in and nurse here." "Send her to Temple Moors," implied that any female requiring seclusion might at one time secure it under the charge of these Christian knights in this their preceptory, and be returned to the world again, probably, in all respects, a better woman. At all events, the world, being in ignorance, did not repudiate the erring sister.

Stories linger over this wilderness of mixed good and evil. The church, which was consecrated to the great cause of saving sinners, has perished. No stone remains to tell us where it stood; and to "send her to Temple Moors," is to proclaim a woman an outcast from society.

THE LEGEND OF TAMARA.

THE lovely nymph Tamara was born in a cavern. Although her parents were spirits of the earth, the child loved the light of day. Often had they chided her for yielding to her desires and visiting the upper world; and often had they warned her against the consequences which would probably arise from her neglect of their advice.

The giants of the moors were to be feared; and it was from these that the earth spirits desired to protect their child.

Tamara—beautiful, young, heedless—never lost an opportunity of looking on the glorious sun. Two sons of Dartmoor giants—Tavy and Tawrage—had seen the fair maid, and longed to possess her. Long was their toil, and the wild maiden often led them over mountain and moor in playful chase.

Under a bush in Morewinstow, one day, both Tavy and Tawrage came upon Tamara. They resolved now to compel her to declare upon which of them her choice should fall. The young men used every persuasion, and called her by every endearing name. Her parents had missed Tamara, and they sought and found her seated between the sons of the giants whom they hated. The gnome father caused a deep sleep to fall on the eyes of Tavy and Tawrage, and then he endeavoured to persuade his daughter to return to his subterranean cell.

Tamara would not leave her lovers. In his rage the gnome cursed his daughter, and, by the might of his curse, changed her into a river, which should flow on for ever to the salt sea. The lovely Tamara dissolved in tears, and, as a crystal stream of exceeding beauty, the waters glided onward to the ocean.

At length Tavy awoke. His Tamara was gone; he fled

to his father in the hills. The giant knew of the metamorphosis, and, to ease the anguish of his son, he transformed him into a stream. Rushing over rocks, running through morasses, gliding along valleys, and murmuring amidst the groves, Tavy still goes on seeking for Tamara—his only joy being that he runs by her side, and that, mingling their waters, they glide together to the eternal sea.

Tawrage awakened after a long sleep. He divined what had taken place, and fled to the hills to an enchanter. At his prayer he, too, was changed to a stream; but he mistook the road along which Tamara had gone, and onward, ever sorrowing, he flows—away—away—away from his Tamara for ever.

Thus originated the Tamar, the Tavy, and the Taw.

THE CHURCH AND THE BARN.

THE Daunays were great people in their day; but many of them bore indifferent characters.

Sir John de Daunay was a strange mixture of ostentatious pride and penuriousness. His Lady Emelyn was as proud as her husband, but extravagant to a fault.

The priests of St Germans persuaded Sir John to build a church on his lands at Sheviock. He commenced the work, and, notwithstanding his great wealth, his heart failed him and he curtailed the fair proportions on which he had at first decided.

Emelyn was enraged at this; and it is said, that, prompted by the devil in visible presence, she resolved to build a barn which should exceed in beauty the house of God.

The barn rose with astonishing rapidity. Stones were laid at night, and the work proceeded as if the most lavish expenditure had been bestowed upon it. The church progressed but slowly, and was, after all, a very inferior structure to the barn. The devil, without doubt, having assisted Lady Daunay in her wicked work.

"There runneth a tale amongst the parishioners how one of the Daunay family's ancestors undertook to build the church, and the wife the barn adjoining; and that, casting up accounts on finishing their work, the barn was found to have cost 1½d. more than the church."*

The Daunay aisle in Sheviock Church still preserves the name of this family, who appear to have possessed at one time nearly all this, and much of the adjoining parish.

THE PENRYN TRAGEDY.

"News from Penryn, in Cornwall, of a most bloody and unexampled Murder."

SUCH was the title of a black-letter pamphlet of eight pages referred to by Lysons. This curious book does not appear to be in existence.

Mr Davies Gilbert, who possessed much property in the parish of Gluvias, was especially interested in the farm of Bohelland, the place which has been rendered for ever notorious, as having been the scene of Lillo's tragedy of "Fatal Curiosity."

From a work entitled "The Reign and Death of King James of Great Britain," Mr Gilbert quotes as follows:—

"He had been blessed with ample possessions and fruitful issue, unhappy only in a younger son, who, taking liberty from his father's bounty, and with a crew of like condition, that wearied on land, they went roving to sea, and in a small vessel southward, took boot from all they could master. And so increasing force and wealth, ventured on a Turk's man in the Streights; but by mischance their own powder fired themselves, and our gallant, trusting to his skilful swimming, got on shore upon Rhodes; with the best of his jewels about him; where, offering some to sale to a Jew, who knew them to be the Governor's of Algier, he was apprehended, and, as a

* Davies Gilbert's "Cornwall."

pirate, sentenced to the galleys among other Christians, whose miserable slavery made them all studious of freedom, and with wit and valour took opportunity and means to murder some officers, got on board of an English ship, and came safe to London; where his misery, and some skill, made him servant to a surgeon, and sudden preferment to the East Indies. There, by this means, he got money; with which returning back, he designed himself for his native county, Cornwall. And in a small ship from London, sailing to the west, was cast away upon that coast. But his excellent skill in swimming, and former fate to boot, brought him safe to shore; where, since his fifteen years' absence, his father's former fortunes much decayed, now retired him not far off to a country habitation, in debt and danger.

"His sister he finds married to a mercer, a meaner match than her birth promised. To her, at first, he appears a poor stranger, but in private reveals himself, and withal what jewels and gold he had concealed in a bow-case about him; and concluded that the next day he intended to appear to his parents, and to keep his disguise till she and her husband should meet, and make their common joy complete. Being come to his parents, his humble behaviour, suitable to his suit of clothes, melted the old couple to so much compassion as to give him covering from the cold season under their outward roof; and by degrees his travelling tales, told with passion to the aged people, made him their guest so long by the kitchen fire, that the husband took leave and went to bed. And soon after his true stories working compassion in the weaker vessel, she wept, and so did he; but compassionate of her tears, he comforted her with a piece of gold, which gave assurance that he deserved a lodging, to which she brought him; and being in bed, shewed her his girdled wealth, which he said was sufficient to relieve her husband's wants, and to spare for himself, and being very weary, fell fast asleep.

"The wife tempted with the golden bait of what she had, and eager of enjoying all, awakened her husband with this news, and her contrivance what to do; and though with horrid apprehensions he oft refused, yet her puling fondness (Eve's enchantments) moved him to consent, and rise to be master of all, and both of them to murder the man, which instantly they did; covering the corpse under the clothes till opportunity to convey it out of the way.

"The early morning hastens the sister to her father's house, where she, with signs of joy, inquires for a sailor that should lodge there the last night; the parents slightly denied to have seen any such, until she told them that he was her brother, her lost brother; by that assured scar upon his arm, cut with a sword in his youth, she knew him; and were all resolved this morning to meet there and be merry.

"The father hastily runs up, finds the mark, and with horrid regret of this monstrous murder of his own son, with the same knife cuts his own throat.

"The wife went up to consult with him, where, in a most strange manner beholding them both in blood, wild and aghast, with the instrument at hand, readily rips herself up, and perishes on the same spot.

"The daughter, doubting the delay of their absence, searches for them all, whom she found out too soon; with the sad sight of this scene, and being overcome with horror and amaze of this deluge of destruction, she sank down and died; the fatal end of that family. The truth of which was frequently known, and flew to court in this guise; but the imprinted relation conceals their names, in favour to some neighbour of repute and kin to that family. The same sense makes me therein silent also."—*Gilbert*, vol. ii. p. 100.

Mr Harris of Salisbury, in his "Philological Inquiries," says of Lillo's tragedy :—

"It is no small praise to this affecting fable that it so much resembles the 'Œdipus Tyrannus' of Sophocles. In both tragedies, that which apparently leads to joy, leads in its completion to misery; both tragedies concur in the horror of their discoveries, and both in those great outlines of a truly tragic revolution, (according to the nervous sentiment of Lillo himself,)—

'the two extremes of life,
The highest happiness the deepest woe,
With all the sharp and bitter aggravations
Of such a vast transition.'"

GOLDSITHNEY FAIR AND THE GLOVE.

ON the 5th of August, St James's day, (old style,) a fair is held here, which was originally held in the Church-town of Sithney, near Helston.

In olden time the good *St Perran the Little* gave to the wrestlers in his parish a glove as the prize, and the winner of the glove was permitted to collect the market toll on the day of the feast, and to appropriate the money to his own use. The winner of the glove lived in the Church-town of Sithney, and for long long years the right of holding the fair remained undisputed.

At length the miners of Goldsithney resolved to contest the prize, and they won it, since which time the fair has been held in that village, they paying to the poor of the parish of Sithney one shilling as compensation.

Gilbert remarks, "The displaying of a glove at fairs is an ancient and widely-extended custom. Mr Lysons says it is continued at Chester. The editor has seen a large ornamented glove over the guildhall at Exeter during the fairs." *

THE HARLYN PIE.

"ADJOINING the Church of Constantine, in the parish of St Merryn, was a cottage which a family of the name of Edwards held for generations, under the proprietors of Harlyn, by the annual render of a pie, made of limpets, raisins, and various herbs, on the eve of the festival in honour of the saint to whom the church was dedicated. The pie, as I have heard from my family, and from more ancient members of the family, and from old servants, was excellent. The Edwards had pursued for centuries the occupation of shepherds on Harlyn and Constantine commons. The last died about forty years ago, and the wreck of their cottage is almost buried in the sand." †

PACKS OF WOOL THE FOUNDATION OF THE BRIDGE OF WADEBRIDGE.

LOVEBONE was the vicar of Wadebridge, and there was a ferry across the river. It was a frequent custom for the farmers to ride their horses and to drive their cattle across

* Vol. iii. p. 309.

† Letter from William Peter, Esq. of Harlyn, to Davies Gilbert, vol. iii. p. 178.

when the tide was low, and frequently men and beasts were lost in the quicksands formed on the rising of the tide. A sad accident of this kind happened, and Lovebone resolved on building a bridge; as Leland says in his "Itinerary," "Then one Lovebone, vicar of Wadebridge, moved with pitie, began the bridge, and with great paine and studie, good people putting their help thereto, finished it with xvii fair and great uniform arches of stone."

Great was the labour, and frequent the disappointment. Pier after pier were built, and then they were lost in the sands. A "fair structure" was visible at night, in the morning there was no trace of the work of the masons. Lovebone almost despaired of success, indeed he was about to abandon the work, when he dreamed that an angel came with a flock of sheep, that he sheared them, let the wool fall into the water, and speedily built the bridge upon the wool.

Lovebone awoke with a new idea. He gathered from the farmers around, all the wool they would give him, he put it loosely into packs, placed these thickly upon the sand, and built his piers. The work remains to this day in proof of the engineering skill of the suggesting angel.*

Quoting Beaumont and Fletcher's "Knight of the Burning Pestle," we find the Citizen saying to the Prologue:—

"Why could you not be content as well as others, with the Legend of Whittington? or the Life and Death of Sir Thomas Gresham, with the building of the Royal Exchange? or the Story of Queen Eleanor, with the rearing of London Bridge upon woolsacks?"

* See Keighton's "Tales and Popular Fictions," p. 247.

THE LAST WOLF IN ENGLAND.

THE extirpation of the wolves, which once existed in every part of these islands, is an oft-told story.

But it is not generally known that the last native wolf lived in the forests of Ludgvan, near Penzance. The last of his race was a gigantic specimen, and terrible was the havoc made by him on the flocks. Tradition tells us that at last he carried off a child. This could not be endured, so the peasantry all turned out, and this famous wolf was captured at Rospeith, the name of a farm still existing in Ludgvan.

CHURCHES BUILT IN PERFORMANCE OF VOWS.

THERE are several churches which, tradition tells us, owe their origin to vows made by terrified men that they would, if relieved from their dangers, build a temple to God.

Amongst these may be named Brent Tor, thus spoken of by Mr Bray:—

"The church of Brent Tor is dedicated to St Michael. And there is a tradition among the vulgar that its foundation was originally laid at the foot of the hill; but that the enemy of all angels, the Prince of Darkness, removed the stones by night from the base to the summit,—probably to be nearer his own dominion, the air,—but that, immediately on the church's being dedicated to St Michael, the patron of the edifice hurled upon the devil such an enormous mass of rock, that he never afterwards ventured to approach it. Others tell us that it was erected by a wealthy merchant, who vowed, in the midst of a tremendous storm at sea, (possibly addressing himself to his patron, St Michael,) that if he escaped, he would build a church on the first land he descried." *

Brent Tor is a very remarkable hill, and can be seen far off at sea. This may possibly lend some support to the latter tradition.

St Anthony, in Kerrier, is likewise stated to be the consequence of a vow. Soon after the Conquest, as some persons of rank and fortune were coming to England from Normandy, they were overtaken by a violent storm, from which they expected immediate destruction. In the midst of their distress, they directed their prayers to St Anthony, and laid themselves under a solemn vow to erect a church to his memory, if he would save them from shipwreck; and that this church should be erected on the very spot where they should first get on shore. Driven by the tempest, they were conducted, by a power fully equal to that which St Anthony might be supposed to possess, into St Mawes' harbour, and happily landed on that very spot where the church now stands. And it appears that the materials with which the tower is built, and the situation which the church and tower occupy, are calculated to give sanction to this tradition.

BOLAIT, THE FIELD OF BLOOD.

TRADITION asserts that it was on the spot, so called in the parish of Burian, that the last battle was fought between the Cornish Britons and Athelstan. This is in some measure confirmed by the discovery of flint arrow-heads, in considerable quantities, from time to time, in and near this "field of slaughter."

* "Traditions, Legends, Superstitions, and Sketches of Devonshire," by Mrs Bray, who gives a letter of her husband's, for some time vicar of Tavistock.

We have little beyond the evidence of tradition to guide us in regard to any of the triumphs of Athelstan in Cornwall. It appears tolerably certain that this Saxon king confined the Cornish Britons to the western side of the Tamar; thus breaking up the division known as Danmonium, and limiting the territory over which the kings of the west ruled.

Scattered over Cornwall, we have the evidence, in the names of places, of Saxon possession. In all probability these were the resting-places of portions of the Saxon army, or the district in which fortified camps were placed by Athelstan, to restrain a turbulent people. Be this as it may, the battle at Bolait is said to have raged from morning until night, and then, overpowered by numbers, the Cornish who still survived fled to the hills, and thus left Athelstan the conqueror.

It was after this fight that Athelstan, seeing the Islands of Scilly illumined by the setting sun, determined, if possible, to achieve their conquest. He then recorded his vow, that he would, if he returned victorious, build a church, which should be dedicated to St Buryana. Of this church Hals writes as follows:—

"BURIAN.

"This church was founded and endowed by King Athelstan, about the year 930, after such time as he had conquered the Scilly Islands, as also the county of Devon, and made Cornwall tributary to his sceptre. To which church he gave lands and tithes of a considerable value for ever, himself becoming the first patron thereof, as his successors the kings of England have been ever since; for which reason it is still called the royal rectory, or regal rectory, and the royal or regal peculiar; signifying thereby that this is the church or chapel pertaining to the king, or immediately under the jurisdiction of him, as the supreme ordinary from whom there is no appeal; whereas other peculiars, though exempt from the visitation or jurisdiction of the diocesan bishop within whose see they stand, yet are always subject to the provincial Archbishops of Canterbury and York, or other persons.

"This church or college consisted of canons, Augustines or regular priests, and three prebendaries, who enjoyed the revenues thereof in common, but might not marry; and the lord chancellors of England of old visited this peculiar—which extended only over the parishes of Burian, Sennen, and St Levan—for the king.

"One of the Popes of Rome, about the time of Edward III., obtruded upon this church, the canons and prebends thereof, a dean to be an inspector and overseer over them,—whom he nominated to be the Bishop of Exon for the time being,—who for some time visited this church as its governor, as the lord chancellor did before; which encroachment of the Pope being observed by Edward III., as appears from the register of the writs, folio 40 and 41, 8 Edward III., rot. 97, this usurpation of the Pope was taken away."

WOEFUL MOOR, AND BODRIGAN'S LEAP.

THE Bodrigans, from a very early period, were connected with the borough of Looe. Otto, or Otho de Bodrigan, was lord of the manor of Pendrim and Looe in the reign of Edward II. Another Otho de Bodrigan was Sheriff of Cornwall in the 3d of Richard II., A.D. 1400.

Sir Henry Bodrigan was "attaynted for taking part with King Richard III. against Henry VII.; and, after flying into Ireland, Sir Richard Egecombe, father of Sir Pears Egecombe, had Bodrigan, and other parcels of Bodrigan's lands;

and Trevanion had part of Bodrigan's lands, as Restronget and Newham, both in Falmouth Haven."

On the Barton of Bodrigan there exists what are evidently the remains of ancient fortifications, and near them a piece of waste land known as the *Woeful Moor*.

Here Sir Henry Edgecombe and Trevanion defeated the great Bodrigan. He fled, and tradition preserves, on the side of the cliff, the spot known as Bodrigan's leap, from which he leapt into the sea, and swam to a ship which kept near the shore. As he leapt the precipice, he bequeathed, with a curse, "his extravagance to the Trevanions, and his folly to the Edgecombes."

These families divided between them an estate said to be worth, in those days, £10,000 per annum.

"At that period in our history when the law of the strongest was the rule, three families in Cornwall were engaged in a series of domestic wars; these were Bodrigan, Trevanion, and Edgecumbe. And when Richard the Third obtained sovereign power, on the division which then took place in the York faction, Bodrigan endeavoured to seize the property of Edgecumbe, with little respect, as it would seem, for the life of the possessor; but in the final struggle at Bosworth Field, where Henry Tudor put an entire end to this contest for power under the guise of property, by seizing the whole to himself, Trevanion and Edgecumbe had the good fortune to appear on the winning side, and subsequently availed themselves to the utmost of belligerent rights against Bodrigan, as he had attempted to do before against them. The last of that family was driven from his home, and seems to have perished in exile. His property was divided between the two families opposed to him, and, after the lapse of three hundred and fifty years, continues to form a large portion of their respective possessions."—*Gilbert*, vol. iii., p. 204.

William de Bodrigan was lord of the manor of Restronget, in the 12th of Henry IV. The family possessed it till the beginning of the reign of Henry VII., when, on the attainder of Bodrigan, it was given to William Trevanion.*

PENGERSWICK CASTLE.

THIS castellated building—for it does not now admit of being called a castle, notwithstanding its embattled turrets and its machicolated gate—is situated in a hollow running down to Pengerswick Cove, in the Mount's Bay, where there never could have been anything to defend; and certainly there is nothing to induce any one to incur the cost of such a building.

Mr Milliton, in the reign of Henry VIII., slew in the streets of London a man in a drunken brawl. He fled, and went to sea. It is not known to what part of the world he went, but we are told that he became excessively rich; so rich, indeed, that "when he loaded his ass with his gold, the weight was so great as to break the poor animal's back." Returning to his country, and not daring to appear in any of the large towns, he bought the manor of Pengerswick, and built this castle, to defend himself, in the event of his being approached by any of the officers of the law.

A miserable man, Milliton is said to have lived in a secret chamber in this tower, and to have been visited only by his most trusted friends. Deeply deploring the crime that had condemned him to seclusion from the world, he spent his

* See Gilbert, vol. iii., p. 293, and Bond's account of the Trelawnys in Bond's Looe.

dreary hours in ornamenting his dwelling. His own story is supposed to be told in the painting of an overladen ass in one room, with a black-letter legend, importing that a miser is like an ass loaded with riches, who, without attending to his golden burden, feeds on thistles. There is also a carving of water wearing a hollow in a stone, and under it the word "Perseverance." Of the death of Milliton we have no account.

There is very little doubt but that Pengerswick Castle is very much older than the time of Milliton; indeed tradition informs us that he purchased the place. The legends previously given, and others in my possession, refer to a much earlier period. This castle was, it is said, surrounded by trees; but John Hals, who inherited the property, had all the timber cut down and sold.

THE CLERKS OF CORNWALL.

I.

"IN the last age there was a familiarity between the parson and the clerk and the people which our feelings of decorum would revolt at—*e.g.*, 'I have seen the ungodly flourish like a *green bay*-tree.' 'How can that be, maister?' said the clerk of St Clement's. Of this I was myself an ear-witness."

II.

"At Kenwyn, two dogs, one of which was the parson's, were fighting at the west end of the church; the parson, who was then reading the second lesson, rushed out of the pew and went down and parted them; returning to his pew, and doubtful where he had left off, he asked the clerk, 'Roger, where was I?' 'Why, down parting the dogs, maister,' said Roger."

III.

"At Mevagizzey, when non-resident clergymen officiated, it was usual with the squire of the parish to invite them to dinner. Several years ago, a non-resident clergyman was requested to do duty in the church of Mevagizzey on a Sunday when the Creed of St Athanasius is directed to be read. Before he had begun the service, the parish clerk asked him whether he intended to read the Athanasian Creed that morning. 'Why?' said the clergyman. 'Because if you do, no dinner for you at the squire's, at Penwarne.'"

IV.

"A very short time since parish clerks used to read the first lesson. I once heard the St Agnes clerk cry out, 'To the mouth of the burning *viery vurnis*, and spake, and said, Shadrac, Meshac, and Abednego, *com voath and com hether*,' (Daniel iii.)"

V.

"The clerk of Lamorran, in giving out the psalm, 'Like a timorous bird to distant mountains fly,' always said, 'Like a timmersum burde,' &c., &c., with a shake of the head, and a quivering voice, which could not but provoke risibility."*

A FAIRY CAUGHT.

THE following, communicated to me on the 8th of August, is too good to be lost. I therefore give it in my correspondent's own words:—

"I heard last week of three fairies having been seen in Zennor very recently. A man who lived at the foot of Trendreen hill, in the valley of Treridge, I think, was cutting

* Hone's Table-Book.

furze on the hill. Near the middle of the day he saw one of the small people, not more than a foot long, stretched at full length and fast asleep, on a bank of griglans, (heath,) surrounded by high brakes of furze. The man took off his furze cuff, and slipped the little man into it, without his waking up; went down to the house; took the little fellow out of the cuff on the hearthstone, when he awakened, and seemed quite pleased and at home, beginning to play with the children, who were well pleased with the small body, and called him Bobby Griglans.

"The old people were very careful not to let Bob out of the house, or be seen by the neighbours, as he promised to shew the man where the crocks of gold were buried on the hill. A few days after he was brought from the hill, all the neighbours came with their horses (according to custom) to bring home the winter's reek of furze, which had to be brought down the hill in trusses on the backs of the horses. That Bob might be safe and out of sight, he and the children were shut up in the barn. Whilst the furze-carriers were in to dinner, the prisoners contrived to get out, to have a "courant" round the furze-reek, when they saw a little man and woman, not much larger than Bob, searching into every hole and corner among the trusses that were dropped round the unfinished reek. The little woman was wringing her hands and crying, 'Oh, my dear and tender Skillywidden, wherever canst ah (thou) be gone to? shall I ever cast eyes on thee again?' 'Go 'e back,' says Bob to the children; 'my father and mother are come here too.' He then cried out, 'Here I am, mammy!' By the time the words were out of his mouth, the little man and woman, with their precious Skillywidden, were nowhere to be seen, and there has been no sight nor sign of them since. The children got a sound thrashing for letting Skillywidden escape."

THE LIZARD PEOPLE.

THERE is a tradition that the Lizard people were formerly a very inferior race. In fact it is said that they went on all fours, till the crew of a foreign vessel, wrecked on the coast, settled among them, and improved the race so much that they became as remarkable for their stature and physical development as they had been before for the reverse. At this time, as a whole, the Lizard folks certainly have among them a very large population of tall people, many of the men and women being over six feet in height.

PRUSSIA COVE AND SMUGGLERS' HOLES.

SMUGGLERS' hiding-places (now, of course, unused) are numerous. On the banks of the Helford river are several, and two or three have lately been discovered on the coast about St Keverne by the falling in of their roofs. In a part of Penzance harbour, nine years ago, a hiding-place of this kind was discovered; it still contained one or two kegs, and the skeleton of a man, with his clothes in good preservation. It is presumed that the poor fellow while intoxicated was shut in, and the place never more opened by his companions. Speaking of Penzance—about fifty years since, in the back of the harbour, was an old adit called "Gurmer's Hole," and in the cliff over its entrance, *on a dark night*, a phosphorescent appearance was always visible from the opposite side. It could not be seen from beneath, owing to the projection of the face of the cliff. A fall of the part taking place, the phenomenon disappeared.

Sixty or seventy years since, a native of Breage called "Carter," but better known, from a most remarkable personal resemblance to Frederick the Great, as the "King of

Prussia," monopolised most of the smuggling trade of the west. By all accounts he was a man of uncommon mental power, and chose as the seat of his business a sequestered rocky cove about two miles east of Marazion, which continues to bear the name of "Prussia Cove," and where deep channels, cut in hard rock, to allow of the near approach of their boats, still shew the determination of the illicit traders. Although constantly visited by the excise officers, the "king" rarely failed to remove his goods, the stocks of which were at times very large, suffering for a long period comparatively little from "seizures." On one occasion his boats, while landing a cargo, being hard pressed by the revenue cutter, Carter had some old cannon brought to the edge of the cliff and opened fire on the unwelcome intruder, and after a short but sharp engagement, fairly beat her off. The cutter was, of course, back again early in the morning, and part of the crew, with the captain, landed; the only traces, however, of the engagement to be seen was the trampled ground. On approaching Carter's house, the officer was met by the "king" himself, with an angry remonstrance about practising the cutter's guns at midnight so near the shore, and disturbing his family at such unseemly hours. Although the principal parties concerned were well known, no evidence could be obtained, and the matter was allowed to drop. Toward the close of his career, Carter "ventured" in larger ships, became less successful, and was at last exchequered. He died, at a very advanced age, in poor circumstances.

CORNISH TEENY-TINY.

MR HALLIWELL gives us, in his "Popular Rhymes and Nursery Tales," the story of Teeny-tiny. In this a little old woman takes a bone from the churchyard to make soup. She goes to bed, and puts the bone in the cupboard. During the night some one comes demanding the bone, and at length the terrified old woman gives it up.

A similar story is told in Cornwall.

An old lady had been to the church in the sands of Perranzabuloe. She found, amidst the numerous remains of mortality, some very good teeth. She pocketed these, and at night placed them on her dressing-table before getting into bed. She slept, but was at length disturbed by some one calling out, "Give me my teeth—give me my teeth." At first the lady took no notice of this, but the cry, "Give me my teeth," was so constantly repeated, that she at last, in terror, jumped out of bed, took the teeth from the dressing-table, and, opening the window, flung them out, exclaiming, "Drat the teeth, take 'em." They no sooner fell into the darkness on the road, than hasty retreating footsteps were heard, and there were no more demands for the teeth.

THE SPANIARD AT PENRYN.

IN the reign of James I. there happened to be upon our coast a Spanish vessel of war. Favoured by the mists of evening and the growing darkness, the ship entered Falmouth harbour unseen. The crew armed themselves, and taking to their boats, proceeded with great caution to the town of Penryn, situated at the head of the harbour. There they landed, formed themselves into proper order, and marched into the town, purposing to plunder the inhabitants and burn the town. With steady tramp they cautiously proceeded up the dark main street, resolving to attack the principal dwellings first. Suddenly a great shout was heard, drums and trumpets sounded, the noise of many feet rushing to and fro fell on the ears of the Spaniards. Believing that they were discovered, and that preparations had been made for their reception, fear seized them, and they fled precipitately to their boats and left the town. The martial music proceeded, however, from a temporary theatre, in which a troop of strolling players were entertaining the people.

BOYER, MAYOR OF BODMIN.

IN the reign of Edward VI., Boyer was the mayor of Bodmin, and he appears to have been suspected of aiding in an insurrection of the men of Devonshire and Cornwall. However this may be, Sir Anthony Kingston, provost-marshal of the king's army, sent orders to Boyer to have a gibbet erected in the street opposite his own house by the next day at noon. He, at the same time, sent his compliments to the mayor, telling him that he should dine with him, in order to be present at the execution of some rebels.

The unsuspecting mayor obeyed the command, and at the time appointed provided an entertainment for his guest. Kingston put about the wine, and when he observed the mayor's spirits were exhilarated, asked him if the gibbet was ready. Being told that it was, with a wanton and diabolical sneer he ordered the mayor to be hanged upon it.

At the same time a miller was ordered to be hanged; his servant was so deeply attached to him, that he went to Kingston and begged him to spare his master's life, even if he hung him in his place. "If you are so fond of hanging," said Kingston, "you shall not be disappointed," and he hanged the miller and his servant together.

A similar story is told of a mayor of St Ives.

THOMASINE BONAVENTURE.

IN the reign of Henry VI., about the year 1450, in the parish of Week St Mary, on the northern coast of Cornwall, was born of humble parents a girl, to whom the name of Thomasine was given. This child was in no way distinguished from other Cornish children; they ever have been, and still are, remarkable for their healthful beauty, and Thomasine, like others, was beautiful. Her father was a small farmer, and the daughter was usually employed in minding the sheep upon Greenamore, or preventing the geese from straying too far from his dwelling.

Thomasine appears to have received no education beyond that which nature gave her. She grew to womanhood a simple, artless maiden, who knew nothing of the world or its cares beyond the few sorrows which found their way into the moorland country of Week and Temple.

Thomasine was watching her flocks when a mounted traveller, with well-filled saddle-bags, passing over the moors observed her. Struck by the young woman's beauty, he halted and commenced a conversation with her. "Her discreet answers, suitable to the beauty of her face, much beyond her rank or degree," says the quaint Hals, "won upon him, and he desired to secure her as a servant in his family." This traveller, who was a draper from London, sought out the parents of the shepherdess, and proposed to relieve them of this daughter, by taking her to the metropolis, promising her good wages and many privileges; and beyond this he agreed that, in case he should die, seeing she would be so far removed from her friends, she should be carefully provided for.

Having satisfied themselves of the respectability of this merchant traveller, the parents agreed to part with their daughter; and Thomasine, full of girlish curiosity to see the city, of which she had heard, was willing to leave her home.

We next find Thomasine in London as a respected servant to this city draper. His wife and family are pleased with the innocent Cornish girl; and by her gentle manners and great goodness of heart, she won upon all with whom she was brought in contact. Years passed away, and the draper's wife died. In the course of time he proposed to make the faithful Thomasine his wife. The proposal was accepted, and "Thomasine and her master were solemnly married together as man and wife; who then, according to his promise, endowed her with a considerable jointure in case of her survivorship." Within two years of this marriage the draper died, and Thomasine was left sole executrix. The poor servant, who but a few years previous was minding sheep on the moors, was now a rich widow, courted by the wealthy of the metropolis. With that good sense which appears ever to have distinguished her, she improved her mind; and following the examples by which she had been for some time surrounded, she added to her natural graces many acquired elegances of manner.

The youth and beauty of the widow brought her numerous admirers, but all were rejected except Henry Gale, of whom we know little, save that he was "an eminent and wealthy citizen." He was accepted, and Thomasine Gale was the most toasted of all city madams. After a few years passed in great happiness, Thomasine became again a widow. Gale left her all his property, and she became, when not yet thirty years of age, one of the wealthiest women in London. So beautiful, so rich, and being yet young, the widow was soon induced to change her state again. She chose now for her companion John Percivall, who was already high in the honours of the corporation.

At the feast of Sir John Collet, who was Lord Mayor in the second year of the reign of Henry VII., in 1487, Percivall was the mayor's carver, "at which time, according to the custom of that city, Sir John drank to him in a silver cup of wine, in order to make him sheriff thereof for the year ensuing, whereupon he covered his head and sat down at table with the Lord Mayor of London." John Percivall was elected Lord Mayor himself in 1499, and he was knighted in the same year by Henry VII. Sir John Percivall and Dame Thomasine Percivall lived many years happily together; but he died, leaving all his fortune to his widow.

Lady Percivall was now advanced in years. She had had three husbands, but no children. The extraordinary accession of fortune made no change in her simple honest heart; the flattery of the great, by whom she had been surrounded, kindled no pride in the beautiful shepherdess. The home of her childhood, from which she had been so long separated, was dear to her, and she retired in her mourning to the quiet of that distant home.

She spent her declining years in good works. Roads were made and bridges built at her cost; almshouses for poor maids were erected; she relieved prisoners; fed the hungry, and clothed the naked. In Week St Mary, Thomasine founded a chantry and free school "to pray for the souls of her father and mother, and her husbands and relatives." To the school she added a library, and a dwelling for the chanters and others, "and endowed the same with £20 lands for ever." Cholwell, a learned man and great linguist, was master here in Henry VIII.'s time; and here he educated in the "liberal arts and sciences," says Carew, "many gentlemen's sons." Such were a few of the benefits conferred on Week by the girl who once had tended the flocks upon the moors;

but who, by great good fortune, and more by the exercise of good sense, became Lady Mayoress.

Dame Thomasine Percivall died, respected by all who knew her, in 1530, having then reached the good old age of eighty years.

It appears probable that the name Bonaventure, by which this remarkable female is usually known, was given to her, likely enough, by the linguist Cholwell, to commemorate her remarkable fortune.

Berry Comb, in Jacobstow, was once the residence of Thomasine, and it was given at her death to the poor of St Mary Week.

THE LAST OF THE KILLIGREWS.

LADY JANE, the widow of Sir John Killigrew, sate in one of the windows of Arwenick House, looking out upon the troubled waters of Falmouth Harbour. A severe storm had prevailed for some days, and the Cornish coast was strewn with wrecks. The tempest had abated; the waves were subsiding, though they still beat heavily against the rocks. A light scud was driving over the sky, and a wild and gloomy aspect suffused all things. There was a sudden outcry amongst a group of men, retainers of the Killigrew family, which excited the attention of Lady Jane Killigrew. She was not left long in suspense as to the cause. In a few minutes two Dutch ships were seen coming into the harbour. They had evidently endured the beat of the storm, for they were both considerably disabled; and with the fragments of sail which they carried, they laboured heavily. At length, however, these vessels were brought round within the shelter of Pendennis; their anchors were cast in good anchoring-ground; and they were safe, or at least the crew thought so, in comparatively smooth water.

As was the custom in those days, the boat belonging to the Killigrew family, manned by the group of whom we have already spoken, went off as soon as the ships were anchored and boarded them. They then learnt that they were of the Hanse Towns, laden with valuable merchandise for Spain, and that this was in the charge of two Spanish factors. On the return of the boat's crew, this was reported to Lady Killigrew; and she being a very wicked and most resolute woman, at once proposed that they should return to the ships, and either rob them of their treasure, or exact from the merchants a large sum of money in compensation. The rude men, to whom wrecking and plundering was but too familiar, were delighted with the prospect of a rare prize; and above all, when Lady Killigrew declared that she would herself accompany them, they were wild with joy.

With great shouting, they gathered together as many men as the largest boat in the harbour would carry, and armed themselves with pikes, swords, and daggers. Lady Jane Killigrew, also armed, placed herself in the stern of the boat after the men had crowded into their places, and with a wild huzza they left the shore, and were soon alongside of the vessel nearest to the shore. A number of the men immediately crowded up the side and on to the deck of this vessel, and at once seized upon the captain and the factor, threatening them with instant death if they dared to make any outcry. Lady Jane Killigrew was now lifted on to the deck of the vessel, and the boat immediately pushed off, and the remainder of the crew boarded the other ship.

The Dutch crew were overpowered by the numbers of Cornishmen, who were armed far more perfectly than they. Taken unawares as they were, at a moment when they thought their troubles were for a season at an end, the Dutchmen were almost powerless.

The Spaniards were brave men, and resisted the demands made to deliver up their treasure. This resistance was, however, fatal to them. At a signal, it is said by some, given by their leader, Lady Jane Killigrew,—although this was denied afterwards,—they were both murdered by the ruffians into whose hands they had fallen, and their bodies cast overboard into the sea.

These wretches ransacked the ships, and appropriated whatsoever they pleased, while Lady Jane took from them "two hogsheads of Spanish pieces of eight, and converted them to her own use."

As one of the Spanish factors was dying, he lifted his hands to Heaven, prayed to the Lord to receive his soul, and turning to the vile woman to whose villany he owed his death, he said, "My blood will linger with you until my death is avenged upon your own sons."

This dreadful deed was not allowed to pass without notice even in those lawless times. The Spaniards were then friendly with England, and upon the representation made by the Spanish minister to the existing government, the sheriff of Cornwall was ordered to seize and bring to trial Lady Jane Killigrew and her crew of murderers. A considerable number were arrested with her; and that lady and several of her men were tried at Launceston.

Since the Spaniards were proved to be at the time of the murder "foreigners under the Queen's protection," they were all found guilty, and condemned to death.

All the men were executed on the walls of Launceston Castle; but by the interest of Sir John Arundell and Sir Nicholas Hals, Queen Elizabeth was induced to grant a pardon for Lady Jane.

How Lady Jane Killigrew lived, and when she died, are

matters on which even tradition, by which the story is preserved, is silent. We know, however, that her immediate descendant, John Killigrew, who married one of the Monks, and his son William Killigrew, who was made a baronet in 1660 by Charles II., were only known for the dissoluteness of character, and the utter regardlessness of every feeling of an exalting character, which they displayed. Sir William Killigrew, by his ill conduct and his extravagant habits, wasted all the basely-gotten treasure, and sold the manor and barton of Arwenick to his younger brother, Sir Peter Killigrew. With the son of this Peter the baronetcy became extinct. The last Sir Peter Killigrew, however, improved his fortune by marrying one of the coheirs of Judge Twisden. Sir Peter and his wife, of whom we know nothing, died, leaving one son, George Killigrew, who connected himself with the St Aubyn family by marriage. This man appears to have inherited many of the vices of his family. He was given to low company, and towards the close of his life was remarkable only for his drunken habits.

He was one evening in a tavern in Penryn, surrounded by his usual companions, and with them was one Walter Vincent, a barrister-at-law. The wine flowed freely; songs and loose conversation were the order of the night. At length all were in a state of great excitement through the extravagance of their libations, and something was said by George Killigrew very insultingly to Walter Vincent.

Walter Vincent does not appear to have been naturally a depraved man, but of violent passions. Irritated by Killigrew, he made some remarks on the great-grandmother being sentenced to be hanged. Swords were instantly drawn by the drunken men. They lunged at each other. Vincent's sword passed directly through Killigrew's body, and he fell dead in the midst of his revelries, at the very moment when he was defending the character of her who had brought dishonour upon them.

This Walter Vincent was tried for the murder of George Killigrew, but acquitted. We are told by the Cornish historian, "Yet this Mr Vincent, through anguish and horror at this accident, (as it was said,) within two years after, wasted of an extreme atrophy of his flesh and spirits; that, at length, at the table whereby he was sitting, in the Bishop of Exeter's palace, in the presence of divers gentlemen, he instantly fell back against the wall and died."

George Killigrew left one daughter; but of her progress in life we know nothing. Thus the Cornish Killigrews ceased to be a name in the land.

Such a tale as this does not, of course, exist without many remarkable additions. Ghosts and devils of various kinds are spoken of as frequenting Arwenick House, and the woods around it. Those spectral and demoniacal visitations have not, however, any special interest. They are only, indeed, repetitions of oft-told tales.

SAINT GERENNIUS.

THIS reached me at too late a period to be included with the legends of the saints:—

"The beacon at Veryan stands on the highest ground in Roseland, at a short distance from the cliff which overlooks Pendower and Gerrans Bay. Dr Whitaker, in his 'Cathedral of Cornwall,' states it to be one of the largest tumuli in the kingdom. Its present height above the level of the field in which it stands is about twenty-eight feet, and its circumference at the base three hundred and fifty feet; but it must have been originally much larger, as a considerable portion on one side has been removed, its summit being now about eighty feet from the base on the south side, and only fifty feet on the north, whilst the top of the cairn which was discovered in it, and which was, no doubt, placed exactly in the original centre of the mound, is at least ten feet still further north than the present summit.

"A tradition has been preserved in the neighbourhood, that Gerennius, an old Cornish saint and king, whose palace stood on the other side of Gerrans Bay, between Trewithian and the sea, was buried in this mound many centuries ago, and that a golden boat with silver oars were used in conveying his corpse across the bay, and were interred with him. Part of this tradition receives confirmation from an account incidentally given of King Gerennius, in an old book called the 'Register of Llandaff.' It is there stated that, A.D. 588, Teliau, bishop of Landaff, with some of his suffragan bishops, and many of his followers, fled from Wales, to escape an epidemic called the yellow plague, and migrated to Dole in Brittany, to visit Sampson, the archbishop of that place, who was a countryman and friend of Teliau's. 'On his way thither,' says the old record, 'he came first to the region of Cornwall, and was well received by Gerennius, the king of that country, who treated him and his people with all honour. From thence he proceeded to Armorica, and remained there seven years and seven months; when, hearing that the plague had ceased in Britain, he collected his followers, caused a large bark to be prepared, and returned to Wales.' 'In this,' the record proceeds, 'they all arrived at the port called Din-Gerein, king Gerennius lying in the last extreme of life, who, when he had received the body of the Lord from the hand of St Teliau, departed in joy to the Lord.' 'Probably,' says Whitaker, in his remarks on this quotation, 'the royal remains were brought in great pomp by water from Din-

Gerein, on the western shore of the port, to Carne, about two miles off on the northern; the barge with the royal body was plated, perhaps, with gold in places; perhaps, too, rowed with oars having equally plates of silver upon them; and the pomp of the procession has mixed confusedly with the interment of the body in the memory of tradition.'"

CORNISH DIALOGUE.

AS the Cornish dialogue peculiarly illustrates a description of literary composition which has no resemblance to that of any other county, I think it advisable to give one specimen:—

DIALOGUE BETWEEN MAL TRELOARE AND SANDRY KEMP.

'Twas Kendle teening, when jung Mal Treloare
Trudg'd hum from Bal, a bucken copper ore;
Her clathing hard and ruff, black was her eye,
Her face and arms like stuff from Cairn Kye.
Full butt she mit jung Saundry Kemp, who long
She had been token'd to, come from Ding Dong;
Hes jacket wet, his faace rud like his beard,
And through his squarded hat hes hair appeared.
She said, "Oh, Kemp, I thoft of thee well leer,
Thees naw that daay we wor to Bougheehere,
That daay with ale and cakes, at three o'clock,
Thees stuff'd me so, I jist neen crack'd me dock:
Jue said to me, 'Thee mayst depend thee life,
I love thee, Mal, and thee shust be ma wife.'
And to ma semmen, tes good to lem ma naw
Whether the words were aal in jest or no."
Saundry. Why, truly, Mal, I like a thing did zay,
That I wud have thee next Chewiden daay.
But zence that time I like a think ded hear
Thees went wi' some one down, 'I naw where;'
Now es that fitty, Mal? What dost think?
Mal. Od rot tha body, Saundry, who said so?
Now, faath and traath, I 'll naw afore I go;
Do lem me naw the Gossenbary dog.

Saundry. Why, then, Crull said jue wor down to Wheal Bog
With he and Tabban, and ded make some tricks
By dabben clay at jungsters making bricks;
Aand that from there jue went to Aafe-waye house,
Aand drink't some leeker. Mal, now there's down souse.
Aand jue to he, like a thing ded zay,
Jue wed have he, and I mait go away.
Mal. I tell the lubber so! I to Wheal Bog!
I'll scatt his chacks, the emprent, saucy dog.
Now hire me, Saundry Kemp, now down and full,
Ef thee arten hastes, thee shust hire the whole.
Fust jue must naw, tes true as thee art there,
Aant Blanch and I went to Golsinny feer.
Who overtookt us in the doosty road,
In common hum but Crull, the cloppen toad.
Zes he to Aant, "What cheer? Aant Blanch, what cheer?
Jue makes good coose, suppose jue been to feer."
"Why, hiss," zes Aant, "ben there a pewer spur.
I wedn't a gone ef nawed ed been so fur.
I bawft a pair of shods for Sarah's cheeld."
By this time, lock! we cum jist to the field.
We went to clemmer up the temberen style.
(Haw kept his eye upon me all the while.)
Zes hem to Aant, "Then whos es thees braa maide?
Come tha wayst long, dasent be afraid."
Then mov'd my side, like a thing,
Aand pull'd my mantle, and just touch'd my ching,
"How arry, jung woman?" zes haw. "How dost do?"
Zes I, "Jue saucy dog, what's that to jue?
Keep off, jung lad, else thees have a slap."
Then haw fooch'd some great big doat figs in me lap.
So I thoft, as haw had been so kind,
Haw might go by Aant Blanch, ef haw had a mind.
Aand so haw ded, aand tookt Aant Blanch's arm.
"Araeh!" zes haw, "I dednt mane no harm."
So then Aant Blanch and he ded talk and jest
Bout dabbing clay and bricks at Petran feast.
Saundry. Ahah then, Mal, 'twas there they dabbed the clay?
Mal. Plaase Father, Kemp, tes true wot I do saay.
And hire me now, pla-sure, haw dedent budge
From Aanty's arm till jest this side Long Brudge.
Aand then zes he to Aant, "Shall we go in
To Aafe-way house, and have a dram of gin
And trickle mixt? Depend ol do es good,

Taake up the sweat, and set to rights the blud."
So Aant did saay, "Such things she dedn't chuse,"
And squeezed my hand, aand loike a thing refuse.
So when we pass'd along by Wheal Bog moor,
Haw jumpt behind, and pok't es in the door.
Haw caal'd for gin, aand brandy too, I think.
He clunk'd the brandy, we the gin did drink.
So when haw wish'd good night, as es the caase,
Haw kiss't Aant Blanch, and jist neen touched my face.
Now, Saundry Kemp, there's nothing shure in this,
To my moinde, then, that thee shust take amiss.
Saundry. No, fath, then Mal, ef this is all aand true,
I had a done the same ef I was jue.
Mal. Next time in any house I see or near am,
I'll down upon the plancheon, rat am, tear am,
Aand I will so poaw am.
Saundry. Our Kappen's there, just by thickey bush.
Hush! now Mally, hush!
Aand as hes here, so close upon the way,
I wedent wish haw nawed what we did zay,
And jett I dedent care, now fath and soul,
Ef so be our Kappen wor to hire the whole.
How arry Kappen? Where be going so fast?
Jure goin'-hum, suppose, jure in sich haste.
Kappen. Who's that than? Saundry, arten thee ashamed
To coosy so again? Thee wust be blamed
Ef thees stay here all night to prate wi' Mal!
When tes thy cour, thee wusten come to Bal.
Aand thee art a Cobbe, I tell thee so.
I'll tell the owners ef thee dosent go.
Saundry. Why, harkee, Kappen, doant skoal poor I.
Touch pipe a crum, jue'll naw the reason why.
Cozen Mal aand I ben courtain bout afe a year.
Hould up tha head, Mal; don't be ashamed, dost hire?
Aand Crull one day made grief 'tween I and she;
But he shall smart for it now, I swear by G——.
Haw told me lies, as round as any cup.
Now Mal and I have mit, we've made it up;
So, Kappen, that's the way I stopt, I vow.
Kappen. Ahah! I dedent giss the case jist now.
But what dost think of that last batch of ore?
Saundry. Why pewer and keenly gossen, Kappen, shure
I bleeve that day, ef Frankey's pair wornt drunk,
We shud had pewer stuff too from the sump.

But there, tes all good time, as people saay,
The flooken now, aint throw'd es far away;
So hope to have bra tummells soon to grass.
How did laast batch down to Jandower pass?
Kappen. Why, hang thy body, Saundry, speed, I saay,
Thees keep thy clacker going till tes day.
Go speak to Mally now, jue foolish toad.
I wish both well, I'll keep my road.
Saundry. Good nightie, Kappen, then I wishee well.
Where artee, Mally? Dusten haw hire me, Mal?
Dusent go away, why jue must think of this,
Before we part, shure we must have a kiss.

She wiped her muzzle from the mundic stuff,
And he rubb'd his, a little stain'd with snuff.

Now then, there, good night Mal, there's good night;
But, stop a crum.
Mally. Good night.
Kappen. Good night.

Keendle teening, candle lighting.
Squarded hat, broken or cracked hat.
Lem ma naw, let me know, tell me.
Wheal Bog, wheal, or, correctly spelt, huel, is old Cornish, and signifies a mine or work.
Doat figs, broad figs.
A cobbe, a cobbler, a bungler.
Bra tummills, brave heaps, large piles of ore.

APPENDIX.

APPENDIX.

(A.)

ST PIRAN—PERRAN ZABULOE.

"IT is rather a curious circumstance," says Davies Gilbert, "that the word *Zabuloe* added to Perran, for the distinction of this parish, is not Celtic, but through the French *sable*, from *sabulum*, a word frequently used by Pliny, as indicative of sand or gravel.

"The encroachments of the sand have caused no less than three churches to be built, after considerable intervals of time, in this parish. The last was commenced in 1804; and in this year, (1835,) a building has been discovered more ancient than the first of these churches, and not improbably the oratory of St Perran himself. The length of this chapel within the walls is 25 feet, without, 30 feet; the breadth within, 12½ feet; and the height of the walls the same.

"At the eastern end is a neat altar of stone covered with lime, 4 feet long, by 2½ feet wide, and 3 feet high. Eight inches above the centre of the altar is a recess in the wall, where probably stood a crucifix; and on the north side of the altar is a small doorway, through which the priest may have entered. Out of the whole length, the chancel extended exactly 6 feet. In the centre of what may be termed the nave, in the south wall, occurs a round arched doorway, highly ornamented. The building is, however, without any trace of window; and there is only one small opening, apparently for the admission of air.

"The discovery has excited much curiosity throughout the neighbourhood; which has, unfortunately, manifested itself by the demolition of everything curious in this little oratory, to be borne away as relics."—*Gilbert.*

"Very little is known concerning the saint who has given his name to the three Perrans. He is, however, held in great veneration, and esteemed the patron of all Cornwall, or, at least, of the mining district."—*Hals.*

(B.)

THE DISCOVERER OF TIN.

BY an anachronism of fifteen hundred years or more, St Perran was considered as the person who first found tin; and this conviction induced the miners to celebrate his day, the 5th of March, with so much hilarity, that any one unable to guide himself along the road has received the appellation of a Perraner; and that, again, has been most unjustly reflected as a habit on the saint.

"It may here be worthy of remark, that, as the miners impute the discovery of tin to St Perran, so they ascribe its reduction from the ore, in a large way, to an imaginary person, St Chiwidden; but *chi-wadden* is white house, and must, therefore, mean a smelting or blowing house, where the black ore of tin is converted into a white metal.

"A white cross on a black ground was formerly the banner of St Perran, and the standard of Cornwall; probably with some allusion to the black ore and the white metal of tin."—*Gilbert.*

A college, dedicated to St Perran, once stood in the parish of St Kevern, (Dugdale's "Monasticon," vol. vi., p. 1449.) This probably had some connexion with Perran Uthnoe. The shrine of St Perran was in that parish, which is said to have contained his head, and other relics.

Lysons quotes a deed in the registry of Exeter, shewing the great resort of pilgrims hither in 1485.

In the will of Sir John Arundell, 1433, occurs this bequest:—"Item, lego ad usum parochie S'c'i' Pyerani in

Zabulo, ad clandendum capud S. Pierani honorificè et meliori modo quo sciunt xls."—*Collectanea Topogr. et Geneal.*, vol. iii. p. 392.

For a full examination of the question, Did the Phœnicians trade with Britain for tin? the following works should be consulted:—"History of Maritime and Inland Discovery," by W. D. Cooley; "Historical Survey of the Astronomy of the Ancients," by Sir George Cornewall Lewis; "Commerce and Navigation of the Ancients," by W. Vincent, D.D.; "Phœnicia," by John Kenrick, M.A.; "The Cassiterides: an Inquiry into the Commercial Operations of the Phœnicians in Western Europe, with particular Reference to the British Tin Trade," by George Smith, LL.D., F.A.S.

(C.)

ST NEOT.

THE following account of this celebrated saint, as given by Mr Davies Gilbert, will not be without interest:—

"Multitudes flocked to him from all parts. He founded a monastery, and repaired to Rome for a confirmation, and for blessing at the hands of the Pope; these were readily obtained. He returned to his monastery, where frequent visits were made to him by King Alfred, on which occasions he admonished and instructed the great founder of English liberty; and finally quitted this mortal life on the 31st of July, about the year 883, in the odour of sanctity so unequivocal that travellers all over Cornwall were solaced by its fragrance. Nor did the exertions of our saint terminate with his existence on earth; he frequently appeared to King Alfred, and sometimes led his armies in the field. But, if the tales of these times are deserving of any confidence, the nation is really and truly indebted to St Neot for one of the greatest blessings ever bestowed on it. To his advice, and even to his personal assistance as a teacher, we owe the foundation by Alfred of the University at Oxford.

"The relics of St Neot remained at his monastery in Cornwall till about the year 974, when Earl Alric, and his wife

Ethelfleda, having founded a religious house at Eynesbury. in Huntingdonshire, and being at a loss for some patron saint, adopted the expedient of stealing the body of St Neot; which was accordingly done, and the town retains his name, thus feloniously obtained, up to this time. The monastery in Cornwall continued feebly to exist, after this disaster, through the Saxon times; but, having lost its palladium, it felt the ruiner's hand; and, almost immediately after the Norman Conquest, it was finally suppressed. Yet the memory of the local saint is still cherished by the inhabitants of the parish and of the neighbourhood—endeared, perhaps, by the tradition of his diminutive stature, reduced, in their imagination, to fifteen inches of height; and to these feelings we, in all probability, owe the preservation of the painted glass, the great decoration of this church, and one of the principal works of art to be seen in Cornwall."—*Gilbert's Hist. Corn.*, vol. iii. p. 262.

(D.)

THE SISTERS OF GLEN-NEOT.

BY THE REV. R. S. HAWKER OF MORWENSTOW.

IT is from Neot's sainted steep
The foamy waters flash and leap;
It is where shrinking wild-flowers grow,
They lave the nymph that dwells below!

But wherefore in this far-off dell,
The reliques of a human cell?
Where the sad stream and lonely wind
Bring Man no tidings of their kind!

Long years agone! the old man said,
'Twas told him by his grandsire dead,
One day two ancient sisters came,
None there could tell their race or name.

Their speech was not in Cornish phrase,
Their garb had marks of loftier days;
Slight food they took from hands of men,
They wither'd slowly in that glen.

One died! the other's shrunken eye
Gush'd till the fount of tears was dry;
A wild and wasting thought had she—
"I shall have none to weep for me!"

They found her silent at the last,
Bent in the shape wherein she pass'd—
Where her lone seat long used to stand,
Her head upon her shrivell'd hand!

Did fancy give this legend birth?
The grandame's tale for winter-hearth,
Or some dead bard, by Neot's stream,
People these banks with such a dream?

We know not! but it suits the scene,
To think such wild things here have been;
What spot more meet could grief or sin
Choose at the last to wither in?

Echoes of Old Cornwall.

(E.)

MILLINGTON OF PENGERSWICK.

IN the reign of Henry VIII., one Militon, or Millington, appears to have purchased Pengerswick Castle. This Millington is said to have retired into the solitude of this place on account of a murder which he had committed. (Mr Wilkie Collins appears to have founded his novel of "Basil" on this tradition.) In all probability a very much older story is adapted to Mr Millington. So far from his being a recluse, we learn of his purchasing St Michael's Mount, "whose six daughters and heirs invested their husbands and purchasers therewith."

That Millington was a man of wealth, and that large possessions were held by his family, is sufficiently evident. St Michael's Mount appears to have been "granted at first for a term of years to different gentlemen of the neighbourhood. To Millington, supposed of Pengerswick, in Breage; to Harris, of Kenegie, in Gulval; and, perhaps jointly with Millington, to a Billett or Bennett."—*Hals.*

(F.)

SARACEN.

THE term *Saracen* is always now supposed to apply to the Moors. This is not exactly correct. Percy, for example, in his " Essay on the Ancient Minstrels," says, " The old metrical romance of ' Horn Child,' which, although from the mention of Saracens, &c., it must have been written, at least, after the First Crusade, in 1096, yet, from its Anglo-Saxon language or idiom, can scarcely be dated later than within a century after the Conquest." I think this ballad, and several others of an early date, prove the application of this term to some Oriental people previous to the Crusades. Soldàin, soldàn, regarded as a corruption of sultan,—

> " Whoever will fight yon grimme soldàn,
> Right fair his meede shall be,"—

is clearly a much older term, applied to any grim Eastern tyrant, and especially to the Oriental giants. It would not be a difficult task to shew that the word Saracen, as used in Cornwall,—" *Atal Saracen !*" " *Oh, he's a Saracen !*" &c., was applied to the foreigners who traded with this county for tin—at a very early period.

END OF SECOND SERIES.

CPSIA information can be obtained
at www.ICGtesting.com
Printed in the USA
LVHW112141080422
715402LV00007B/59

9 783752 589375